OTHER EVOLUTIONS

a novel

REBECCA HIRSCH GARCIA

Copyright © Rebecca Hirsch Garcia, 2025

Published by ECW Press
665 Gerrard Street East
Toronto, Ontario, Canada M4M 1Y2
416-694-3348 / info@ecwpress.com

All rights reserved. No part of this publication may be reproduced, stored in a retrieval system, or transmitted in any form by any process — electronic, mechanical, photocopying, recording, or otherwise — without the prior written permission of the copyright owners and ECW Press. The scanning, uploading, and distribution of this book via the internet or via any other means without the permission of the publisher is illegal and punishable by law. This book may not be used for text and data mining, AI training, and similar technologies. Please purchase only authorized electronic editions, and do not participate in or encourage electronic piracy of copyrighted materials. Your support of the author's rights is appreciated.

Editor for the Press: Jen Albert
Copy editor: Peter Norman
Cover design: Jessica Albert
Cover artwork: Elizabeth Ranger

This is a work of fiction. Names, characters, places, and incidents either are the product of the author's imagination or are used fictitiously, and any resemblance to actual persons, living or dead, business establishments, events, or locales is entirely coincidental.

LIBRARY AND ARCHIVES CANADA CATALOGUING IN PUBLICATION

Title: Other evolutions / Rebecca Hirsch Garcia.

Names: Garcia, Rebecca Hirsch, author.

Identifiers: Canadiana (print) 20250213699 | Canadiana (ebook) 20250213710

ISBN 978-1-77041-726-7 (softcover)
ISBN 978-1-77852-470-7 (ePub)
ISBN 978-1-77852-471-4 (PDF)

Subjects: LCGFT: Novels.

Classification: LCC PS8613.A715 O84 2025 | DDC C813/.6—dc23

This book is funded in part by the Government of Canada. *Ce livre est financé en partie par le gouvernement du Canada.* We acknowledge the support of the Canada Council for the Arts. *Nous remercions le Conseil des arts du Canada de son soutien.* We would like to acknowledge the funding support of the Ontario Arts Council (OAC), the City of Ottawa, and the Government of Ontario for their support. We also acknowledge the support of the Government of Ontario through the Ontario Book Publishing Tax Credit, and through Ontario Creates.

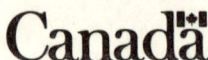 

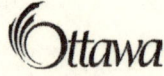

PRINTED AND BOUND IN CANADA   PRINTING: MARQUIS   5 4 3 2 1

 Purchase the print edition and receive the ebook free. For details, go to ecwpress.com/ebook.

To my mother, Trudi Hirsch Garcia,
who taught me how to keep the dead alive.

The future is perhaps a wave that will wash us away.
—*Agnès Varda*

PART I
VANISHING

NOTHING EVER HAPPENS IN OTTAWA

I ALWAYS FEEL too human at parties. By which I mean parties begin at the point at which I am my most artificial: plucked, shaved, and made up, and all the effort reminds me that threatening to burst through all this grooming at any moment is my natural self. She is always there waiting for me at the end of the night: hair frizzing, dress stained, the smell of sweat, familiar, claiming dominion over the sweet, fading notes of perfume.

Parties are always a disappointment too. In the movies of my youth, which always took place elsewhere, impossibly gorgeous women in beautiful gowns were always being romanced by impossibly handsome men in tuxes. At real parties no one, even at their best, can compare to that soft-lens movie magic. I always see the flaws: the lines of undergarments underneath the silky sheen of polyester satin; the men's shoes, stiff and shiny from disuse, announcing their owners' arrival with little mousey squeaks. Women's powdery makeup gathers in the folds of their wrinkles, men's carefully curated stubble doesn't quite cover the acne scars left behind from teenagedom. There's always a dead ant floating miserably in a bowl of flower arrangements and the tablecloths aren't made of linen or any sort of natural fabric; instead they are scratchy to the touch polyester, the easier to wash the inevitable stains out.

This inability to ignore the uglier side of things is why I never go to parties, and yet recently Marnie called me to beg me to go a wedding as a favour for the brother of a friend.

I said no, because I always say no, even though I knew that Marnie would, as she always does, get her way in the end.

I also said no because I couldn't remember if this brother of a friend remembered about my arm or if, when he showed up to collect me, his face would twist in disgust before it would correct itself, smoothing into the placid look of neutrality that Ottawans are so good at. Then we would have to spend a whole dreadful night together pretending both that his face hadn't betrayed him and that I hadn't seen it.

He remembers, Marnie told me.

And when he showed up at my doorstep there was absolutely no disappointment when he saw me.

You're saving me, Alma, he said, lifting up my left hand and holding it tight.

For hours I stood beside him and introduced myself over and over again to people whose names I didn't bother trying to learn.

I averted my eyes from the cracks and did my best at playing the role of Guest.

But then my feet began to burn in my heels and I noticed the smallest snag in the fabric of my dress, a favourite of mine, and I noticed people kept sliding their eyes over to me and then sliding their eyes away as soon as they noticed me noticing.

I felt an itch running down my spine, unbearable, and muttered my excuses and walked away, very slowly.

There was nowhere really to go, the dance floor and dining area all one. So I circulated in the true meaning of the word, ambling in a loop around the room, trying to get as far away as possible from my companion, knowing that every step only brought me closer to him and his friends and their stares.

And then I was spared, for a minute, when I saw another friend of Marnie's, whose name I could not recall but who, seeing me, smiled at me and drew me into the sphere of people she was talking to with the warmth of her gaze.

There are people who meet you when you are a child and who always, forever after, see you that way even when you are an adult. That was the way it was for this friend of Marnie's. She brought me close to her body, to the soft swell of her chest, and the smell of alcohol and sweat and perfume all in one, ushering me close to her as if I was a child.

Alma, beloved, they are saying that Ottawa is boring. The most boring place on earth. Tell them it isn't, Alma, tell them.

And the man beside her said, Ottawa is where fun comes to die, and everyone made noises of amusement, shadows of laughter at this truism.

And I thought of how everyone I had ever loved lived within the borders of the city, this city I had been born in and raised in and would likely die in, had laughed and cried and loved and hated and nearly died in, and I said, Oh, absolutely, I agree.

Marnie's friend laughed a real laugh at that and because she had just taken a swig of champagne it was glorious. Alcohol droplets misted out of her like a fountain and everyone in the little circle either screamed in horror or laughed themselves and backed away and went in search of napkins and in the chaos I excused myself and went back and found my date and was somehow able to bear the night a little better.

At the end of the night when we were all in line to get our coats at the coat check I noticed that the man who said Ottawa was where fun came to die was behind me.

He blushed when he saw me looking at him.

Hello there, he said.

Hello.

I didn't mean to offend you, he said.

You didn't.

I'm sure lots of interesting things happen in Ottawa. For example— and he gestured at my arm.

Or rather, he gestured at the prosthetic arm I was wearing.

He was a lot older than me, this man. He had reached that age when all old men begin to look a little like old women and all old women begin to look a little like old men. Somehow, though, they never look like each other.

Not everything is a story, I told him. Goodnight.

It felt as though the very house was asleep by the time I got home. So as not to wake it I didn't turn on the lights. In the dark I abandoned the prosthetic and stripped off my dress and let it fall to the floor where it would wrinkle helplessly. It didn't matter to me. I had already ruined it with my sweat, with my being, when I was careless and looked away and had let it snag. It was ruined, like all things were in the end.

In the dark I scrubbed off my makeup and then in my sulky, feral, undressed state, I sat in my favourite chair in the dark.

My arm was aching where it wasn't, phantom pains that I couldn't rub out.

I thought about the old man at the party, the one I had not wanted to converse with, and in the dark I talked to him.

I told him:

Everything *is* a story.

But not everyone deserves to hear it.

THE STORY OF MY ARM

FOURTEEN WAS THE last age when I had two arms. After that I had one.

When I am in a decent enough mood and the person asking is not particularly offensive the story I tell them about my arm is this:

When I was fourteen I was in a car accident.

And that is all they need to know.

ANOTHER STORY, FOR EXAMPLE, WHICH NOT EVERYONE DESERVES TO HEAR

IF I WERE to tell someone the story of my life, I wouldn't start with my birth. I wouldn't start with the birth of my parents either, or their parents, or their parents, whose names have been lost to me, are as untouchable, as untraceable, as if they never lived.

I would start the story of my life with the birth of my older sister.

I would start with Marnie.

When my mother was pregnant with Marnie she had been in Canada long enough to know that it would be better for the baby if the baby was white. My mother, Merced, was an immigrant from Mexico, never able to slough off a thick accent which marked her as being Not of This Place. Despite her bronzed skin, there lurked inside her murky connections to the white-skinned Spaniards who had colonized and raped upon their arrival in her mother country. She hoped that between her Jewish husband (brown-haired but fair of skin) and the shame in her past it would be enough to give the baby a good life. A white life.

When the baby was born she was a mottled dark berry colour. My father counted baby fingers and toes, which added up every time to a perfect set of ten of each. His mother was pleased with the baby. She was an immigrant herself, a survivor, a refugee. Her entire family had been murdered, leaving her to create a new one with her own flesh. She cried every time she saw Marnie, the baby named for the favourite sister, the one she remembered as a naughty teenager who wore lipstick when she was too young for it and took out her violin at parties, the sister who didn't survive.

At her birth my father Aaron's sister, aunt Eshkie, prophesized that Marnie would turn browner than my mother.

But Marnie lightened up day by day.

By the time my father and mother sat at the kitchen table of their tiny Toronto apartment, which I would never see in life, only in pictures from that happy time, and decided that they needed to move to Ottawa to take care of my grandmother—still years away from dementia but already an old woman—by that time Marnie's skin had lightened to a pale and luminous white. Her eyes were still an unsettling steel-grey that would eventually morph into a soft moss-green that belonged to no relative in memory, and the first of the bright blonde strands of her youth had begun to appear upon her formerly bald dome.

My parents cried hugging friends they would lose touch with and gave away, sold, or packed up everything they owned, and travelled by car to Ottawa, where nothing ever happens and I was finally born.

I was born into a different world. I was born to parents who were five years older, and were tired. My mother especially. She was tired of trying to teach Marnie the language of her colonizers when Marnie was learning the languages of the Canadian colonizers, English and French seeping into school, home, play. She was tired of taking care of my father's mother despite loving her, loving her with all the misplaced affection of a daughter separated by that great big ungovernable country, America, from her own mother. But mostly she was tired of walking with the child she had grown and fed from her own body and being constantly mistaken for The Help. The women in her new Ottawan neighbourhood assumed she was a babysitter or a nanny or a friend. When they were corrected they blushed, the pink coming through under their patchy makeup. They were so sorry. They hadn't meant to assume. Once or twice some supposedly liberal-minded woman called my mother Marnie's stepmother. My mother, a lapsed Catholic married to a conservative Jew, the word *divorce* unthinkable for either of them, bristled at the thought of being anyone's second anything.

So when my mother found out she was pregnant once more, she wished again. For a child who would be hers and would look it. And once again her wish came true: I was born with black hair, full and thick already, and mottled skin that lost its purple sheen but stayed a convincing brown, all the melanin from her past reasserting itself in my body.

My mother told us, that is Marnie and me, this story all the time when we were growing up. It made us sound like the princesses in the storybooks my father read to us at bedtime. Sisters were always different, one taking after the moon, the other the sun, one golden-haired and one with hair black as night (though they were always white, the princesses in these books). When I was a little older I thought of the story a bit differently. It seemed that my mother was claiming witch-like powers though I had never known a woman less like a witch, a beautiful woman, a tidy woman, a woman who still crossed herself every time she passed a church but who had long ago abandoned the practical aspects of Catholicism.

One day it occurred to me to ask her what she was trying to say when she kept telling me this story. She pinched my earlobe for asking.

But what's the point?

She looked at me like she couldn't believe she had raised a daughter so stupid.

That you were always so wanted.

BLOOD EVERYWHERE YOU LOOK

MARNIE AND I, the loved children, the wanted children, grew up side by side as Ottawans, as Glebites, on a street named Linden Terrace. We were raised in the house that my grandparents—my zaide, who died long before I was ever born, and my bubbe—had purchased when the neighbourhood was rundown, before civil servants took over and the prices skyrocketed and it turned into a home that neither Marnie nor I would have ever been able to purchase but that we would inherit anyway one day when everyone we loved or who had loved us was dead.

My grandparents bought the land to replace that other land in those other countries where they came from. Countries, whole swaths on the map, that they could not look at without feeling bites of pain, countries that my father, who had been expressly forbidden to do so, would never visit, where Marnie and I (who had not been expressly forbidden) would never choose to visit, where everyone they had previously loved had lived and then, for no reason I could ever understand, had been rounded up, tortured, and murdered. They bought the new house and they bought another and they hoarded it, afraid that someone would come and claim it one day.

Oh but in this land, my mother said, away from my father's ears. On this land they are the colonizers.

Maybe she didn't say *colonizers*. It was a word that would have felt strange in her mouth, in her accent. She would have said it in a more euphemistic way, sifting through the second-hand language for the right words for her meaning.

She would have said something like, All this land, it was stolen too.

Or maybe: Remember Alma, that this land used to belong to someone else.

Or maybe: No one ever forgets the land they have lost.

She didn't need to say that last bit. Marnie and I learned those lessons as infants, aware of the injustice of the other people living shadow lives on the other land, the land that should have been ours by right.

We didn't even know where it was but we wanted it.

When someone steals something the stolen-from never forget.

Someone, somewhere, is always waiting to get it back.

In the recent past and the far—all through the carefully curated neighbourhoods where city planners had parcelled lots and planted trees and cut through the earth and eliminated all traces of the original caretakers—everywhere under everything if you looked hard enough, if you bothered looking at all, there was genocide.

You have everything to be grateful for, aunt Eshkie shouted at me once after I lost my arm. Why can't you be happy?

AN INTRODUCTION TO DEATH AND THE CONCEPT OF UNHAPPINESS

MY GRANDMOTHER DIED when I was four and Marnie was nine.

This was incredibly difficult on both my parents. My mother loved my grandmother. When my father asked if they could move back to take care of her, my mother couldn't understand why it was phrased as a question.

My grandmother loved my mother back, unquestionably, as a second daughter. They had so much in common. They were both immigrants. They had both chosen to make Canada their home, though for my grandmother, the refugee, it was less a matter of choice than of survival. They were both very traditional women in that they deferred, or pretended to defer, to their husbands, always wore skirts, never swore, prayed to God daily, and thought sleeveless tops were something only loose women wore. They were both exactly the type of people to understand and use the phrase *loose women*. And of course my grandmother, who had lost her whole family in the war and then created a new one, venerated my mother for bringing her grandchildren.

I learned later on in biology classes what this had cost her. That babies are like parasites, taking the nutrients they need from their host bodies, and the host will give up anything, no matter the cost to themselves, to protect their invader. Women who have experienced pregnancy have fewer teeth than other adults because their babies leach the calcium from their bones. My grandmother had a gold tooth that glinted in the light. My mother a porcelain one dyed to match her extant set.

They were thick as thieves, both of them laughing across their versions of English. It was not that either of them was particularly funny or that either understood what the other was trying to say in particular, only that each knew that the other was trying to make a joke and the other laughed in appreciation of the spirit in which the mishmashed words had been intended.

I was never old enough to appreciate this camaraderie. As she aged the English drained away from my grandmother. By the time I knew her she frequently reverted back to Yiddish, the language she used in the kitchen in Canada where she raised her children with her husband, a little island of Jewishness.

In our kitchen, in the Glebe, she spoke a mixture of German and Yiddish to me, her little kluge mädchen, her bubbeleh, and I answered back in English.

By the time I was old enough to have conscious memories Marnie was at school and my mother's charges had dwindled down to two: myself and my grandmother. My mother found it easier to treat us as if we were both children, one small and strong, one adult-sized but weak.

When we went out we were given instructions to hold each other's hands and look both ways before we crossed the street. We were served our lunches at the same time and reminded to wash our hands before eating and clean our plates. We each took a seat on either side of my mother during the daily ritual of soap opera watching. If we sat and watched quietly and if I refrained from sucking my thumb and my grandmother refrained from trying to wander off, then we were each rewarded later with a cookie, which we chewed over quietly at the kitchen table.

In many ways my grandmother was more like a sister than a grandmother, my first conspirator, my equal, whereas Marnie was like a third grownup, one who, like my father, went away mysteriously during the day and returned in the evenings armed with new stories, scraps of French, and tales of people who seemed as elusive as movie stars for all I saw of them.

But I only know this from the little bits I've pieced together over the years, fragments of fragments of someone else's memory.

Before I could really affix my grandmother in my mind she died.

A SHORT NOTE ON MARNIE AND MARNIE

MARNIE, NOT TO be confused with *my* Marnie, was my only Canadian cousin, birthed shortly after my sister by my father's only sibling, Edith, called Eshkie. For reasons which no one in the family ever understood, and to the great embarrassment of all involved, Edith was a bigot. I suppose there is one in almost every family, bringing shame upon all their relations.

No one ever explicitly called aunt Eshkie a bigot and she was careful not to be something as unfashionable as an outright racist, but she always treated my mother and me as inconvenient intruders in the family circle. Even my Marnie, for all her fair skin and blonde hair, was viewed as fruit from the poisoned tree. Aunt Eshkie liked her best, acknowledged her as her niece even, but treated her with a cold indifference.

Everyone in the family tried their best to shelter my mother and me from aunt Eshkie as much as possible. So if there were any more explicit acts of bigotry they were kept well away from my ears though Marnie (my Marnie) once told me that aunt Eshkie had once told my mother to go back to where she came from, after which both my father and uncle Bobby, Eshkie's husband, sent the Marnies away to play and they were not let back for what seemed like hours. When they returned they found aunt Eshkie with red-rimmed eyes, completely mute, and my mother sipping tea, a catlike smirk on her face.

But the most loathsome and dishonourable thing aunt Eshkie ever did was tied to my sister's birth.

She named her daughter Marnie, even though my parents had claimed the name for my sister at her birth five months earlier.

This was something that was simply not *done*. It was such an obvious affront to my mother and to Marnie—a statement that Mama and Marnie were no family of Eshkie's, that Marnie was no rightful heir to that family name, to that legacy. It was an act so blatant in its cut that my grandmother did not talk to aunt Eshkie for a year afterwards, and even after they began to talk again—a peace brokered by my father and uncle Bobby, the two appeasers forever trying to reconcile a family ruled by irreconcilable, ungovernable women—even after everyone in the family had reached a kind of fragile accord, my grandmother never, not once, referred to cousin Marnie by that name. To her my Marnie was always Marnie and cousin Marnie was referred to by her middle name, something no one else ever called her.

THE STORY OF A DRESS

WHEN I THINK of my grandmother's death I don't remember it with any particular sadness. Someone must have told me she died and explained death to me but it didn't seem important at the time. What did seem important was that it was decided that I should have a new dress, having nothing appropriately funereal to wear.

While the planning and the grieving happened uncle Bobby ushered Marnie and Marnie and me to Marks & Spencer and left it to us to choose our dresses.

The Marnies chose complimentary black dresses with white Peter Pan collars, puffed sleeves, and satin sashes. The only difference was Marnie (my sister) had a dress with black sleeves that trailed to her wrists and Marnie (my cousin) had short ones that pinched her upper arms. (My other grandmother, my abuela, would have called my cousin gorda, which is what she called me the first time she met me, pinching my upper-arm fat in a way that made my eyes water and made me repent of all the times I had never defended cousin Marnie when aunt Eshkie told her to put down that piece of cake for God's sake.)

Left to my own devices, uncle Bobby hovering unhelpfully at the border of the little girls' section, I quickly located a pink dress with a smocked bodice and a skirt of tulle that puffed out like a fluffy cloud.

I cannot, for the life of me, remember my grandmother's face but by God, I can remember the exact pink of that dress, the soft pastel of cotton candy. Earlier that year I had declared pink to be my favourite colour and my sister had told me it wasn't, it was *her* favourite colour and mine was blue. Then to seal this decision she had repeated it to my parents. Now everything bought for me, from shoes to toothbrushes to backpacks to the wooden *Alma* nameplate hanging from my door, was blue. I had white-and-navy-blue saddle shoes. I had blue-and-yellow cat's eye marbles. I had a gingham quilt in shades of blue, and a fluffy beige teddy bear on my bed in a blue knit sweater. I was stuffed so full of blue that I would have been shocked to find out that the colour of my blood was red. I was so sick of blue I felt a physical pinch of dis-ease every time I was gifted something in that colour.

I saw that dress, pink like a blush, pink like bubble gum, pink the forbidden favourite colour that I kept in my heart. I wanted it.

It was of course a completely inappropriate choice for a funeral. But uncle Bobby, who was a nice man, who gave me chocolate when no one was looking and called me bubbeleh, was also one of those men who, through concentrated pretense, avow to know absolutely nothing about fashion except that little girls wear dresses and like pink, and I was a little girl. I was also a little girl who had just lost her grandmother, though I wasn't particularly feeling the loss at that moment. He would have bought that dress for me, I know he would have, if I had asked.

I never got the chance.

Fortunately for uncle Bobby and less fortunately for me I was persuaded away from my cloudish choice by Marnie, my Marnie. Perhaps *persuaded* is too gentle a word for what she did. I was fondling the pink dress between my fingers, feeling the scratchy way the tulle felt on my soft skin, at odds with how insubstantial it looked, when Marnie came and pulled me away. She had already chosen her dress and there was another one—in my size, and cream—tossed over her arm.

I knew who that dress was for and I balked at the idea of wearing it. When I wore white, adults told me how lovely and tan my skin was, stressing the word *tan*. I hated wearing white. I felt my eyes welling up, I felt myself preparing to put up a fight for pink and then I felt Marnie's firm hand encircling my chubby child's wrist, ushering me close against the bony flat of her chest in what, to adult eyes, would have seemed like a comforting embrace.

The planes of her poked at all my softness in a way that hurt but before I could wriggle away or protest she whispered in my ear, I will snap your arm like a twig if you try to get uncle Bobby to buy that dress.

I whimpered and tried to pull away from her; her grip tightened. I looked to uncle Bobby who was no longer looking at us but overwhelming a sales assistant by telling her that his mother-in-law had died and none of the children were coping with it very well.

I could see that the situation was helpless. My tears dried up, Marnie put a look of solemnity on her face, and together we went over to uncle

Bobby, the forbidden pink dress abandoned on the rack, the white dress clutched in my hands as if it had been my idea. We lined up beside him and Marnie said, Excuse me uncle Bobby, and saved the sales assistant who was embarrassed by our grief, so fresh and large and inappropriate in that well-lit store where everything was New! New! New! and had yet to die, and he gathered up our dresses in his big hands and went and paid for them.

If he noticed the sadness on my face, it was easily attributable to my dead grandmother.

The welts on my wrist were less easily explained but uncle Bobby, never one to cause strife, conveniently overlooked them.

Poor Marnie. Even though at the time she seemed terribly grown up, she was a child, just old enough to feel the loss of our grandmother in a way that was profound and real. I didn't see it that way at the time. I was at that age when I thought that because she was five years older she was akin to a god. At that age, at all ages really, I was easily seduced by beauty and Marnie was, even as a child, extremely beautiful. Other parents were always remarking on Marnie's fair hair and pale skin, the pretty slope of her nose that was a little wide, the only trait carried from mother to child. No one, I thought, no one that beautiful could ever be unhappy.

There are no pictures directly from that time of loss, but in the years afterwards, Marnie's green eyes reflected a sense of tragedy, giving her a serious look that was uncanny and striking on a child's face.

Poor Marnie.

The dresses purchased, we went home to begin the long and complicated process of mourning. Tags were cut, dresses hung in the closet. The white dress, like a ghostly spectre, waited for me to merge with it. At night lying in bed I vibrated with the excitement of knowing that sometime very soon we would put my grandmother in a box in the ground and I had an appropriate dress to wear for this occasion.

TACTICS

WHAT I REMEMBER from the day of the funeral was all the preening.

I was dressed first, by Marnie, who wrestled me into my white dress and, at my insistence, tied the white sash of the dress in a pleasingly large bow.

If you keep touching it, she told me, I won't retie it no matter how much you cry.

Then she set about dressing herself, a private ritual which I was not allowed to witness. I was booted from Marnie's room, just managing to remove my pudgy fingers from the door frame as she slammed it shut and narrowly avoiding an accident which would have left me, if not fingerless, in possession of several broken fingers.

There were no mysteries in my own bedroom except the ones I had placed there: A secret flashlight tucked between the mattress and the bedframe that I sometimes used to look at books in the dark. A hoard of candy left over from last year's Halloween, growing staler by the minute, that migrated from my winter boots to my rain boots depending on where it was less likely to be discovered. But today the candy seemed unpalatable. Not because my grandmother was dead but because the white dress would surely stain with the signs of my candy crimes.

I made my migration across the hall to my parents' bedroom.

My father was missing which I didn't mind. Since his mother's death he had become an unpredictable mix of sulky and overly affectionate. There were times when it seemed he was looking past me and there was nothing I could do to bring him back. Even pinching him with all my five-year-old force would only cause him to reluctantly turn his misty eyes in my direction, pat me on the head, and then float off to another room to continue misting in private.

And then sometimes he would come to my room and sit on the edge of my bed and tell me how lucky we were to have each other.

Life is so precious, he would tell me, looking at me intensely, his eyes no longer misty but a clear and fierce brown.

It's a miracle we have the time we have together. You know the Nazis shot children your age. Younger than you. They took babies by the ankle and they bashed their heads into the wall.

I nodded and tried to look sad about the babies, even though I had heard versions of this story before.

Come sleep, I would say, patting the side of the bed and moving to make room for him.

Sometimes he would lie down with me but more often than not he would stay up and smooth my hair and cradle me in his arms and continue to talk about the war and about his father who had died when my father was a little older than Marnie and how he would do his best to not do that to Marnie when she reached that age.

I wanted to ask him to stay alive for me too but already I knew such a thing couldn't be promised. Death was lurking around every corner. It was a minor miracle that I, at the age of five, had been permitted to live so long.

In my parents' room my mother was sitting at her vanity in her slip, trying to do her makeup in the mirror of a compact because the mirror of her vanity, like all the mirrors in the house, had been covered with black cloth.

Is that allowed? I asked.

I don't know, Almita, she said.

I also got the sense that she didn't care.

She was a woman who cared about appearances, my mother, both her own and that of others. When we came in with the white dress, she had picked up the cloth between two fingers and rubbed it. She did this with all the clothes we bought. She always insisted on natural fabrics, cotton and linen and silk, soft on the skin. Polyester and synthetic blends to be shunned at all costs.

She made a little murmur of approval when she touched my white dress.

Who picked this for you? she asked. Your uncle?

Marnie, I said, meaning our Marnie, which she immediately understood to be so. We didn't say it aloud in our family, but though we liked cousin Marnie a little of our distaste of aunt Eshkie had rubbed off on her. There was nothing wrong with her really; she was a very ordinary little girl with thick glasses and dull brown hair that frizzed in the rain. But that was the problem. Marnie, my sister, was like the sun. We all paled in comparison to her. At least I was different in every way, being younger, being browner, and having a name of my own. In our family cousin Marnie was the shadow of someone who was quite extraordinary.

My mother with the white cloth in her fingers had looked at Marnie and then tilted her chin in a slight nod.

Very good, she had said.

Now she drew me onto her lap, something she seldom did when she was fully dressed, wanting to keep my sticky child hands as far away from her beautiful clothes as possible. But that day, the day we were putting my grandmother into a pine box and lowering her into the ground, she let me sit on her slippery silk slip and press my ear into her breast where I could hear her heart beat, clattering to let me know that she was alive.

Mama, I said. Another word for love.

I reached up to touch the gold oval pendant of Guadalupe which she always wore on a chain low enough so that the pendent slipped between the valley of her breasts, keeping her faith hidden and close to her.

I need to tell you something, I said. Obligingly, she lowered her ear to my mouth and I whispered to her, I'm not upset Bubbe's dead.

My mother sighed. She lifted her head and dropped the point of her chin onto my crown, letting the weight of her head rest on mine. It hurt, but I didn't want to tell her. I wanted her to make me feel better about not feeling bad.

But she didn't.

It doesn't matter, Almita. One day you'll be as old as I am and you won't even remember this conversation.

I'll remember everything, I said petulantly. I really thought I could. Time was still a confusing concept to me, stretching out infinitely long. I remembered so much of what had happened in the past. It was forgetting that seemed a foreign concept.

Never tell anyone what you told me, my mother said.

She slipped me off her lap and while I tried to resist, tangling my fingers in the chain of her necklace, the silkiness of her slip was too much and I was sloughed off, my feet on the floor, my arms bereft of her, before I really understood what was happening.

Like a secret?

But my mother wasn't tricked by this. She knew that at that age I was so excited by secrets that I spilled them in every direction at everyone who came near me whether they asked about them or, more often, did not. The mailman, for instance, knew that my mother's hair was mostly grey and she had to have it dyed to maintain that glossy black.

Not a secret, my mother said carefully. Just tact.

I was feeling quite well about myself as I descended the stairs of our home and saw aunt Eshkie wearing a dingy black suit that was not really black but off-black, the kind of faded black that comes from washing a fabric too many times. Aunt Eshkie was pacing at the bottom of the stairs and biting at a fingernail, something I had been trained out of.

My mother, after saying the word *tact*, had had to explain what, exactly, tact was. My vague understanding was that tact was withholding information from people who were too delicate to understand hard truths.

Normally I was the one who was too delicate to understand things. Whenever something was too complicated to explain, like why some people starved and I never would, my parents would tell me I would understand when I was older. Marnie made a habit of teasing me for my stupidity, my inability to understand cursive or read the big books in the family library. Being the tactful one, the one who understood a truth and kept it coiled carefully in the folds of my brain, made me feel smugly superior.

I was superior to my father who was rattled by my grandmother's death. I was superior to aunt Eshkie who, like my father, had lately been possessed by a grief that made her memory fog. Days earlier, after one of aunt Eshkie's visits, Marnie had opened the fridge to pour me a glass of milk and had found, outside its native habitat, a gently cooling stapler perched atop an egg carton. Marnie had placed the stapler with a thunk down on the kitchen table and we had contemplated it as we ate cookies which, under normal circumstances, we would not have been able to eat so liberally.

Remembering that she was losing her mind, I greeted aunt Eshkie with my most charitable smile.

Hello aunt Eshkie, I said. Are you looking forward to burying Bubbe today?

Even being an adult, and knowing what I know now about grief and loss, I find it hard to understand what Eshkie did next and completely impossible to let go of my own personal resentment to approach anything like forgiveness.

WHAT AUNT ESHKIE DID

WAS GRAB HOLD of my child's elbow and drag me off the steps where I went sailing through the air, light enough to be guided into a swirling flight that propelled me off the upper steps, heavy enough so that gravity disappointingly ended my twirl in a crash and I smashed clumsily onto the carpeted floor. By some miracle I landed like a cat, on my feet. I had avoided being broken. Intact I survived to be dragged again, to the kitchen, at this point squirming with my child's might against the bruising grip of her bony fingers into my fleshy arm. By this point I knew she had evil intentions, but I was only able to do so much, no part of me a match for an adult woman.

In the kitchen the Marnies and uncle Bobby, all dressed for the funeral, were sitting waiting for the rest of us. Their eyes widened in shock to see aunt Eshkie (snarling) and me (squealing as I tried to wriggle free).

At this point uncle Bobby should have intervened, separated wife from niece and tried to rescue the situation. Instead he gaped like a fish as he tried to work out what was happening, giving aunt Eshkie, one claw still holding me in place, time to reach the other claw into the drawer where we kept the kitchen scissors (for cutting string, unwieldy packaging, and the tips of milk bags). Everyone in the kitchen, including myself, let out a gasp as she brandished the scissors. I had been told enough Nazi stories to know that truly crazed people don't mind hurting little children. Was aunt Eshkie angry enough to stab the hitherto innocent kitchen scissors through my chest into my beating heart, stilling it forever?

She was not.

The closer the scissors got to me the more aunt Eshkie slowed down. She adjusted her grip, letting go of my arm to grab me by the dress and then, wielding the scissors, took a vicious snip into my white sleeve. Then she dropped the scissors, wedged her hands into the cut she had made, and proceeded to rip it further, rending the fabric so that the right side sleeve of my dress was torn from cuff to seam. It was unmendable.

I think everyone in the kitchen was so relieved that aunt Eshkie hadn't murdered me that there was, at first, a sense of calm. I was aware that previously everyone had been screaming and shouting and arguing only because it was now quiet enough that I could hear my own breath coming in short huffy bursts.

Uncle Bobby and the Marnies pushed their way past aunt Eshkie and formed a semicircle around me, assessing the rent. Marnie lifted one flap of my sleeve and rubbed the fabric between her fingers.

Aunt Eshkie was the one to break the silence.

Almita, aunt Eshkie said, I may have lost my temper a little.

She never called me Almita and the Spanish diminutive sounded wrong in her anglo accent. In that moment I could see she was a small woman. Not just small of stature but small of spirit. A weak, pathetic bully who had taken out her anger on a child. Her face was turning red from the humiliation of being exposed this way and she was already pasting on a smile, trying to act as if nothing had happened.

Marnie (my sister) was the first to react.

She turned away from me and towards aunt Eshkie, her shoulders squared. She had the dignity of a woman, the dignity of my mother, as she walked up to aunt Eshkie and, with no warning, clawed her in the face.

Aunt Eshkie screamed.

She moved away from Marnie and covered her face and when, for a moment, her hands came away I could see there were shaky red scratch marks all down her forehead and cheeks. Marnie hadn't quite drawn blood but it was impressive nevertheless. It may sound strange but I had never realized before that Marnie loved me. That she, with her teasing and her pinching and her bullying, would move to protect me if someone else took the liberties against me which she took every day.

I had never loved her more.

Marnie (cousin) began to cry.

My Marnie went back a second time, grabbing aunt Eshkie by the wrist and trying to pull her hands away from her face so she could get at her again.

Uncle Bobby, choosing this moment to become effectual, walked over to Marnie and pried her off his wife, lifting her up by her waist. Propelled by rage and now lifted a good foot off the ground, Marnie started kicking her legs into aunt Eshkie's stomach, succeeding in getting in at least one kick hard enough to knock the wind out of Eshkie and causing her to double up onto the floor. The backing soundtrack to all this was a stream of curse words which were coming from both aunt Eshkie and Marnie and which up until that moment I had never heard before in my life. My parents had succeeded in convincing me that to tell someone to shut up was the vilest thing that could be said to another human. Now my little ears were awakening to a whole new world.

At this moment my father came in, misty eyed as usual, and took in the disaster that was his family. His sister on the floor clutching at her face, his beautiful and dignified daughter now red-faced and spitting foul language like nails, his other daughter wailing in a long unending wall of noise (at some point I had started and simply kept going). The adults in this situation were clearly incompetent. My father turned to (cousin) Marnie and she, white-faced and frizzy-haired, pointed a finger at her own mother and said, It's all Mummy's fault. She cut Alma's dress.

I had never realized Marnie (my cousin) could be so just. I had never loved *her* more.

My father might have, at this point, restored calm and rescued the day, only this was now the moment that my mother made her own entrance.

Black was not her colour. She usually favoured the rich jewel tones which she had told me looked so inviting on our warm skin. But even in the black of mourning, a true black, an all-encompassing colour which made her look sickly, she was dazzling.

She had arrived in a black skirt and black pumps and a black knit sweater over which lay a simple gold chain, her Guadalupe nowhere to be seen. She was ready to grieve.

Instead she saw me (distressed, ravaged). She saw Marnie (still in the grips of our uncle). My dress was ripped. Marnie's careful braids, which at my arrival had been neat and tidy, now had wisps of blonde escaping, giving her a frizzy haloed effect.

My mother was, in many ways, not a perfect woman, but the primal way in which she descended into absolute violence, no explanation required, was something close to perfection. She grabbed my uncle by the hair (well, what little of it he had left) and pulled him down to her level. She was at this point letting loose in English and Spanish, a total linguistic loss of control I had never seen before.

Everyone started screaming and fighting and pinching and pulling all over again.

It was chaos.

And I simply chose to evade it.

THE FIRST DISAPPEARANCE

ALL FAMILIES HAVE their own private jokes. They also have their own private myths and lore. In my family the joke is that I have a habit of vanishing. The joke originated from the day of my grandmother's funeral when I disappeared for approximately three hours and sixteen minutes, plunging the entire family into chaos and forcing a delay in the ceremony.

For years I didn't tell anyone where I went, not even Marnie. This was because when I came back I was so resentful over what had happened to my dress that I didn't want to tell them. Then, in an act that only inflated my sense of importance, my family began deliberately not to talk about it when they talked about my bubbe's funeral. They would give me glances out of the corner of their eyes and then quickly look away when I caught them peeping. This was a mistake too. It made me feel like the secret of where I had been made me important. I felt as though I had an eerie and uncanny aura about me. I felt like a girl in a fairy tale who had ventured out in the woods and come back changed. And even though I was very much the same, my family could never be sure I was actually still myself, Alma Alt, sister, daughter, cousin, niece, or whether I was a changeling only pretending to be Alma (Alma Alternate), waiting patiently until an inopportune moment when I could finally reveal my truest self.

Later, I realized that no one thought of me as eerie at all.

They thought, as was logical to assume, that a stranger had molested me.

They were just waiting for me to reveal it in my own time. I realized this finally when I was an awkward, lumpy tween. But to admit to my previous pretensions would have been as devastating to me as a revelation that I had been molested would have been to my parents. And later still when I was an adult and finally tried to tell them the truth—well, by that point no one believed me.

Who would hold on to nothing for so long?

A PORTAL TO THE UNKNOWN

ACCORDING TO EVERYONE in the kitchen (mother, father, sister, aunt, uncle, cousin) who were all interviewed in a messy clump by the police, I had run through the kitchen, down the hallway, and slipped through the front door. This mass interview was a fatal flaw in their detective work. If something had happened to me and I had become one of those little girls on the news (though, let's be real, I wasn't a blonde white girl and would never have made it onto the news) THIS jumble of interviews would have been the moment when the investigation, like a Dalí clock, slipped out of shape.

Cousin Marnie was the first to notice my flight and went running after me. When she went through the front door she expected to immediately see me and be able to call me back inside. When she didn't, she thought she had been mistaken, turned back, and began to search the rest of the house.

After failing to find me, (cousin) Marnie returned to the living room. The physical violence had, for the most part, abated at this point. The men were sitting silently (uselessly) while their wives continued to snipe at each other, panting from chairs situated at opposite ends of the kitchen. Marnie sat in our mother's lap and wrapped her long child arms protectively around her, punctuating each point our mother made with a nod of her head.

Everyone claimed that cousin Marnie was not to blame for what she did next. But because of this one decision, in years to come my mother would sigh at everything she did and say, You know, your cousin Marnie isn't very smart.

What cousin Marnie did was sit down on her father's lap, and in imitation of my Marnie, put her arms around him and listen to the argument.

Minutes, the import of which the family failed to appreciate, passed, each more precious than the last.

Eventually enough time had passed that though everyone was still angry it became necessary to temporarily set aside what had happened and act as a family so they could bury my grandmother who, God forgive us, was at least no longer alive to see her own daughter act like an *animal* towards her beloved youngest grandchild.

The bickering started again.

It occurred to my mother that I would now have to wear my navy play dress to the funeral. It was not as smart as the white dress, which conveyed purity and served to make my skin look bronzed and healthy, but it fit me well and was respectable as a second choice. It occurred to my mother to change me. It occurred to my mother I was not there to change.

She began to look for me. I could not be found. My father and Marnie joined in the search. Still I could not be found. Uncle Bobby joined in. Fear began to creep into the thoughts of everyone present. At this point cousin Marnie tugged on uncle Bobby's sleeve and whispered in his ear that she had already searched the house and she was sure that I wasn't in it.

Everyone was convinced they had seen me run down the hallway towards the front door. Now they became convinced I had walked through it.

The adults went round the block and then the neighbourhood in increasingly wide loops.

The Marnies stayed behind and held each other and cried.

The adults met up at home, absent one Alma.

My father threw up.

The police were called.

In an act of penance, which still did not negate all that she had done, aunt Eshkie, aware that my father was a wreck and that she would be taken more seriously by the police than my accented mother, handled everything.

WHAT ACTUALLY HAPPENED

THE ABSOLUTE FROTH of adults kicking and screaming each other blocked me from the hallway, and the front entrance. They were an unpredictable mass and I was, even then, aware of how tiny I was, how easily my body bent to external pressure and manipulation. Even Marnie (my sister), who was not quite adult-sized, could (and sometimes did) pick me up by the ankles and turn me upside down, threatening to drop me on my head when she was annoyed. And hadn't I just had proof that aunt Eshkie was more than willing to injure me according to her own wicked desires?

So no, the entrance that led to the hallway from the kitchen and then out to the front door was barred to me.

However there were multiple doors in the kitchen. One led to the basement, a dead end they surely would have immediately checked. The others were a set of glass-panelled French doors that led to the back garden.

These doors were very beautiful and filled with a particular kind of bubbled glass which dappled the light. Even though they were impractical, letting the cold bleed inside in the winter and roasting us alive in the summer, and even though my parents were always threatening to replace them with more functional sliding doors, they were too beautiful to be rid of. They were worth their daily inconveniences for the pleasure they gave our family whenever we were in the kitchen.

They were made of a not very thick varnished wood, and though a century of handling had worn them down it was still possible to see the pattern of flowers and unfurling leaves embedded in the original brass handles.

They were tricky, these doors, they often dragged on the floor when opened, and the knobs would sometimes turn and turn uselessly, the latch refusing to catch so that the doors would refuse to lock or unlock as the case may be.

The knobs were also smaller than a standard knob and set very low on the door so that adults always found them difficult to handle. It gave the impression that the original occupants of the house were child-sized.

I believed that the doors had been created for me, as if the craftspeople who made them, long dead, with names washed away by time, had known that one day in a moment of desperation I would need to use them to escape the madness of my family and had fitted them with this idea in mind.

It was all over in an instant. One second I was in the kitchen with the anger and the flailing limbs, and the next I was on the patio.

The knobs had turned for me, the lock had unlocked, and for once the door had opened and shut as smoothly as if it were new.

Behind the bubbled glass my family were mere outlines of people. It was amazing how little noise passed through the door, how quickly the sounds of the world, of wind, birds chirping, leaves rustling, my own panting breath, drowned out their angry voices.

I floated mournfully down the steps of the patio into the garden proper.

I could feel the cool of the air hitting my arm on the side where my sleeve was in tatters. The sensation triggered a fresh round of crying.

Although I had not wanted the dress at first, I had been so hopeful when Marnie put it on me that morning. She had braided my curls into neat plaits and tied the sash of the dress in a voluptuous bow and I had imagined that I was, if not as beautiful as Marnie, imbued with the kind of beauty that all newness brought, like fresh untrammelled snow glittering on the sidewalk. But now I was like the dirty grey slush after the snow had been salted and everyone had dragged their boots through it. I was wrecked. I wanted to be more wrecked. I wanted to be low.

I followed that instinct by going as low as I could. I threw myself on the grass and when that wasn't enough I went to the edge of the garden where persistent and mysterious bushes grew near the fence. There was almost enough space among the branches for a little girl and I slid in amongst them. When I had situated myself with my front pressed into the dirt, the cool smell of earth invading my nostrils, a branch poking my hip and others tangling in my hair, I began to wail.

The wailing I did for two reasons. The first being that it felt good and the second being that I wanted to be found and petted and comforted. I had visions of someone, preferably my father because I knew my mother simply *wouldn't*, crouching outside the bush and taming me slowly, until I came to settle in his lap, like a cat. Perhaps food would be involved as he coaxed me out, one hand extended, offering a treat. Perhaps he would promise me a new dress and I could go back and get the pink one. Perhaps, and here the fantasies in my head began to spin out of control and my little heart beat ever quicker from the sheer lust of the thought, perhaps they would buy me two dresses, a white one to replace the one that aunt Eshkie had ruined and the pink one. The white dress would certainly need replacing now. It was covered in green grass stains and all sorts of dirt and when I tried to rub the marks off I only succeeded in rubbing them in. Now I was as guilty as aunt Eshkie of being bad and destroying the dress. I wailed some more, really pouring my heart into it.

At first the wailing was organic and I was simply obeying the pain which came in waves when I thought of aunt Eshkie, the rip, the stains. But slowly, without wanting to, I began to calm down on my own, my sobs turning into little hiccups, the pain in my heart dulling. Gradually it became difficult to scream. I had to push myself to do so. It became a performance. A performance I was acting out for myself alone because very quickly it became apparent there was no one observing me but me.

Through the bushes I looked towards the house. It seemed unoccupied—at least there were no longer any angry shapes visible through the kitchen doors—and it occurred to me that maybe they had forgotten about me and gone to the funeral.

This triggered a fresh round of sincere crying. I could not believe that, aunt Eshkie aside, they had all abandoned me.

I would have to become a feral child now and live in the bushes and eat the little red berries that my father always warned me not to eat because they were poisonous. I would have no one for company but the pampered fluffy cats of the Glebe, who sat on porch steps and occasionally moseyed out to the sidewalk to be worshipped by passersby. None of this appealed to me at all.

The way some cats are indoor cats, I was very much an indoor child. I was timid and easily tired and, as Marnie enjoyed reminding me, not very mature for a five-year-old. I couldn't braid my own hair or tie bows as well as Marnie. I had yet to master drawing necks on humans; in art class all of my smiling figures had roundish heads placed directly atop squared shoulders in a way I knew was wrong but couldn't fix. Even though I proudly told my mother I had stopped I still secretly sucked my thumb at night and was pleased each time I was able to transgress this way without her noticing.

Thumb-sucking was a secret nighttime habit, but having realized that I was to become a garden urchin I decided to reward myself with a daytime suck. I was just starting to slow my cries, readying myself to stuff my thumb into my mouth, when I heard a voice asking me if I was alright.

It wasn't just asking in a general way either. It was asking after me, Alma, the crying child in the bushes, specifically.

Alma, the voice said again. Are you alright?

The voice, I realized, had been asking me this for a while.

This meant that the voice had been watching me possibly from the moment I first flung myself on the grass and crawled into the bushes. The shame of knowing that someone had been watching as I threw a tantrum, the shame of knowing I had been such a poor representative of the Alt family (even though it was unclear whether I was still a member of the Alt family) was so humiliating that my tears dried up and my wails petered off into a noisy sigh.

The voice, I came to see, was attached to a person. I could only see this person in fragments, as they could only see me in fragments, the both of us doing our best to stare at each other through gaps in the shadowbox fence that separated my backyard from them.

But I could see enough: a freckled nose, an ear too pink for the porcelain of its face, a blue eye. These fragments made up Oliver Jentsch.

I couldn't recall how I had met Oliver, the same way I couldn't remember when I had begun to live in our house on Linden Terrace. He simply existed. Sometimes when I looked out the big window in Marnie's room in the summer I could see him playing in his backyard which bordered our backyard. Sometimes I saw him in the big-kids' playground at school which was separated from the little-kids' schoolyard by a black iron wrought fence.

He was the same age as Marnie but, in the way that was true of all of Marnie's peers, he had always been much nicer to me than she was. He said hello to me when he saw me. He had once tied my shoe when my lace had come undone. My parents had bought us a huge beach ball to play with in the backyard and one summer when Marnie had accidentally spiked it over the fence, Oliver, by some miracle of timing, had immediately sent it sailing back. They got the idea of playing volleyball that way, or rather their version of volleyball which was to deliberately pass the ball back and forth for as many rallies as they could without it ever hitting the ground. Oliver had tried to let me join in the play, occasionally lobbing the ball gently in the direction of my voice. Most of the time the ball simply plopped to the ground in front of me and the few times I did manage to smack it back into the air I could never get it over the fence.

But Marnie and Oliver rallied back and forth between them for what seemed like hours, ignoring the sticky sweat of summer in favour of the joy of competition. They played long past the point when I gave up and sprawled under a tree. I watched Marnie running back and forth, her face flushed red with heat and a burgeoning sunburn, and listened to Oliver's voice counting back to us. They played until they achieved a perfect synchronicity between them, and remained undefeated until our mother called Marnie and me back inside and Marnie caught the ball neatly in her hands.

Goodbye, Marnie, he had said.

Goodbye, little Alt.

Even then he hadn't forgotten me.

I'm sad, I told Oliver through the fence.

I never would have guessed, he said. He made a sad face back at me, pulling his mouth down in an exaggerated frown like a clown. It didn't feel mocking though. It felt sympathetic. At first I didn't realize it was you, he continued. I thought you were an animal.

I was excited by this because I had felt like an animal when I was crying and I was charmed by the prospect that Oliver had felt this too.

What kind of animal?

I was hoping for something magical like a unicorn, but Oliver told me he thought I was an injured dog, keening in the bushes, before he had pressed his face against the fence and found that the type of animal I was was girl.

As he was talking he tried to poke his fingers through one of the slats. I reached through and brushed them. It was nice, being there like that, the soft skin of his fingertips worth reaching for even if it meant pressing myself against the wooden slats of the fence and tangling further in the pokey underbrush.

Don't you want to go back inside? Oliver said. Maybe Marnie can help you be less sad.

He clearly didn't know anything about sisters.

No, I don't think so, I sniffled. I never want to go back. I hate my family. I'm going to stay here forever.

Forever is a long time, Oliver said. While you're thinking about it why don't you come over to my backyard?

I can't climb the fence.

There's a secret hole over there, he said pointing. You can't see it from your side because of all the shrubs but on this side you can see there's a huge chunk missing. The wood's rotted away. I think it will just about fit you.

I had to crawl out from where I was and then crawl back under a new set of bushes to find the hole in the fence. Even with Oliver's voice guiding me it took awhile to find. This was time in which anyone from the house, coming into the yard, could have found me, reached for me, brought me back home. But no one did.

Instead I was left with enough time to find the gap in the fence, the gap that should not have been there because if my parents had noticed it they would have fixed it immediately, my mother being house-proud, my father being orderly.

It was just the bottom of one board rotted away, just a little gap where a boy was able to stick his arm through and beckon to a little girl, a little girl who was, with a little wriggling and only one tear, able to fit her whole body through the gap and tumble from her home into another's.

My parents loved their backyard; they had a contract with a landscaper who planted lavender for the bees and tulips just for us. My mother liked to barbecue and throw parties and sit in the back, baking in the sun with a drink in one hand and a book in the other. Every year there was a discussion as to whether a pool that we could use for only three months of the year was worth it though every year my parents always decided it wasn't. A year ago they had finally promised Marnie and me that soon they would build the tree house we both so desperately desired. But Oliver's backyard wasn't like ours at all.

The earth was sandy and hard, the kind of crumbly stuff from which nothing could grow; if there had ever been grass it had dried up and died.

Instead of plants there were some toys and broken plastic buckets and sharp metallic half-rusted pieces of metal strewn about. There was a radiator leaning atilt against the side of the house, its rust turning a patch of the building the same rust colour.

There was, also, to my undying envy, a swing set with metal chains that squeaked noisily as they were pushed about by the breeze and a sort of dilapidated shed with a charming door half open. It was not quite a tree house, but it was more than what I had in my yard.

This, I thought, was where I could live out the rest of my feral days. It was just large enough to hold one Alma and, my head full of visions of living, cozy and catlike, in this one-room wooden structure, I started towards it only to be gently tugged away by Oliver.

Hey, he said.

Instead of leaning down to my height the way adults I didn't like did, he put an arm around me and brought me close to him.

Do you want to see something cool?

I *did* want to see something cool. I made a whimper of assent, my eyes darting to the shed, my future home. But this wasn't what Oliver wanted to show me. He took my hand gently in his and tugged me along and I, used to a lifetime of obedience and being tugged, this way and that, by people twice my size, followed him.

We went up a set of cracked stone steps that led to the back door of the house.

The first thing I noticed was the smell.

We loved old movies in our home. We watched black-and-white films where men with strong jaws and women wearing fox furs endlessly lit each other's cigarettes and slowly exhaled smoky ribbons back and forth. So I knew, theoretically, what a cigarette was. But neither of my parents smoked and I had never been in the presence of a cigarette.

The air in Oliver's home tasted ashy.

It was more than my little body could take. My eyes watered; my lungs burned. I began to gag, choking on the taste of the air, and Oliver thumped me on the back. The backyard door had led directly into the kitchen and he sat me, still coughing, down at the kitchen table where it took everything I had not to run back out the way we had come. I hoped he would open a window but instead he poured me a glass of water from the tap and then rubbed me soothingly on the back, his hands making circular motions as I choked it down. I finished what I could of the water and tried not to breathe through my nostrils and when Oliver asked me if I was better I nodded. He had been so kind to me, I didn't want to disappoint him. And he had promised me something cool.

Again, my hand was taken into his and he led me patiently further into that smoky house. In some ways, I remember, it was so much emptier than our own house. Ours was a home which was always filled with Mother and Father and Marnie and me, all of us collectively living on top of and around and in front and back of each other. At Oliver's there didn't seem to be anyone aside from him and me inside of it. It was so quiet it almost felt as though the house was stuffed up with silence and we were invading it. And at the same time there were so many more *things* in the house itself. It overwhelmed.

There was nowhere for my eye to alight: I couldn't have picked out any pieces of furniture because if they were there they were obscured. There were boxes stacked precariously on top of one another and half-torn-apart microwaves and radios vomiting their metal parts out in little heaps. Piles of books cluttered half the steps of the staircase we ascended.

A door was half opened to reveal a room filled with stacks of what looked like binders.

And then of course there was the smoke, which was worse on the second floor. This far up it seemed to have a shape. I almost felt that if I reached out I could touch it.

Oliver brought me inside another room which, to my relief, had a large window that was propped open. And though it didn't feel much better than the rest of that ashy house, the curtains fluttering with the breeze promised fresh air and I began to try to breathe real lungfuls of breath instead of inhaling shallowly through my mouth.

Though the room was full of things—an unmade bed, a battered wooden desk with scratches both intentional and accidental, a chair piled with clothes, shelves with books and plaques mixed in among them—it was less crowded than the rest of the house. It had not been stretched beyond proportion. I could still tell it was a boy's room. I could tell it was Oliver's.

The room also felt less empty than the rest of the house. There was the sense that its disorder came from life and not abandonment. And a beat was running through it, steady and comforting as the pitter-patter of rain.

I began to look for the source of the noise and saw, sitting on Oliver's nightstand—beside a lamp, a baseball glove, and an open copy of *A Wrinkle in Time*—a wooden hand cut off at the wrist, with flexible joints so that the fingers could articulate. Every second the fingers of the hand would drum, lifting and then hitting the surface of the nightstand one at a time. Then they would pause for a moment as if in rest before beginning to drum again and again.

Oliver saw where I was looking.

You like this?

He picked it up and brought it over to me. The sound of the drumming went away but the fingers kept moving, gracefully wheeling over and over again in the air.

It's a perpetual motion machine, Oliver said. My mother makes these.

He offered it to me to hold but I flinched away.

Up close there was something frightening about it. It reminded me of mannequins in stores, the way that even with their dull painted-on faces and the plastic shine of their limbs there was just enough suggestion of life that I believed if I turned away from them they might strangle me.

For a second I felt a deep disappointment that this was the thing Oliver had brought me inside to see. I would, I realized, have to pretend to like it to appease him, so that he would still be my friend and maybe leave dishes of milk and small parcels of food scraps outside my door in the shed.

But I had underestimated him.

He saw I didn't like the hand and he opened the drawer of the nightstand and tossed it inside. And then, because it was still beating its fingers against the drawer, as if it wanted to get out, he opened up the drawer again, wrapped the hand in a sweater to mute the sound, and threw the makeshift bundle in his closet.

I always forget what a noisy bother it is, Oliver said, smiling at me.

The hand wasn't what Oliver wanted to show me. What he wanted to show me was a small personal computer set up on his desk. We didn't have one at home yet, though my parents had one at the accounting office. I had seen it when my father unboxed it and let me run my hands over the keys on the keyboard and look at my own reflection in the black of the screen. The Marnies had also been there and he had told us that this thing was the future and one day we would learn to wield it with ease. He sometimes let the Marnies type out their assignments on the computer. Though I didn't know how to write very well I had tried to imitate the clacking of fingers on keys, my fat fingers unable to move quickly enough, so that my version of text was just strings of *A*s and *L*s and whatever other letters I was typing.

I couldn't see how that machine could be the future. I hadn't been impressed with it then and I wasn't impressed now when Oliver showed me his version of the same machine, similarly bulky and black and mute.

I've played with one of these before, I said.

Ah, of course, the little expert.

Oliver took my finger in his hand and leaned forward and we pressed the start button together. We watched ourselves in the black of the screen till the machine flickered to life and we disappeared from view.

I was already somewhat charmed by this but then Oliver took a disk of hard square plastic and handed it to me.

Can you help me put this in?

He helped me guide the disk into a slot I hadn't noticed that made a hard clicking noise when the disk was fully inserted, and a little blue button I hadn't noticed popped out, like a turtle sticking its neck out of a shell.

Oliver pulled me onto his lap. His knees were bony, and I settled against his chest.

Now watch the screen, Alma, he said.

It was unnecessary. I was already watching the screen.

I felt myself stiffen in his arms and cry out in surprise as a little pixelated car appeared.

I was still at the stage where I had to sound out letters until they became words, the meaning becoming apparent on a delay which is why I was grateful when Oliver said the name of the game for me.

SkyRoads.

We'll play together, he said.

In the game a little car had to travel along a series of blocks that were laid out in a path, floating freely in the sky. The car was manipulated with the arrow keys and was able to move left and right and jump up. The further you advanced in the game the more difficult the roads became, with large gaps and holes and tunnels. Perhaps this doesn't sound impressive now, but to my five-year-old eyes it was the most amazing thing I had ever seen in my life. I watched Oliver play with relentless skill, the skill of a maestro, and when he finally died, his car sliding off the curved dome of a roof before tumbling into oblivion, he did something Marnie would never have let me done. He let me play.

I was terrible at *SkyRoads*. Even after Oliver explained the rules to me slowly, even after he demonstrated for me, I was always too excited when I took control, mashing the keys too quickly, flames celebrating my demise every time I accelerated into a wall. Oliver was patient with my failures. He was unwilling to accept that I was years away from gaining the hand-eye coordination to master the game. He let me try again and again. He wasn't willing to give up on me.

In the end I gave up on myself.

When, in my frustration, I became perilously near tantrum, he switched tactics. He took over the controls again but asked me to put my hands over his as he manipulated the keys.

Good job, Alma, he would say every time he ascended to another level. And though I knew that I wasn't really the one making the car fly through the pixelated air I really did believe that, on a profound and most importantly *true* level, I was helping.

Oliver was very good at the game and we played like that for a very long time.

Perhaps we would have stayed like that forever, safe, entranced, outside of time, if another strange voice, my second that day, hadn't interrupted us.

What is that? the voice said.

That being me.

Though Oliver was a familiar body to me his mother, Mrs. Jentsch, wasn't.

She was terrifying in the way that my mother was terrifying to other children—my mother who loved Marnie and me, but loved us sternly, treating us as fussy, delicate, and sometimes annoying pets that needed to be toughened up. But that *was* warmth from my mother. I saw the way she treated other children as hostile, her lip curling up into a grimace instead of a smile every time someone dumped their baby into her arms, the way she was always rolling her eyes at other people's children, never impressed by the markers of success, the fact that they knew how to spell their own names, or were potty-trained, or could skip.

Oliver's mother was like that. I recognized her as a woman who would not instinctually bend to talk to children, lower her voice into a singsong secret, tease, caress, or care about me.

Is that the neighbour girl? she asked.

She took out a cigarette from a pocket and lit it and began smoking, in front of me, undeterred by the cough I immediately let out.

The police came and knocked on the door looking for her. They think she's been kidnapped. I told them I didn't know anything and now this—

She gestured at me like I was a crime.

I could feel Oliver's arms tightening around me, a panicked squeeze, not a comforting embrace.

I just found her— Oliver began.

But whatever Oliver's explanations or excuses were didn't seem to matter.

His mother cut him off with a look. She took another drag from the cigarette. Alright then, she said and gestured for me to get down from his lap.

After a moment's hesitation she held out her hand to me and I took it, though we both seemed reluctant to touch each other, she because I was a grimy little child, I because I was afraid her dislike of me would translate into physical roughness, a pulling of my self that I couldn't abide after that day's tussle with aunt Eshkie.

But she was not a violent person. She was brisk as she guided me, but she never dragged or pulled me and when, on the stairs, I hesitated over a large pile of books she waited patiently for me to find my way around them.

She led me to the front door, allowed me to walk through it alone, and then said, You know your way home don't you?

I did actually. Though I was disoriented from walking out the front when I had entered through the back I knew I had only to follow the rectangular contours of the city block we were located on and eventually I would wind my way to my house. But even if I hadn't known, the rush of euphoria I felt upon exiting the house and smelling Clean! Air! I would have said anything to get away from the smoke.

Yes, ma'am, Mrs. Jentsch, I said.

Well go on then, she said.

I tottered down the front walkway and then began to skip, elated at going home knowing they had missed me after all. I would not have to be a street child. I did not spare a backwards glance at that massive house, which had seemed so small and cramped from the inside. It was already a part of my past, forgotten in my joy.

DISCOVERY

UNLIKE MARNIE I was not old enough to have a key to my own home. I did know where the spare key was kept (inside a little box tucked inside the mailbox), but even though I had had this secret carefully pointed out to me by both my parents neither one of them had ever realized a crucial fact that made this information useless to me: I was still too short, even on my tiptoes with my arm extended and my little fingers grasping, to reach the inside.

So when I returned home to Linden Terrace, filthy from my adventures but becalmed from watching Oliver conquer *SkyRoads*, I had to ring the doorbell to my own home and wait to be let in.

The man who answered the door was completely unknown to me.

For one wonderful instant I believed in the possibility that the hole in the fence I had crawled through had brought me into a sideways world. A world which looked just like the one I was from but which was otherwise completely different. Perhaps in this world my parents had stayed in Toronto and this strange old man with the grey beard and the kippah was now the occupant of the house. I was very excited by this possibility.

But the man seemed familiar with me, or at least the concept of me.

Alma? he asked and when I nodded he bent down and picked me up, cradling me high up against his chest so that I was able to wind my arms around his neck.

He took me into the living room where everyone was gathered, along with a police officer. The strange man, who turned out to be the cantor who was there for my grandmother's funeral, surrendered me into the arms of my parents, and they wrapped me in a hug between them, pressing together so hard my bones hurt and gathering Marnie up into the hug, her hand resting on my little Mary Jane–encased hoof.

No one chastised me about my dress, or my general condition of filth. They seemed in all quite happy to see me and I was petted and kissed repeatedly.

Where were you? they wanted to know.

Playing, I said, because it was true. I was so pleased with the attention that I couldn't find the words to explain *SkyRoads* and how much I wanted them to buy it so that when I visited their office, instead of playing with paper clips and calculators and building little towers out of the single-use creamer cups, I could make cars fly through the sky.

But telling them the truth was the wrong move. It transformed the relief that my deliverance had brought into anger.

While they had been suffering (We thought you were dead, sister Marnie whispered) I had been enjoying myself, playing for hours.

And didn't we tell you never ever to cross the street when you're by yourself? What were you thinking, Alma? How could you be so irresponsible?

The smiles were sliding off the faces of the police officer and the cantor. Even traitorous aunt Eshkie had the good sense to look discomfited.

Weren't we all supposed to be happy? Wasn't my arrival—touched perhaps, but generally unharmed—supposed to signify a kind of triumph of life, unlike the alternative where I was dead in a ditch somewhere? But no. We were not happy. It became clear to everyone that my parents were not satisfied with my continued life. I was the wayward child who had profited while they were in misery and they would punish me, if only with a crushing sense of guilt.

Both my parents, I could tell, wanted more than anything to boot out the police officer, boot out the cantor, and hold me tight to their chests for the miracle of still being alive while yelling at me for my thoughtlessness. Unfortunately for them however there were still, delayed as they might be, respects to be paid to the dead.

On account of the exhausting day I had had (but really because I was filthy from top to toe and there was no time to wash me) I was allowed to stay at home. An adult needed to be left behind to care for me and though it was obvious from the start it would be uncle Bobby there was much discussion and delay before my parents accepted that he would.

He was an alright man, uncle Bobby. Even if he was married to aunt Eshkie. His weakness was in his overly deferential nature, a willingness to shirk responsibility that led him to defer to me even though I was clearly the child in our relationship. When I told him I didn't want to take a bath he didn't make me and when I told him I wasn't tired and didn't want to go to sleep he allowed me to sit in the kitchen in my pyjamas and scooped ice cream out into my favourite bowl, the one with Peter Rabbit running round the rim of the porcelain.

As I licked happily at the ice cream, my mind already working on how best I could persuade uncle Bobby to provide me with a bonus scoop, he tried to talk seriously with me.

You know I love you very much, Alma. You know your aunt would never really hurt you and she's sorry she made you cry?

We both knew she wasn't.

There had been yelling and fighting and my arm still ached. There had been smoke and also *SkyRoads*. The ripping of the dress seemed so far away.

He had my no-longer-white dress in his hands.

It would end up in the trash at some point, but for now it was still mine.

He picked me up and sat me down and pointed at the rip.

Do you know what this is?

A rip, I said.

Not just a rip. It's what we do at funerals, uncle Bobby said. The rabbi or in this case the cantor comes and rips your clothes because when someone dies you are never whole again, not the same way.

Do you have one?

No, Alma, it's only for direct descendants and ascendants. Like you. Like your aunt Eshkie.

Did the cantor do it to Daddy?

Yes.

And Mama?

No, she's not . . . It's a different relationship. But he did it for Edith and the Marnies.

Aunt Eshkie didn't tell me it was for a purpose, I pouted.

Well, Edith wasn't supposed to do it to you. The rabbi is. And besides, you're really too young. You'll understand when you're older, uncle Bobby said.

That phrase. When I was older I would understand. When I was older the understanding would corrupt me so that I would be a completely different person and betray the child I had been and none of my current opinions would hold.

But I already did understand. The dress had been something joyous and new; it had had the potential to turn me into a beautiful better person perhaps like (my) Marnie. And instead it had been ruined, first by aunt Eshkie and then by my own actions. There was nothing in this world that could be kept safe and pure. There was rot and death around every corner. Everything was always changing and only for the worse. And I would not only never see my bubbe again, I had been robbed of the catharsis of seeing her put into the ground.

Ice cream was one of the treats my grandmother and I got when we were good for my mother and now I was here, without my bubbe, eating it alone and she would never have ice cream again, never sit beside me and show me her empty bowl, every scrap eaten, and wink at me, her little bubbeleh.

I was very, very sorry.

I put down my spoon and buried my face in uncle Bobby's chest and together we cried.

PART II
ABSENCE

FOURTEEN

BY THE TIME I was fourteen, even with two arms, I am sorry to say that much of what made me attuned to the wonderful, the weird, the eerie had been stamped out of me by life, brutal and ordinary.

In the years following my grandmother's death I had shucked off the grief as only a child could. I had begun school where French replaced everything I might once have known about Yiddish. I folded myself in with the little village of my peers, little white Canadian girls of Scots-Irish descent who I knew from pre-K playgroups and after-school programs.

I forgot everything I ever knew about my grandmother. I was, for a while, completely fine.

And then, in middle school, for the first time I left the comforting bubble of the Glebe. For grades seven and eight I mingled with outsiders.

I was faced with a sudden influx of others who came from different schools, who co-opted my friends, who thought I was a snob, a designation which baffled me as I had spent my whole life up to that point barely aware that there was life outside the Glebe.

These petty territorial distinctions made my middle school years hellish. Everyone else was in hell too, only I didn't know it, and so I felt isolated and embittered.

But by the time I turned fourteen these two bizarre years were almost over.

I had hopes that high school would be better.

It wouldn't be, but I didn't know that at the time.

The future, and that fixed date when I would lose my arm and forever lose the ability to be ordinary, was rapidly approaching. Like an idiot I stumbled along optimistically towards it.

I was doing all this suddenly as a de facto only child. Because the year I entered high school was the year Marnie left us to go to university.

IN WHICH A DRAWING IS FOUND, THEN LOST

IF MY CHILDHOOD, from my grandmother's death to the loss of my arm, could be marked as my trudge towards mediocrity, Marnie's journey during that same period was a swift ascent to genius.

I always felt that there was something quite special about our family. That my father was very thoughtful in a way that was clever and my mother very practical in a way that was genius. They were my two infallible north stars and if one did not have the answer to whatever was troubling me, the other would. And if I thought they were both wonderful it was nothing to how I felt about Marnie. I worshipped her as I would a goddess.

When she deigned to take notice of me, to help with my homework or to fold little origami figures for me, it was as if the sun itself had reached down to kiss me with her touch. When she sent me away from her or ignored me in favour of her friends it was as if I was buried in an eternal, unending dark which sent me into a sulking mood which only Marnie could bring me out of.

I loved her.

Somehow though it was surprising to me when other people began to think of Marnie as special too.

Marnie and I attended the same elementary school, the same middle school, but when it came time for her to go to high school she announced that rather than returning back into the fold of the Glebe, to attend the high school that was only a few short blocks from us, she would be going somewhere else entirely.

We didn't have much reason to go to that part of the city often, but during the summer before she went to high school my father drove us through the bungalows of Alta Vista, till we arrived at the squat sprawling building where Marnie would be going every day for the next five years.

It was not architecturally impressive, but even then Canterbury was locally famous as a selective high school that had churned out a dozen or so nationally semi-famous artists, musicians, writers, and actors. It functioned almost as a private school within a public system and to get into the school children had to audition or present portfolios.

Upon her admittance Marnie had to write a letter to the principal of the high school she would not be attending asking for permission to be redistricted. He sent her back a very nice letter releasing her with pleasure and wishing her well in her academic pursuits.

I was as impressed as if the prime minister himself had written to Marnie, and when no one was looking, I licked the signature to see if it bled. It did.

The arts high school had various programs, but if I had been asked to pick out where Marnie was going I believe I would have thought it was the Dramatic Arts program.

We loved the movies. Almost every weekend since my mother decided we were old enough to behave, my parents liked to put Marnie and me in dresses to sit in a dark theatre and watch movie stars fall in love and die over and over again on the silver screen.

On the occasions we didn't go out my father would take us to the video store and let Marnie and me pick out a movie each while he perused the classics section, gave us a VHS education on Hitchcock and Bergman and Truffaut.

My mother liked big action movies and romantic comedies, movies as formulaic as possible so that all the jibber-jabber of confusing English dialogue didn't slow her down. Sometimes, seated on the couch, her arms around me as I was forced to watch *Casablanca* for the umpteenth time, I would look over at her and see her eyes wide as saucers, tears fluttering to the surface, her mouth trembling in a half smile.

But it was impossible to believe that any of those beautiful actors on screen were any better looking than my Marnie, whose blonde hair darkened to a honey hue that gleamed gold in the sun and was wavy and thick, a genetic gift from both our Mexican and Jewish ancestors.

I never dreamed of fame for myself. I never saw myself in any of the hundreds, perhaps thousands, of movies I watched in those years. Even in the rare Mexican movies we watched, mostly Buñuel's in his exile period, the actors shone white, white, white.

But I would have liked Marnie to be a movie star. It would have suited me to have a rich, famous, well-connected sister. Poring over *YM* and *Seventeen* magazines borrowed from my friends, I counted down the days when Marnie would no longer be hindered by age restrictions and I would be able to submit her into modelling contests where surely, surely, even though she was Canadian and the American magazines never let Canadians win, surely someone would see her face in a pile of faces and realize she was the most beautiful.

Anyway none of that happened.

Marnie had no interest in being an actress. Had not even thought to audition. To my absolute bafflement Marnie had submitted an art portfolio, under the direction of her seventh-grade teacher who believed in her talent absolute and who kept in contact with Marnie through eighth grade and encouraged her to go to Canterbury, even though she no longer directly taught her.

You know how Marnie loves to draw, my father explained as my visions of Marnie the Oscar winner evaporated in the air.

I did not know that.

I was allowed to see her portfolio. Marnie laid out a big black case on the dining room table and pulled out pieces of paper here and there while I sat between my father and my mother, one of my mother's hands heavy on my thigh to remind me to look but not touch Marnie's important work.

Marnie would spend the next five years with her hands stained with paint, charcoal, graphite. She would develop a bumpy callous on her right ring finger from holding paint brushes and pens and pencils, and another hidden one on the pad of her right thumb from the summer that she took up photography with a film camera and was constantly manually adjusting her aperture to the light.

But right before high school her unpractised, uncalloused hands were only working in pencil.

Maybe they were good, the drawings that took Marnie away from me. Maybe they weren't.

The only drawing I remember was of a little girl staring soulfully out at the viewer. The girl in the picture had thick, wavy, windswept hair, which gave the impression of motion, but she herself, with her dark eyes staring sincerely out at the viewer, looked very still. The little girl looked as if she had suffered, I decided. As if she knew, in a profound and true way, what pain meant.

The little girl was me and she was not me.

I liked the girl in the picture because Marnie had made her interesting to look at, but I did not like the picture because I was not sad. I was not a sad child. Everyone always told my parents that I was a happy, playful, laughing girl.

I was normal.

Look, Almita, my mother said, pinching my thigh extra hard so I would remember myself and not reach for the picture. Look at how beautiful your sister has made you look.

You can have the picture if you want, Marnie said.

I don't want it.

Well, I want it, my father said. This is beautiful work, Marnie. When are you going to draw me this way, eh? Am I not handsome enough for you?

You're too bald to be handsome, Marnie said tartly and even though my mother reached to pinch her earlobes, it was clear she was only joking. My father clasped his hands over his heart in mock agony.

I think, my mother said when they had all calmed down, we should frame this one.

No one noticed that I had said nothing.

My parents had Marnie date and sign the picture.

It resurfaced, one day, framed in a tasteful black metallic frame in the hallway amidst our old school portraits, the gold foil portrait of Our Lady of Guadalupe, the image of whom is ubiquitous in Mexican homes, and a picture of Bubbe, half turned away from the camera, which had gone up after she died.

Marnie's drawing of the girl who was me and not me stayed there for many years until one day, years later, it occurred to me that I could do what I wanted and I took it down.

I had never liked it, and I was no longer willing to be mocked by that little girl's sad smile. But I couldn't bring myself to destroy it like I would have if it had been made by any hands but Marnie's. So I didn't throw it out; I slotted it between some books in the bookshelf in my father's study and allowed myself to forget about it. At some point, even later than that, looking for something to read, I searched among the books. Eventually I realized that the portrait should have been among those books and was not. Not among the books and not in the filing cabinets that held our old report cards, passports, and decades' worth of old tax returns.

I asked my parents, individually, if they knew where it was and both were surprised to find it wasn't still where they had hung it though it had been many years since I had moved it.

Like so many things in life, the portrait became a mystery. It had winked out of the world and could no longer be found.

A MURAL

HER FINAL YEAR of school, I wasn't even aware that my time with Marnie was dwindling away, that the end of high school would be the end of us as sisters as we knew it. That final year she was barely there, consumed, like all the other art students, with the making of her grad mural.

The grad murals were legendary. They stayed in the hallways long after the students who had painted them had moved on, a kind of legacy, a touch of immortality, though presumably the oldest of the murals was only about ten years old.

All throughout those years of school, as I did my homework, and ran out to play with my friends, and bickered with my parents over how much time I spent on the computer, Marnie had been in the background. She was hunched over the table in the dining room or hunched over the desk in her room or hunched over the computer, ignoring my pleas for time on the internet and our mother's pleas to think of her posture and stand up straight.

Sometimes, between hunching, Marnie would rip up whatever she was doing, tearing paper or photographs in smooth dispassionate sections of four before binning them completely, deleting files with a click before clicking on the Trash icon and deleting them a second time, rendering them beyond recovery. Between these failures Marnie would announce she had won a prize, been accepted in another publication, awarded a grant, invited to speak at an arts centre in Toronto where my parents were only too happy to drive her and I had to spend my Saturday in the hallway of a museum, being quiet in the back of the room, trying to finish a book I wasn't interested in, longing to be home or near a computer, talking with my friends.

Though she was as nervous about the exhibition of her grad piece it seemed to me one with all the other Marnie events in which she was told over and over again that she was special, special, special.

Every day that school year Marnie had worked in her corner of the stairwell, and while she apprised us of every development, we had never, because of geography, been able to see the miracle of her work which every pimpled unspectacular student, whether an art student or a general one in the school because of simple districting, had the privilege of seeing.

I was not in a pleasant mood when we arrived on a cold spring day an hour or so after school had ended.

That winter I had developed breasts and I was not happy about it especially now that the weather meant I could no longer hide myself in my large duffle coat or the oversized sweaters my friend's Ukrainian mother knitted for me out of imported New Zealand wool. My parents, firmly in denial that their youngest had any breasts at all, had neglected to take me bra shopping. The night before, my mother had tried to wrestle me into the nicest dress I owned, an empire waist silk dress from Marks & Spencer which had been immense on me when they purchased it in a sale when I was ten and which, now that it finally fit me lengthwise, could not be induced to close over my chest.

My mother kept insisting it would fit, telling me to suck in my gut despite the fact that it was my chest that was the problem.

You're not trying, Alma, she kept saying as she wrestled with the zipper.

She has breasts, Mother!

It was Marnie who had spoken the truth we were afraid to.

I felt myself flush red, as my mother turned to Marnie and said, She's a baby!

I pushed them both out of my room, humiliated that Marnie had named that unnameable thing: my body.

My mother should have been the one to, discreetly, and without using the word *breasts*, take me shopping for something that actually fit, instead of trying to force me into a little-girl dress that never would.

And yet later that night, when I had cried myself calm, Marnie knocked on my door, walking in before I could tell her to go away.

I was thinking it might be nice if you wore one of my dresses tomorrow, Marnie said. There's going to be a lot of people and it would be so much easier to spot you if you were wearing something recognizable. You could wear this. She held up a stretchy velour blue dress from Le Château. Or this, holding up the plaid Jacob minidress which I coveted.

Until then the only thing preventing me from sneaking into Marnie's room when she wasn't there and stealing the dress for myself was that I believed it wouldn't fit. It didn't quite, but in the opposite way than I imagined: rather than being too loose, the dress was tight across the chest. It zipped up, was the ultimate thing. It zipped up all the way.

Could I wear your Docs too? I said as I admired myself in the mirror. My feet were still smaller than Marnie's but I figured I could wear my thick winter socks to pad them out.

Don't push it, Almita, Marnie said, and tweaked my nose.

Marnie was only one of several students exhibiting their grand murals that night.

They had started in ninth grade with some twenty-odd students and gradually, between those who couldn't hack it and those who moved and those who had lost interest, they had dwindled to a group of twelve.

A large crowd was there to see the murals. Though they looked terribly grown up to me, I could tell they were mostly students by the way Marnie kept waving at them. A sprinkling of younger siblings, of whom I seemed one of the oldest, and a handful of frazzled-looking adults, parents holding bouquets, moved as one. Again and again we smushed ourselves into alcoves and under staircases, while a nervous-looking student stood in front of a large black curtain, gave a little speech, and then unveiled their piece to rapturous applause.

Your husband must be so proud of Marnie, a woman was telling my mother near the back of the room. The woman was leaning close to my mother and touching her on the arm. I knew my mother disliked the overfamiliar intimacy of strangers. I slipped in beside her, dragging her arm away from the stranger's hand and putting it, possessively, around my own shoulders.

And is this your daughter? The woman smiled at me and patted me on the head like I was a dog.

Does she go to Canterbury too?

She couldn't have picked a sorer subject. I had wanted to go to the school. In fact, ever since Marnie had been accepted there, I thought I was fated to follow in her footsteps.

That winter I had tried out for drama, memorized one of the six obligatory monologues they had girls audition with, gone to the group trials where I did my best to dance and play and shout so that I could stick out in the mind of the adjudicators. But I knew when the mail came, a thin white envelope instead of the thick welcome packet that Marnie had received, that I was a reject.

Three other girls in my class, including my former best friend, Evie, had gotten into the drama program. Evie now went to the off-campus Dairy Queen to eat lunch with the other girls, as if it were already high school and she had already forgotten me.

I felt my mother's hand tighten reflexively against my arm.

Alma's going to Glebe next year, my mother said. She's not special.

The woman's jaw dropped a little.

Excuse me, I said. I want to see the other works.

ORDINARY

EVEN THOUGH THE high school was pretty small I immediately got lost, which was sort of the point. My skin itched with humiliation. I wanted to die.

Over and over again I heard my mother saying, She's not special, and the woman's face looking horrified.

It wasn't myself that I was burning for. It was my mother.

That woman, whoever she was, didn't understand my mother, thought she was some harsh brute. And my mother could be harsh in so many ways, but not in this one.

Not being special was what she and my father wanted to be above all. They had spent their whole lives pushing Marnie and me into the best schools they could, making us take all the extracurriculars like dance, piano, and ballet where we competed fiercely against other children who were all desperate to be the best, to be special.

But the second Marnie had shown that she was special I realized how different my parents were from everyone else's: special wasn't something they had wanted their children to be. They were proud of her but they feared for her. They didn't understand how to take compliments from Marnie's teachers, my father freezing up, my mother lowering her head and muttering in a way that made those hateful others think that she couldn't speak any English at all.

The more Marnie won awards the more they praised me for the Bs and Cs I brought home.

They feared Marnie's beauty and her talent in that they marked her as different. They were proud of my own ordinariness, not understanding, or rather refusing to understand, that I *was* different, often the only girl in my classes who was decidedly not white, the only one who wasn't a McKay or a McLeod.

They wanted us unrecognizable and mediocre. My mother was raised a strict Catholic, my father a conservative Jew. They had raised us as nothing. They wanted us to be like the other Canadians, not understanding that the white Canadians they viewed as accent-less blanks were coloured by their own backgrounds, their vague European roots, their veneer of Christianity whether they went to church or no.

They were exhausting. Hopeless. I turned down another hallway and found myself beside a fire exit. I pushed my way out and was relieved that the fire alarm didn't ring. Rather than the flat front of the building with the wide lawn and the arching driveway I was facing a wide field, one I had never seen before. Disoriented, I started to follow the contours of the building I had just left. If I walked enough I would find the parking lot we had parked in and I could wait by the car until someone, Marnie or my parents, found me and we could all go out for a celebratory dinner and then go home.

Instead I found Oliver.

I didn't recognize him at first because he was kissing a girl. Their shameless intimacy, the way their bodies were pressed together with a casualness I hadn't learned yet and was terrified I never would, made it difficult to distinguish them as individuals.

And then I became aware that the sandy-brown hair of the boy was familiar to me, that the forward fall of his shoulders was one I knew, that the arms that cradled this girl had once cradled me.

I started to back away but the girl, without removing her lips from Oliver's, opened her eyes at the exact moment that I was looking directly at her.

She frowned.

I cannot for the life of me remember her face. She had brown hair. She was not uniquely pretty nor uniquely ugly. She was not notable in any way. My parents would have loved her.

Oliver turned to see what she was looking at, and saw me.

Little Alt, he said. He smiled at me. What's up?

OLIVER REDUX

OLIVER WAS STILL our backyard neighbour.

For a few years after he had rescued me, whenever I checked our backyard fence the gap still existed. And then one day, in the fall, when the leaves on the bushes were sparse but we had yet to tuck them into burlap for their hibernal rest, I saw that when I wasn't looking the fence had been repaired.

For a few years after that I sometimes saw glimpses of him at school as we wandered through the hallways. Occasionally he would end up in Marnie's class and then he would come into our home in conversation. Oliver got in trouble for his penmanship. Oliver and I got the top marks on the math quiz.

Mostly though Marnie did not mention Oliver. Mostly Oliver did not exist to me.

The last time I had seen him he and Marnie had been walking together around Patterson Creek, tracing a loop around the edge of the canal. From the O'Connor bridge I saw them in miniature. They weren't touching or even looking at each other but something about the two of them together made them look like a couple and for the first time I wondered if they were. Marnie looked up at me and I raised my hand and waved. When I did Marnie abruptly turned from me, and Oliver, who hadn't seen me, followed her motion, turned, and began walking with her back the way they had come.

Were you embarrassed by me? I asked her later.

What do you mean?

And when I explained about the wave and her turning she said, I didn't even see you there. I would have called you over if I had.

There was no suggestion of a lie in her attitude but even still I doubted the veracity of what Marnie was saying. I wondered if she was keeping Oliver-shaped secrets from the family.

It made me realize that though we lived a few metres away from each other and interacted with similar people Oliver and I didn't really know each other anymore.

I knew that he was one of the people who went to Canterbury, like Marnie, but for what I didn't know.

I knew that he had a car, because sometimes Marnie would tell us he had given her a ride even though she usually took the bus.

It was surprising to see him now, quite near me, and realize that he was much taller than I remembered, but that I was tall too, nearly as tall as Marnie, tall enough that I was embarrassed by how much of my legs were showing in her plaid minidress.

The girl with Oliver was eyeing my legs and I tugged self-consciously at my hem.

It's Marnie's grad exhibit, I said.

Oh, that's today? You can show it to me.

He reached over and put an arm around my shoulders, guiding me gently to his side. With his other hand he tugged along the girl he had been kissing.

It was the strangest feeling being pulled against his torso. I could remember, abruptly, what it had been like to be smaller than small and be sitting in his lap, feeling like he would keep me safe.

And he did keep me safe.

With embarrassing ease he took me to Marnie's mural where my parents and Marnie had all convened.

I felt disoriented for being with Oliver, but I hadn't even been gone long enough for anyone to notice my absence. I barely had time to glance at Marnie's mural; Oliver and I were folded into the circle of conversation where my father's unrelenting questions gave me an excuse to admire the sandy-brown colour of Oliver's eyelashes.

I had lost myself in the slight cleft on the tip of his nose when suddenly I heard my father joke, You be sure to bring her back in one piece, and Oliver answer back, I'll take good care of her, sir.

I realized that my admiration for Oliver's form had left me adrift in the conversation.

What's going on? I asked, but, as was typical for my being a younger child with a soft voice, no one heard me.

It was all over. I would never see the mural again and it remained hazy in my mind, a picture I was secretly glad not to have to praise. We were all drifting away to the parking lot. Marnie and Oliver and his girl were heading in one direction, Marnie having begged off her own celebratory dinner to eat pizza with some friends. It was all happening too fast; suddenly I was in the back of the car and I was asking my parents, What was going on before?

Marnie's going out to dinner.

No, before that. Where is she going with Oliver?

He'll be at McGill with Marnie, my mother said. It's good that she'll have someone to look after her in the fall.

Yes, it's nice, I said.

It didn't feel nice.

Marnie had already promised that when she finally left for university I could have her room, a spacious sprawling proper room that faced the backyard, and she would take mine, a glorified closet, on the rare occasions when she would come back and grace us with her presence.

I suppose somewhere in the back of my mind I had imagined that I could look out the window some nights and see Oliver in his room, which faced Marnie's former room. I had already worked out we could use flashlights to signal to each other. I had found an old book on Morse code for two dollars at the Book Market and was trying to teach myself the dash-dot system. Oliver, with his strange mechanical hand and his *SkyRoads*, seemed like the sort of person who would be into codes, Morse or otherwise.

But that didn't happen.

Oliver didn't want to stay in Ottawa and neither did Marnie.

GOODBYE MARNIE

THE DAY MARNIE went to Montreal we made the hectic journey in two cars, the second one borrowed from uncle Bobby and aunt Eshkie. (Cousin Marnie was only going to Ottawa U. Poor Marnie, my mother said on the drive up repeating that old familiar refrain: she isn't very smart.) My Marnie's things were squished up in a suitcase and garbage bags and cardboard boxes. There was travel and tears, my parents' tears and my own. Marnie was dry-eyed, hurrying us out of her dorm room as soon as we finished lugging up all her things. She was already making friends and making plans with these friends. But before we left she gave me a hug and buried her face in my hair and said, Now you'll have somewhere to run to.

It struck me as an odd thing to say. I was quite happy at home; I didn't want to run to anywhere. In fact on the way back from Montreal to Ottawa my parents and I sat in a diner booth, me on one side, them on the other.

Looking over my plastic menu I saw my parents looking for something semi-edible. They already seemed sad and shrunken and small from missing our Marnie and I realized with a bloom of satisfaction growing in my chest that I was now effectively an only child, to be petted and adored.

THE PHONE CALL

PERHAPS MARNIE KNEW more than I did about what life had in store, because by November of that year I was in Montreal, pouring quarters into a public phone and dialling the number to Marnie's cellphone, the one my parents had purchased for her as a special present for getting into McGill.

Everything is awful, Marn, I began as soon as I heard the quarters drop as the call clicked through. I want to die.

What is it now?

The strange thing was that in the previous life, the one in which Marnie and I saw each other every day and lived in the same house, Marnie had no time for me. When I came to her with my problems she would tell me to grow up or get a life. If I had talked about wanting to die she would have told me not to be so crass, turning up her broad nose and telling me that suicidal impulses were a real problem people with actual depression had and I should stop being a brat. But being away had softened her, made her indulgent.

Sometimes when she called to chat with my parents and wheedle more money out of my father she would end her calls by asking them to put me on the phone. Or rather, she would ask for her little darling, her Almita, to be put on.

It was baffling, it was wonderful. It only made me long for more attention, more adulation, more, more, more.

It's Mama, I said.

Everything was always Mama.

When Marnie was in the house her shine had made me ordinary and thus forgettable in my mother's eyes. But with her gone I became something less than ordinary. I became flawed.

I ate too much. I was getting too dark. My clothes were too loose or too tight or too old (and whose fault is that? I would mutter as my traitorous father slunk out of the room only to later come put his arm around me and suggest we go shopping for something nice).

In public my mother would loudly tell me to say please and thank you like I was a four-year-old instead of a fourteen-year-old.

I wanted to murder her and told her so all the time. She told me I was acting like aunt Eshkie, the greatest of insults.

Almita, Marnie sighed.

Don't interrupt, I told her. What I'm saying is, I'm *here*.

There was a pause and then I could hear not Marnie's voice but the voice of the Older Sister, the second mother, the What Have You Done This Time voice.

Where is here, the voice said even though it already knew.

That morning, on my way to school, I had kicked at the autumnal leaves and thought how I was going to fail my math test. I was barely into my first semester and I was already failing math, which had never happened before. I had always pulled out solid Bs and this semester it simply wasn't happening. I walked in the gutters, listening to the swish, swish, swish of the leaves being kicked up by my ankles. At the crosswalk at Bank and Glebe I ran into some of my friends and we walked together the few blocks to school and I forgot about how I was failing math and I forgot about the test right up to the point where I was sitting in math class with the quiz in front of me. I didn't understand graphing. I could never plot the points correctly. I looked up at the rest of the students, their heads bent in concentration, their mechanical pencils scratching the soft paper. They would all get As, or at the very least pass, while I would fail and have to present my failure to my parents, who would be annoyed at this inability to be ordinary, at this mark on the Alt name.

I raised my hand and asked to be excused to the bathroom and got up. I walked through the halls and kept walking, walked right out the front doors of the school, walked out past the front campus and down Glebe Avenue, the route I usually used to go home, but at Bank I turned left and kept walking to Catherine Street, to the Greyhound, to Montreal and Marnie, my salvation.

Even though I was trying hard not to, the whole time I was walking I was already picturing it in my head. Me in Montreal with Marnie.

The Greyhound station was an unimpressive building, one level high, with the same bureaucratic mica flooring and fluorescent lighting of all buildings built in the '70s. An overflow of people milled about, mostly students with backpacks on their way to Montreal for the weekend, looking to party with their friends or go visit their parents.

I went to the kiosk and paid full price for my ticket. I paid with the emergency cash my father insisted I carry around in my Hello Kitty wallet. I could have gotten a student ticket, but my student ID would have indicated I was in high school and at fourteen I wasn't supposed to be travelling on my own. No one questioned my ticket, and I was allowed to get on the bus, grabbing a window seat and not looking as a girl with large headphones settled in beside me. I felt a thrill as the bus pulled away from the station. I was getting away with something I shouldn't, pulling off another Alma vanishing act.

THE GREYHOUND

WHEN WE ROLLED into the Montreal Greyhound station two and a half hours later much of the romance of running away had dissipated. I was hungry, cramped, and felt disgusting from sitting next to fifty or so unwashed bodies all breathing the same stale air in and out.

If the Ottawa station had seemed nondescript, its Montreal sister was a smaller, seedier version that exposed how well tended-to and clean the Ottawa version was. I scrambled off the bus desperate to escape its smell and came crashing into the more revolting scent of urine and dirt.

But it was well-organized, well labelled. I found the pay phones beside the lockers. I called Marnie and told her to come get me and after what felt like forever I looked up and there she was.

It hadn't been outright said, but there was the vague impression that we were to give Marnie time to be alone, to establish herself as a semi-adult, before we could visit her. I hadn't seen her since early September, the longest we had ever been apart. I had forgotten how beautiful she was, my sister, standing there looking strong and tall and disapproving but there all the same, ready to rescue me.

I rushed to hug her and buried my nose in her neck. She didn't smell the way she used to smell when we lived together, like home, like nothing. But she smelled clean and floral and like someone who had bathed recently.

Okay, that's enough, she said patting me. I couldn't stop, I clung to her harder. You're scenting me like a dog, she said kicking me in the shins, breaking the illusion of Marnie maternal.

Let's get out of here.

I would have followed Marnie to the depths of hell. This was partially because she was Marnie and partly because at that moment I was vulnerable as only someone without money can be vulnerable, with nothing but a handful of change left over from my ticket. But even so, what compelled me to follow Marnie so faithfully was that Montreal as viewed from the Greyhound bus station was a confusing city. There were so many people, more than there ever seemed to be in Ottawa. A lifetime of walking nowhere but the Glebe had left me inept at navigating new streets and new buildings. I clung to Marnie's hand, feeling like a yokel, staring at people openly doing drugs in the park and at buildings that reached much higher than the ones we had at home.

But the more we walked and the farther we got from the bus station, the nicer the streets became and the more the people started to look like the sort of people I knew, dressed in a grunge that was more aesthetic than circumstantial.

And there was Marnie, holding my hand. At a certain point she stopped dragging me and began pointing out streets and signs and businesses, making everything a story.

For some time we walked along Saint-Catherine Street and then Marnie turned us into a side street where there was a deli and I sat at the window, people-watching, while Marnie ordered us Reubens that she paid for with her new credit card, a symbol of adulthood paid off each month by Mama and Papa.

Tell me everything, she said.

After months only hearing her voice on the phone it felt so good to see her face to face. She had always had light bluish marks under her eyes but they had deepened slightly since she went away. Was it my imagination or had her hair bronzed a little, some brown lurking in with the gold? She was wearing a blue top and so her eyes that day looked blue instead of the green I knew they were, and that was another thing I had forgotten about Marnie, her mercurial eye colour in addition to her unwavering good looks.

In front of her, digging into a sandwich, overwhelmed by the strangeness of the city and of what I had done, I didn't have a single complaint left in me.

You came all this way and now that you're here you don't want to kvetch? she said, rolling her eyes. Who are you and what have you done with Alma?

The more we talked the more her mood softened.

That should have been the first sign that something was wrong.

After I had eaten my Reuben she asked me if I wanted anything more. I didn't, but after she paid the bill she kept sitting in the booth, folding and refolding the receipt until the cheap paper tore apart. When she had worried it into confetti she abruptly stood up.

Come on, she said. Let's go get ice cream, I know a place.

And so we went trudging in a different direction, to a bright and well-lit shop even I could tell was a tourist trap, where they dipped their cones in chocolate. Marnie, restless, didn't want to sit at the tiny bar tables.

I know a place, she said again, and again I followed her.

She led us to the brightly lit steps of a museum where we ate up our ice creams. It was fall and night was falling quickly. But somehow it seemed like the street lights and the lights from the museum kept the night cool off us. We sat there together, not quite cold, and watched boys do skateboarding tricks as the breeze ruffled our hair.

In fact so much light was bleeding from the buildings and the street lights that when I looked up the sky was a navy sort of grey and I couldn't see a single star. I leaned against Marnie's shoulder and I felt so happy, so at peace, my eyelids beginning to flutter down easily as I was pulled towards sleep. I waited for Marnie to suggest we go home and when she didn't I finally said it myself, reluctantly breaking the mood.

Let's go home, Marn, I'm exhausted.

But Marnie didn't want to go home.

Come on, she said. It's still early. Let's go for a walk along the Old Port. It's a great place.

She stood up, dislodging me from her shoulder, and began to walk away and I scrambled to keep up.

I was not familiar enough with the city to realize that this was a devastatingly stupid plan that would take me hours from sleep.

Instead, I plodded after Marnie. For a good long while I felt placid and like I would follow my sister forever. But forever ended more quickly that I might have imagined. I became increasingly skeptical as we walked down dark downwards-sloping streets. And still, no matter how far we walked, no matter how the street levelled off, it seemed like only a matter of time before we were plunging downwards again.

Can't we go back, Marnie? I finally ventured to ask. Or do this tomorrow?

No we could not.

My sister no longer seemed kind and indulgent.

It was sister Marnie back again. Don't be a child, she said as we descended yet again. It's beautiful by the water; it's the best place in the whole city.

And as we walked the buildings turned from boring glass-and-steel ones to ones made of stone, ones that looked as if they had been made a hundred years or more in the past, as if we were falling backwards in time.

They call Old Montreal the Paris of North America, Marnie said, and even though I had never been to Paris, except when I visited it in movies, I couldn't imagine that being true.

I was increasingly beginning to think that we were lost when suddenly we turned from an empty street to a filled one. I could see lines and lines of restaurants brimming with customers out on the terraces enjoying the evening. There was a long drive, unmarked by stoplights, running parallel to the terraces and Marnie grabbed my hand and we walked across, cars stopping for us, as we jogged towards the quay. We had only a little farther to go, past some bushes and a sandy patch, before we were on a boardwalk abutting some water.

Here it is, Marnie said.

Here it was.

It was awful. It was dark and stunk of weed. In the distance by the water there were old collapsing buildings, former factories it looked like. The water was water I supposed, a long channel of it. It did not compare favourably to the bodies of water I had grown up beside. It lacked the delicate fineness of the Rideau Canal, or the unbridled rush of the Rideau River.

Marnie wanted to walk along the boardwalk but at this point it really was cold in a way she could no longer ignore. And as we were walking we kept passing bodies in the bushes. Whether they were the bodies of the unhoused, the dead, or predators waiting to jump out and attack us I didn't know or want to find out.

After a minute or two of this I was tugging on Marnie's arm.

I want to go, I said to her. Not in my wheedling little-sister whine but in a serious no-nonsense tone.

I was prepared to argue that staying out was insane but Marnie looked at her watch and, defeated at last, finally acquiesced and began to guide us towards home.

It was worse on the way back, is all I have to say. Ottawan girls aren't made to climb hills. We grow up in the lush comfort of a flat valley where the muscles we need to walk upwards or downwards simply atrophy. But what made it worse was that by the time we got to McGill and I thought we were free, Marnie pointed to where we were going and I realized that her dorm was located up a steep incline.

Marnie, I can't, I said.

At that point I was willing to consider lying down on the ground and sleeping right there on the street.

Oh come on, Marnie said. Yes, you can.

And though I couldn't believe it, somehow between her coaxing and threatening I did somehow make it up that hill.

It was Friday night and busy, and by the time we reached her building most of the students seemed to be leaving for the night. We were the only ones going up in the elevator.

Marnie's room was smaller than I remembered, a shoebox really, one-third taken up with her bed, the opposite third taken up by a desk and wardrobe.

I collapsed onto Marnie's twin, exhausted beyond relief, suddenly filled with a great love for her. She was insane and seemed to have a sudden uncanny ability to climb mountains but now that I no longer had to ascend or descend anything she seemed alright really.

You know we're going to have to share that bed, Marnie said laughing as she shucked off her coat, her shoes.

No, I said. I'm going to die here. I can't possibly move enough to accommodate your gruba tuchus.

She had to peel off my boots and coat and roll my body towards the wall so there was enough room to accommodate the both of us. I refused to brush my teeth but while she slipped away to brush hers I undid my bra. I still had enough energy for that dignity.

When she came back I was already half asleep. I couldn't believe I had run away. I couldn't believe I was with Marnie again.

I love you, Marnita, I said my eyes burning with the relief of being shut. You're my favourite, favourite, favourite sister.

That's another thing, Almita, Marnie said. No one here can know you're my sister okay?

We were pressed together and her breath tickled my ear. If only one of us had been a shorter we might have had more room.

Okay, I said, and then I really was asleep.

NOT A SISTER

I WAS BORN second which meant I was born to follow. I was born to share.

I had no concept of what it was like to be not a sister.

Marnie used to tell me, I've lived without you before and I could do it again.

I believed her.

But who was I if I didn't have Marnie?

THE FRIEND

I WOKE UP the next morning feeling decadent and exhausted the way I felt only after a particularly heavy and satisfying sleep. I was sprawled across the bed, now its sole occupant, half my arm hanging off it. The sun poured down, unconstrained by curtains or blinds, but that wasn't what had awoken me. It was the sound of Marnie's voice, low in deference to my sleep but coming across as exasperated all the same.

I have to go, Almita's awake, she said, hanging up and then throwing her phone on the mattress.

It was Mama, she said.

You told her I was here?

I didn't want to admit it in the moment, but part of the secret motivation for getting on the bus and coming to see Marnie was hoping that my mama would think I had been kidnapped or raped or murdered. When I showed up on Monday for school she would sink to her knees in gratitude, praying to the God I didn't believe in, giving thanks for my deliverance.

She wouldn't ask about my math test and when the results came back she would still be in a fog of gratitude.

Marnie had robbed me of that.

Idiota, she said, tugging my hair affectionately. I called her yesterday right after you hung up. Of course she knows you're here. Do you want to give her a heart attack?

Yes, I said spitefully.

Anyway, who do you think would be the first person she would call if you went missing? Me and then the parents of all your friends and then maybe in a few days the police. If I tried to secrete you away somehow she would know and she would come here and drag you back by your ears. You're very lucky, Marnie said, that I convinced her to let you stay.

This seemed brutally unfair Marnie logic because now I was going to be in horrific amounts of trouble for leaving and Marnie would be vaunted as the good child.

The bathrooms here are shared, Marnie said, rolling out of bed and stepping over me towards the door. It's gross so wear your shoes.

The bathrooms were indeed gross, the kind of gross that comes from a space being used too carelessly too often by too many bodies. It was worn down and covered in a grimy residue which no amount of scrubbing could disperse. Even that early on a Saturday there were girls in the washroom, girls primping in front of bathroom mirrors, and girls showering in the stalls and girls with hair like the matted fur of a streetwise raccoon shuffling with tilted faces and half-shut eyes towards the stalls where they let out streams of piss and full-bodied indelicate farts that the rest of the girls in the bathroom pointedly pretended not to notice.

All the girls seemed to know Marnie and she stopped before every one, exchanging a few words about classes before introducing me to everyone as her friend Alma.

It seemed too incredible a lie to ever be believed because for one I was sure, absolutely sure, that I looked nothing at all like these beautiful sophisticated eighteen- and nineteen-year-old women. And yet every time she said it, those same women looked at me and smiled. A few bothered to ask me where I went to school and before I could answer there was Marnie saying, Alma's from Ottawa, and I watched the eyes of these girls glaze over.

It was strange to be this other Alma, this Alma who was nearly the same height as Marnie, who had her long limbs and the same thick hair that waved just enough to not be straight and frizzled in the rain. We had our father's too-wide eyes which widened even further in surprise or joy. Eyes that held no secrets and could have been on the silver screen back when movies were called shows and played on reels accompanied by piano players and no dialogue.

I had lived my whole life as an Ottawan—no, not even an Ottawan, as a Glebite—and within the confines of that neighbourhood, partially bordered by the Rideau Canal, which wrapped, serpentine, around the avenues, within those confines I was always Marnie's sister. Everyone knew me as such. And yes, as my mother had wished it, Marnie was light and I was dark, but we were the same. We were Alts. I felt the people at her new school were very stupid not to notice these similarities and before I slunk into a stall I looked at Marnie and caught her eye and rolled my eyes and she bit her lip and tried her best not to smile.

It was like that wherever we went that day. She snuck me into the cafeteria using someone else's meal card and we sat with her friends and there I was introduced again as Alma, from Ottawa. Alma who apparently didn't talk much because every time someone bothered to ask me a question Marnie would pull focus from whoever she was talking to and answer for me.

We were childhood friends, she said. We had gone to the same school. I was studying English. All of these answers were technically true and every time they came out of Marnie's mouth I admired my beautiful clever sister for her ability to obfuscate, to dance circles around these people without ever actually lying. It was a game of verbal dexterity, one played apparently for my benefit alone because it was I alone who could appreciate both the truth of Marnie's answers and the skill with which she plucked these truths from her mind and bent them to her will.

When lunch was over she took me on a walk away from the dorm and down to the Cinéma du Parc, a place that played the type of foreign films we loved so much. Along the way we passed beautiful brick low-rise buildings. Marnie told me this was the McGill Ghetto, the place she would move to next year when she outgrew the dorms, and she already had vague plans with three friends to find a place together next year.

You know Oliver lives on this street, she said suddenly as we were about to cross. There was a mix-up with the dorms or he thought he was too good for them or something.

Which building, I said. Where?

Marnie gave me a look, but still she walked me up to a building and pointed to it.

I think that one, she said. I was there once between parties, I don't know.

The rest of the way to the movie theatre I memorized the numbers on the building and the name of the street, pressing them into my mind like sacred flowers between the pages of a book, safekeeping them for later when I could take them out and examine them at my leisure.

THE PARTY

THAT NIGHT, AFTER the movie and after dinner, we prepared to go out with some of Marnie's friends. A few of the girls in the bathroom had mentioned the party that morning. While Marnie tried to deflect by saying we had our own plans I was all too eager to tease her. I said it sounded fun and we would love to go, knowing that Marnie could not well say that her friend Alma was actually her sister Alma and only fourteen and too young to go to adult parties.

Without prompting Marnie allowed me to borrow a party-suitable short skirt and black tights. It didn't even take much pleading for her to lend me her square studded belt.

Her makeup, of course, did not suit me. We went into the bathroom where her white dorm mates also had makeup that did not suit me but sent messages up and down the floors until someone came down with blush and a lipstick for someone darker than me but close enough to make it work. I sat perched on the counter between two sinks, my legs dangling down, while a girl I did not know did my makeup and told me I was beautiful and had gorgeous eyes.

In private Marnie gave me a lecture that was not so much a warning to behave myself as an increasingly hostile diatribe on how to act. I was not to drink, not even a little bit. I was not to mix drinks. (How could I mix drinks if I wasn't having any was a question I wondered but did not bother to ask.) I was not to talk to boys at all.

Some of them are old, Almita, she said. Some of them are grad students and are like twenty-three, twenty-four. Don't be shy about calling them perverts and telling them to fuck off. And if we get lost you come back here, okay?

Okay, I said. I don't want to drink. And I'm not interested in creepy old men.

She fixed at me with one of her haughty Marnie looks. The girl who had done my makeup had done Marnie's as well, giving her the same wing-tipped liner that graced my face, and had said the same thing about gorgeous eyes without noticing that, while they were different colours, Marnie's eyes and mine were the same shape.

You have a thing for *one* older guy, Marnie said.

Whatever fascination a real grown-up party might have held for me, I was disabused of it as soon as I walked through the door. There was an overwhelming rush of bodies. The smells—of those bodies, of spilled beer, of pot—overpowered my senses, leaving me heady and weak. Men kept draping their arms around my shoulders in a too-familiar way and even as I shrugged them off they tried to entangle me in slurred conversations I couldn't make sense of.

Marnie allowed me to walk around with an opened beer in my hand but her large eyes narrowed into points and followed me all around the room. She needn't have worried. I had tried beer before, same as she had, under the supervision of my mother, who drank sometimes on hot summer days, the sweating beads of water on the glass bottles making the drink look deceptively appealing. The taste did not agree with me. I found it rather revolting.

Still, it would have been nice to have something to do, or feel, something other than boredom, as I walked from room to room witnessing increasingly drunken idiots flail about as they tried dancing or talking or playing.

The place was a large three-bedroom apartment and the doors were thrown open so that people could keep circulating in and out, with the added benefit of flushing out the heat and bringing in the cool winds of November.

As time wore on and Marnie, who was drinking, let her concentration slip, I took the opportunity to fade into the kitchen and post myself near the back door. There was a boy there, a harmless-looking one with glasses.

It's hot in there, eh? he said.

For half a second I thought about Marnie and her warnings about boys and almost told him I wasn't allowed to talk to him. Then I realized how ridiculous that sounded and sat down beside him and agreed and we talked for a while.

He was nice, that boy. We didn't introduce ourselves by name but fell into talking easily the way people do, telling each other their favourite books or their secret annoyances, speaking of intimacies without bothering with the basics.

I told him I lived in Ottawa and was here on a visit (performing my own verbal gymnastics as I couldn't bring myself to say I was visiting a friend). He was perhaps the only person I had ever met who was excited that I was from Ottawa. He was from a small, predominantly French-speaking town located somewhere in northeastern Ontario and he had once won a prize, in an essay-writing competition, to visit the nation's capital where he had toured Parliament Hill and met his MP. That all sounded dull to me but he was so happy about it, so genuinely pleased, that I felt his happiness too, a kind of second-hand glow warming me on that cold night.

Do you know Marnie? he said suddenly. Marnie Alt. She's from Ottawa too, I think.

I was opening my mouth to say yes, to confess to this dweeb with glasses who was excited by politics that Marnie was my sister, when Marnie herself appeared.

There you are, she said, and her voice was a kind of happy with steel hidden underneath and I could tell that whatever she had been drinking she was sober enough to want to throttle me for talking to a boy against her explicit instructions.

Here we are, the boy said and then, looking back and forth between us, he said, You know you two, you kind of look alike.

Marnie and I looked at each other then, a secret sister look and the boy caught it too because he started to say, more confidently now, You two look like sis—

And I wanted to laugh, to have Marnie laugh, the game over because we had been caught out by some nobody who had recognized that we were sisters when even her own friends hadn't. Only Marnie's eyes flicked away from mine in embarrassment, and she was the one who laughed, tossing her head back and rolling her eyes, a perfect movie-star eye roll, and she said, Are you drunk? We don't look *anything* alike, and the boy blushed and I blushed too and he started apologizing saying, Oh no of course not I'm so dumb, but I was the dumb one.

Because I hadn't realized till that moment that Marnie was ashamed of me, that pretending I was her friend and not her sister wasn't some game we were playing together, it was a game she was playing alone, the game where Marnie Alt didn't have a Mexican mother or a sister who looked like she was Mexican, where Marnie Alt was just another white Canadian who was maybe Scottish, even though Alt was a German Jewish name, though I would have bet my life in that moment she didn't tell anyone she was Jewish either, that she had disappeared into whiteness and I had made her angry by coming here, by asserting myself where I wasn't wanted, and I wanted to say, How could you, Marnie? or Why would you, Marnie? or better yet, What the actual fuck, Marnie? and instead I stood up and all I could think of to say was Excuse me, I have to go to the bathroom, my voice trembling as I said it and without waiting for them to acknowledge me I walked into the house and across the length of the apartment and out through the open door, out into the night of an unfamiliar city, not caring that I had nowhere to go, only knowing that my heart was broken and I was sisterless and I needed to get away from Marnie.

CONSTANTINE

AT THIS POINT I only confidently knew my way around three places in Montreal, one of which was the dorm where Marnie lived. The other was the piss-scented bus station. The wonderful thing about Montreal being so hilly was that I knew that everything west to east was flat and everything north to south was either upwards or downwards. In this way I headed in what I hoped was the general direction of the bus station. I wasn't really thinking but I assumed that, as in movies and books when down-and-out heroines needed a place to stay, it would be open all night.

It wasn't, but I didn't find that out until years later because as I walked, a second sneaky thought occurred to me. I decided that rather than sleep under the harsh lights of the bus station, inevitably one of the first places where Marnie would look to find me, I could go to Oliver's apartment and throw myself at his mercy.

Of course this was easier said than done because while I had memorized Oliver's street name and number I had passed it exactly once during the day and it was nighttime and I was cold and tired and somewhat unsure of where I was at the moment.

I decided to head to the familiar territory of Marnie's dorm and then try to make my way back to the cinema tracing the same route and find Oliver's apartment. The whole time I did this I was terrified I would run into Marnie. I knew that if I saw her I would lose control and start sobbing and possibly even screaming at her in the street and this would enable Marnie to assume her superior older-sister attitude. She would look down on me and somehow the night would become all about how I had run off yet again. It would be all about Alma the drama queen, Alma the runaway, instead of the fact that Marnie was pretending that her family didn't exist.

I found Oliver's street and there, where Marnie had pointed it out, his building.

I tried the entrance door, locked of course, but there was a set of old-fashioned buzzer buttons and I mashed my palms against them unceasingly until someone finally buzzed me in.

The mailboxes were newer, uglier things than the building itself but they had useful information. Handwritten beside one of the apartment numbers was Kowalski/Jentsch and so I went looking for my Oliver, wandering through the halls of the building, the noise of TV and laughter, other people's lives, much happier than my own, bleeding out into the hallway.

I knocked on the Kowalski/Jentsch door, practising in my mind how I would present myself to Oliver. I would explain the situation coolly in a way that would impress him with my maturity, ask him to lend me money for the bus, and calmly tell him he mustn't tell Marnie, above all not Marnie.

I heard a shuffling on the other side of the door and as I heard the noise of someone peering through the peephole and then working the locks I suddenly felt my lips begin to tremble and I knew with dead certainty I was going to cry and as the door opened I did begin to cry, to wail really, and not in a pretty, delicate way like I imagine Marnie in similar circumstances would have, but with snot shooting out my nose. It was really most unfortunate that I did this because it wasn't even Oliver who happened to open the door, but Kowalski.

Constantine Kowalski turned out to be the second nice boy I met that night.

He was very tall, pointy, lanky, not an inch of fat on him. He looked very much as if someone had pinched his head with one hand and pinched his feet with the other and then stretched him out like gum. He was pretty, really, his bones naturally carving the light. Despite his last name being Kowalski, which at the time I thought might be Jewish, he was also clearly mixed, like me. Half Asian. Japanese, as I later found out. Half Polish Catholic. But all this came later in my acquaintanceship with Constantine Kowalski.

Seeing me weeping he asked if I was okay and when I said I was looking for Oliver he ushered me inside almost without my knowing it.

Suddenly I was in boyland, a place where they didn't have any tissues but they did have toilet paper, a half-used roll of which Constantine found and shoved at me. I tore off a strip and stuffed it up the spigot of my nose.

I'm sorry, he said. I shouldn't say this really, he said lowering his voice. But whatever he's done to you, it isn't worth crying over. You're very beautiful. There are other guys.

He blushed.

I blushed.

Jesus fuck, I thought. What kind of life has Oliver been living here?

I wanted to tell Constantine that Oliver hadn't done anything and also, before he got any ideas, that I was fourteen, when Oliver appeared. He didn't look at all surprised to see me even though we hadn't seen each other in months, not since that night at Marnie's grad exhibit.

Little Alt, he said. What's up? He smiled like he was genuinely glad to see me, as if the little sisters of his acquaintances showed up crying on his doorstep all the time and he was delighted that they thought of him in their time of need.

I was so relieved to see him, this little bit of home in this strange place, that I forgot all about acting mature. I started to cry again.

Oliver's smile slid of his face and Constantine put one bony hand on my shoulder. It was like being comforted by a skeleton and as he tentatively patted me I felt shivers up my spine.

Soon both boys were seated on either side of me, offering me things with increasing desperation. Did I want water? A sweater? A hug? Some cocoa? A beer? (She is NOT drinking, Oliver said with a firmness that reminded me of Marnie and made me sob harder.) Paper towels? Real tissues? Some eggs?

Do you want me to call Marnie? Oliver said and it stung that they were close enough that he had her number, that he must have known what she was doing at school, how she was lying about me, about our family. He knew. He knew, he knew, he knew.

I held my hand over my mouth so I wouldn't scream.

I want to go home, I said. I don't want to be here, I want to go home.

To Marnie? Oliver asked.

No, I said. Back to Ottawa.

Sure, Oliver said. I can do that. I can get you home.

He offered to drive me back to Ottawa.

I wish now that I had been too proud to accept his help. I should have stuck to my original plan. I should have got him to take me to the Greyhound and put me on the bus. But it was late and I was tired and I wanted to go home and walk into my room and sink into my own bed and begin the long process of never talking to Marnie again. And the fastest way I knew that would happen was if Oliver took me from his apartment to my doorstep.

So I nodded at Oliver, and Oliver nodded at Constantine and disappeared into his room for a few minutes, a room I never got to see. I was left with Constantine, the two of us not talking, too shy to look anywhere but away from each other until Oliver came back with his car keys, dressed for the cold night and with an extra jacket for me that he draped over my shoulders.

Okay, he said, let's go.

I felt relieved now that I was in Oliver's safe hands. Relieved and a little embarrassed by my tears now that my problems had resolved so quickly.

I'm so sorry, I said to Constantine, trying to give him back the toilet roll.

Oh no, he said modestly. Please keep it.

We ended up shaking hands goodbye as Oliver watched with amusement.

At least in a night of humiliations I would never have to see Constantine Kowalski again, I thought.

IN BETWEEN PLACES

I READ ONCE that time doesn't really exist in a linear fashion even though we, as humans, experience it that way. That in my worst and saddest moments I should remember that there is a part of me out there floating eternal in my happiest slice of time. I think some people might find this a comforting thought but it made me think instead of how if I am thin-sliced into moments of eternal happiness then I must be thin-sliced into moments of eternal grief, trapped in pain forever.

What is more peaceable to my mind is imagining all the neutral, lost moments in life. For example the hours spent on a plane or a train during a trip. We know that the journey is x hours long. We know that we experienced it. But outside of a few moments, the time compresses down to nothing and then, as more time passes, even those few memorable moments of the trip slide away till maybe the fact of the journey itself is all we can remember. Sometimes not even that. If I could choose, that is where I would like to spend eternity. In those safe pointless moments not worth remembering. Or in my case the short two-hour trip between Montreal and Ottawa I spent with Oliver on that November night.

There was the hum of the engine vibrating through the bottom of the car up into my feet. There was a seemingly endless stream of trees rushing by, illuminated by the headlights of Oliver's car before falling into darkness, just another shade of midnight as we rushed past.

Now that it is all over it seems like we were going fast even though I know we weren't, even though I remember that at one point Oliver stopped to buy a coffee for himself and a donut for me. He didn't make me talk about Marnie or how I had come to be in Montreal or why I wanted to go home.

He talked about himself, not in a selfish way, just talking to talk, and then asked me questions about how I liked it at Glebe, confessing that a part of him had always regretted going to school at Canterbury and losing so many of his friends that way.

It was nice to stop there and as he finished his coffee and we stepped outside I saw it had begun to snow, in thick perfect flakes.

We both looked up at the sky and Oliver stuck his tongue out and caught a flake and then looked at me and straightened the collar of his jacket.

I felt a little in love with him in that moment. I had always been a little in love with him.

Do you mind if I smoke? he asked me, already fishing out a cigarette.

It surprised me. I hadn't known he did that. I still didn't know anyone who did aside from his mother.

I watched him light the cigarette with a heavy silver lighter, the lighter of someone who has habitual use for such a thing.

He exhaled the smoke and I exhaled air and they looked almost the same, the heat of my breath reaching out to touch the ash from his lungs.

Can I try? I said reaching out my hand.

His eyes crinkled with amusement as he reached out to hand me the cigarette and then dropped it and stubbed it out.

Not for you, Almita.

Don't call me that, I snapped. That was a family name. A Marnie name.

It's a filthy habit, he said, ignoring my anger. Come on, let's keep going.

But that's not even the moment I want to stay in. I want the moments after, all those lost minutes when we hurtled towards our final destination.

We saw the Welcome to Ottawa sign.

In another version of this life he would have offered to let me stay in his apartment and I could have slept in his bed, looked at his things, touched his books, his sheets, his desk, while he, a gentleman, would have been left to the inconvenience of the couch.

More trees.

We saw the all-too-familiar lights of St. Laurent shopping centre, which was to me the true marker that we were almost home.

He could have taken me back to Marnie's dorm room where she would have been white with fury that I had run away and we could have had the screaming fight she owed me.

We pulled up off the highway, the car following the familiar swoop of road that led off the highway to the streets of Ottawa proper, pulling past the police station, curling off towards the Glebe.

He could have given me the money to go to the Greyhound. He would have stayed with me until the bus came. He would have let me try my first cigarette on the pavement while we waited and laughed as I coughed my lungs out swearing never to touch a cigarette again, telling him he, and the entire cigarette industry, were cracked-out weirdos before stepping on the bus, the taste of ash in my mouth the entire ride home.

But no.

Oliver would never have done that. He would never have put a fourteen-year-old girl on a bus by herself no matter how close she lived to the bus station, no matter if he could have called her parents to go pick her up.

Maybe there were no choices. Maybe in this life and every other he would have done what he did, which was to secretly call Marnie and tell her I was with him and then secretly call my parents and tell them that Marnie and I had some sort of fight and if it was alright with them he was going to bring me home. He would deliver me straight to their waiting arms.

In another life, where there was no drunk driver, he would have said, I'm sorry, Alma, as we drove up to my door and I saw the lights were on, and knew my mother was inside waiting to yell at me.

I would have said, I'll never forgive you for this, and slammed the car door.

I would have forgiven him anyway, and grown up and never touched a cigarette and lost touch with him. I would have forgotten his name and remembered him with kindness as the gentle boy who did me a favour once. Whatever became of him?

CRASH

I WAS WEARING my seatbelt is the thing.

Seatbelts aren't actually made for women. They're tested on male-sized crash test dummies who are bigger than the average woman and have no breasts.

That's why women are more likely to die than men. Or, if they don't die, are more likely to sustain injuries.

But I didn't know that. My parents always told me to wear my seatbelt and I did. Always.

Was Oliver wearing one too?

I would have bet anything that he was. I remember him wearing one, or I think I did. But then we stopped for that coffee. Had he put it back on after the coffee? Had he unbuckled it when we entered the Glebe knowing we were so close to our destination, so close to not needing a seatbelt at all? My father did that sometimes, as we slid between streets, as the car slowed, anticipating pulling into the driveway, hurrying to the house.

He must not have been wearing a seatbelt. I must have remembered it wrong. Which is why, when the car hit us, his head hit the windshield with a dense thud, leaving behind a smear of blood.

THE HOSPITAL

THE WORST PART of getting into the car crash was that all I wanted to do was go home and die, quietly and in peace and surrounded by my own things, but no one let me do that. Everyone was so determined to force me to live without considering whether I wanted to or not.

I know I felt every moment of sitting in that car, my chest burning and raw. I felt like I was a toothpaste tube squeezed out by a miser till there was nothing, not even any dregs, to push out.

But my mind can't hold on to that time. Memory compresses in on itself so that even though I lived many minutes all I remember is the remembering of the thud, and the pain and then some kind people who had heard the sound of the crash running out of their houses in their pyjamas and trying to open the car, trying to get me to work the door from my side. And I couldn't, but then the firefighters were there and they were taking me out and the ambulance was arriving and my breath was back bringing with it a rush of pain and I was trying to tell them I lived just around the corner, just around the corner, please, I want to go home, please and they were trying to get Oliver out of the car and I could see nothing because the smear of blood and the darkness were obstructing my view and the other car, the one that had hit us, was a little further off, smashed into a tree. A tree that was older than the neighbourhood, a tree they would paint a neon X on and then cut down, taking away its trunk and glorious branches and leaving behind the platform of its stump that remained forever after.

But at that moment the tree was still there and they were bundling me up into the ambulance, the paramedics the most beautiful people I had ever seen in my life, like Hollywood's version of paramedics and not the real thing. It was hard to believe that such angels could live in Ottawa and I contemplated this as they drove me to CHEO and there was no transition between the dark of night and the fluorescent and white of the hallways and I closed my eyes against the burning and when I opened them the smiling social worker told me she had a surprise for me and Mama and Dad were there.

I'm sorry, Daddy, I said, I think Oliver's dead.

I hadn't thought it before I said it and even as I said it, it sounded like a lie.

There goes Alma, I imagined Marnie saying. Exaggerating again.

Don't worry about that, bubbeleh, he said. Don't worry about any of that now.

It is a sorry business being alive.

And I was very much alive even though I was starting to ache all over. There seemed to be a fear I might have internal bleeding. Then a worry I might have a concussion or whiplash.

I was interrogated by a triage nurse and then a nurse and then a doctor, and then another doctor, each interview sandwiched between long stretches of time my parents and I were forced to fill.

I should tell Eshkie I won't be in today, my father said at one point. I should let Marnie know what's going on.

Don't tell Marnie, I mumbled at the same time that my mother said, We don't need to bother Marnie with this. Not yet.

We were still there when the outside light shifted to the startling grey brightness of morning. My mother was stroking my hair and telling me I needed to cut it again and I was already thinking of what it would be like to be back at home, how when I was alone I would strip down in front of the mirror to see how bad the bruises were.

At some point one of the doctors told me to make and close a fist with each of my hands and when I couldn't with my right one he made me close my eyes while he placed his pen on my left arm, over and over again.

Can you feel the pen, now? he said.

Yes.

And now?

No.

And now?

Yes.

Hmmm, the doctor said, like I had said something interesting.

I opened my eyes. He was still looking at me.

Do you feel any pain in your right side?

I didn't. I felt pain in my chest. But I did feel something unusual, a tingle, that I was suddenly aware had been there for a while.

My upper arm feels like it's falling asleep, I said.

Then they wheeled me away and they brought me to a room where there was a bed with another girl and beside her, snoring rather loudly, was what I presumed to be her mother, a woman with her mouth agape folded into an armchair beside her.

THE GIRL IN THE BED

WAS A CHILD. She was three and my predominant memory of our time together was that she never spoke, never cried, just sat there with her body completely tense, breathing shallowly through her mouth in noisy little gulps. Her legs had been burned and there was no way to effectively stop that pain. Everyone did everything they could to try to help her, even me, but we couldn't get her to smile or speak or even get her to eat most days.

To fill up the silence her mother had commandeered the only TV in the room and had, playing on a loop, a VHS tape of *The Wizard of Oz*, which was the girl's favourite movie. Sometimes, at night, I would wake up to the familiar whirr of a tape being rewound, the girl's mother pressing the button so that the witch was resurrected and the monkeys flew in reverse and Dorothy rose up to Kansas, all the way back to the MGM logo with the roaring lion at the beginning.

When it was time for me to finally leave the hospital, I asked my parents to buy a toy for her, something related to *The Wizard of Oz*, and they came through with a stuffed lion that looked like neither the Cowardly Lion in the movie nor the MGM logo but had to do anyway. My mother had found a beautiful red bow and wrapped it around the lion's neck and we presented it to the little girl.

I knew right away when we gave it to her, wedging the thing through the door, that it had been a terrible mistake. The size of it only emphasized that child's smallness, drowning in her hospital bed.

Her mother performed thanks to us, acting over-awed to make up for the fact that her own child, glassy eyed and unfocused, stayed tense and staring off into the distance the same way she always did.

Say thank you, her mother said and then, realizing that what she asked of her daughter was impossible, she thanked my parents instead, saying her daughter was a lucky, lucky girl.

While our parents were talking I went to say goodbye to my roommate, that little child who in all the time I had been there had never looked at me, not once. I took one of her hands in my good one and with her little child's paw she squeezed my hand. It held a tremendous amount of force for being so small. I knew that if she could have she would have, without question, given me every inch of her suffering and even more, if only it abated her own pain, and I knew, without a doubt, that if I had been offered the opportunity to take it from her I would not have done so.

I had to bite my nails into her a little to get her to let go.

Then she went back to clutching her hospital blankets as tightly as she could.

Maybe at a different time I would have gone back to that hospital after I was released and visited her. Seen her come back out of the pain and heal and relearn to walk and talk, and become friends of a sort. But

I was fourteen and embarrassed to exist and I just wanted to go home and shower and forget everything that ever happened. So I left.

THE DOCTOR SAID I COULD LIVE A PERFECTLY NORMAL LIFE WITH ONLY ONE ARM

HE WAS A young doctor and he said it the evening after the accident.

My parents were looking for reassurance and instead of telling them I would be perfectly well he told me that amputation wasn't the end of the world.

Not the end of whose world? Certainly the end for the flesh and bone that was, at that moment, still attached to me. The end of that world.

I kept expecting that at any time I would be allowed to go home and instead I had to spend nights in the hospital, sleeping fitfully, waking up with my heart beating rapidly, slowly calming myself down, and then remembering that I had been in a car accident and that Oliver was dead.

It kept coming back to me, the crunch of metal on metal, the thump of Oliver's skull hitting the windshield, the smell of blood that somehow, impossibly, I could still taste.

I still couldn't feel or move my right arm and so more tests needed to be done and no one wanted to release me.

I really did believe that everything would be alright—until Marnie came to see me.

One minute my parents were trying to fluff some life into my hospital-issued pillows; the next, Marnie was hovering in the doorway. She still looked beautiful, even in her distress. She hesitated just a moment, and we locked eyes on each other and I could see the shame of our last encounter written all over her face. And then she came rushing towards me, embracing me quickly, burying my head in her shoulder and holding me there with a grip too strong to be loving so that my mouth was mashed up against her collarbone and I couldn't speak.

I could see now what I couldn't have seen before, that if vanishing was my trick, acting was Marnie's. She was now playing the role of doting elder sister. The way she brushed the hair from my forehead and the way she lay a comforting hand on my right shoulder, which was still pins and needles, this was all designed for my parents so that they would believe this calculated lying Marnie, this Marnie whom I found repulsive, was the same Marnie we all used to adore. I shrugged Marnie's hand off my shoulder using the fact that it still ached as an excuse.

Oh of course, she said.

My parents knew that something had gone awry between us in Montreal but either they thought it wasn't serious or they had forgotten about it in all the commotion of the accident. Either way they did not rush to separate us which was why Marnie was there when another doctor came in.

He had the bloodshot eyes of an alcoholic and he sat down and in a booming voice introduced himself to the family.

The father, the mother, and the sister, he said. A full set.

Then he explained that while there were still tests to be done they believed the impact of my right side hitting the car had injured my arm so severely that it would have to be amputated.

Who were *they*, I wanted to know, and could they be serious for a minute and go in the back where they apparently made decisions and make a different one for me.

The doctor began to explain what would happen next. We were in my shared room with the burned girl and even though the curtain was drawn for privacy every time the doctor paused for breath I could hear my roommate breathing shallowly, trying not to scream.

Eventually my father and Marnie tried to rally. They asked if we could get a second opinion or what would happen if we simply left my arm as it was, left the limb to dangle fruitlessly by my side.

But the more my father tried to bargain, the more I felt a sense of calm. As the doctor continued to discuss the possibility of sepsis, shock, the necessity for blood transfusions, I felt the surgery was inevitable. I didn't want a second opinion. I wanted to be out of the hospital as soon as possible and if my arm was the price to be paid then I would pay it.

To my surprise my mother backed me completely.

From the moment the doctor said I could live a perfectly normal life with one arm she knew that, going forward, one arm was all I was going to have.

PREPARATIONS

IT WAS ALL very quick after that.

There was a second opinion even though I didn't want it. There were consultations. But before I had much time to think I had to mark my dead arm with an X with a black Sharpie and my parents had to sign forms.

Then they wheeled me into an operating room with a table that had a kind of extension on it and I watched as they unfurled my damaged limb and taped it with medical tape to the extension.

I tried my best to look at my arm before they put me under but they told me I had to keep my head straight and look up, so I didn't even get a last goodbye.

The only question I had before they cut me in two was if I could keep my arm once it had been severed.

No.

Once we were parted my arm was considered medical waste and would be disposed of properly.

HOME AGAIN

ON LINDEN TERRACE my family tried to throw me a Welcome Back party. The decorations and balloons were ones we kept in the closet and brought out for birthday parties, bright and beribboned.

No one could quite keep a smile on their face and no one knew what to say or how to act, giving the whole room a funereal air.

It was made even worse by the fact that Marnie, now on extended leave from McGill, was there, as was aunt Eshkie who kept making fake sad faces and saying things under her breath like Such a shame. Cousin Marnie was my one salvation; she made faces when aunt Eshkie wasn't looking and finally dragged her mother off into the kitchen so I could have a break.

What I really wanted to do was go upstairs and shower, but instead I was forced to interact with my miserable family and pick at the Black Forest cake aunt Eshkie had brought.

I didn't even like Black Forest cake.

No one had bothered to invite any of my friends even though they knew that I had been in the hospital and why. Once, when Marnie and I were alone together in my hospital room not talking during one of the interminable waits between consultations with doctors and nurses, I had plucked her phone out of her bag and called a friend, telling her I had gotten into a car accident. We talked till Marnie's minutes ran out and even though her jaw tightened in annoyance Marnie couldn't say anything and didn't because I was in the hospital about to be hacked apart.

The party was also awful because, around aunt Edith and uncle Bobby and cousin Marnie, I felt embarrassed of my body and wore my temporary prosthetic.

It was a terrible thing to wear. It didn't quite fit properly and badly chafed me where my scar was, the flesh still purple and swollen where it was stitched together. The prosthetic was supposedly flesh-coloured but it was a pale sort of beige that didn't come close to matching my skin, or the skin of any human I had ever seen. And yet. When I didn't have it on I was aware that when people looked at me they wouldn't see me at all, only the absence of my arm. More than that, more than being self-consciously aware of how I looked to others, there was something that no avoiding mirrors or avoiding other people would have altered. When I didn't have my prosthetic on, my right side felt wrong, felt light. I felt the imbalance profoundly; it caused me to resent my left arm, to be all too aware of its weight and feel like it was yanking me to one side. I kept thinking that I needed to grab a weight or something and hold it in my right hand to redress the balance, only every time I had that thought I had a second awful correcting thought: there was no hand on my right side to hold that weight.

Eventually the forced nature of the festivities and my own pain wore me right through. I went up to my room, not even bothering with excuses, and tore off the fake arm, flinging it into a corner and lying down on the bed in my room, Marnie's room, which I had indeed taken over when she went to university.

I was careful to position myself on my left side, arranging myself so as to jostle my injured arm as little as possible. There was still pain; I began counting hoping to reach a number where it would become bearable.

In my room, like in my hospital room, the noise of stertorous breathing, this time my own, lulled me to sleep.

The door opening must have woken me up, because suddenly I couldn't hear the knocking of Oliver's head against the glass play over and over in my ear like a metronome.

Instead there was the noise of Marnie's movements in the dark. She picked up the arm from where I'd dropped it.

The next one will be better, I promise you that, she said.

Fuck off, Marnie.

It didn't feel as good to say as I thought it would. It didn't come close to hurting her the way I was hurt, still bleeding and in so much pain.

Are the Eshkies still here?

Yeah, Marnie said.

I wish they'd leave. I didn't ask for them to be here. You could have at least told Mama and Dad to invite my friends.

They did, Marnie said after a while. They called them when you were in the hospital and begged them to visit. You know the way Mama is. She even offered them money. They didn't want to come.

She placed the arm gently on my dresser and walked out.

THERE IS NO LIMIT TO SUFFERING

HOW DID PEOPLE walk around after a death? How did they brush their teeth and laugh and work and go to brunch and tell stories and listen to people tell them stories in return?

It wasn't that I thought my pain was greater than theirs. On the contrary, I knew that there were unspeakable losses that were worse than mine. What worried me was the weakness in my spirit, my inability to move forward, to go on living. I was afraid that like a pinned butterfly, helplessly flapping my wings, I would be immobilized by my grief, unable to move on.

NEW WOUNDS

I MAY HAVE lost an arm but I found, in the coming months, that I had gained a disproportionate amount of power within our family unit. I told my mother I didn't want Marnie around anymore. She went back to university.

I told my father I wasn't ready to go back to school and he went and talked to the faculty and came back with workbooks and readings, telling me I didn't have to go back until after winter break.

He asked me once how the schoolwork was going and when I said I didn't know, he never brought it up again.

It occurred to me at one point to ask to go to Oliver's funeral. My father told me he had been buried weeks ago. This turned out not to be true, but I didn't know it at the time. This was also how I found that my grandmother had been buried not within days or weeks as I remembered it but within a day of her death as was the custom in Jewish law.

But I remember, I stubbornly insisted to my mother as she changed out my bandage in the kitchen, peeling away the layers.

She was the one to do it; my father couldn't bear it.

At first the closer she got to the wound the dirtier the layers became, the snow-white outer layer gradually giving way to a pad of cotton gauze wet with my blood. Every time we changed the bandage there was a little bit less blood, a smaller amount of pus.

It was healing well but still, on that occasion, my wound was weeping.

It was within the day, my mother told me. Jews bury their dead immediately.

It was strange to reflect on how elastic my memory was, how it had stretched out the time between my grandmother dying and her burial so that I could have sworn it had happened over a longer period. I was so convinced of this I actually asked my father for confirmation.

Of course, Alma, he said. That's why Bobby was the one to take you for dresses. Eshkie and I were picking the coffin, your mother drove us there. It was a mess, the whole thing. A blur.

A VISITOR

A BLUR WAS how I would describe the haze between my surgery and my return to school after the winter break.

The only places I had to be were doctor's appointments and in between I dressed in nothing but sweatpants and huge oversized cotton T-shirts, boyfriend shirts I called them because they were the sort of T-shirt a girl got from her boyfriend and wore around the house to remind her of his smell.

Our laundry machine appeared to vomit one up every now and then, these strange masculine mysteries. What was a Euro Final? Who in my family cared to have a promotional T-shirt for Labatt beer?

Maybe somewhere along the way Marnie had had a secret boyfriend and they were hers, though she always denied it and they kept appearing even after Marnie had moved away.

They were my uniform that late fall and early winter. They were what I wore to my medical appointments even though they embarrassed my mother. They were what I wore to sleep. They were what I wore no matter what I did.

Mostly what I did in those clothes was watch old movies.

Movies were easy. I had finally figured out how to pirate them and that's what I did all day, slowing down the internet connection to the point where other pages wouldn't load.

While I waited for my illicit material to download percentage by fragmented percentage, I sat in front of the TV watching old movies on TCM until my eyeballs burned. I developed ludicrous and painful crushes on Gary Cooper and Franchot Tone, their kind eyes and genteel manners obscuring the fact that in their real lives they were wife-beaters.

I watched Technicolor garbage that all bled together, the studio work shoddy, the stars forgettable, the only thing particularly notable sexism or racism atypical even for the period.

In the evening, when my parents came home from work, I went to my room, passed out for a few hours, and then in the early hours of the morning, when they were asleep, woke up and snuck down to the den. That was where our family computer was located, in the most public space in the house, so that my parents, just by walking by, could conveniently check to see if any online predators were trying to groom me. They needn't have worried. I wasn't interested in any sort of social interaction.

Instead I watched what I had downloaded during the day.

It would have been an alright, aimless sort of existence if not for the fact that sometimes I reached with my right hand for the computer mouse or a snack, my hand felt nothing, and when I looked down, I realized it was not because those things weren't there but because my hand wasn't.

Because my parents no longer had any sort of control over me and my habits they didn't protest as I slunk further into isolation.

One day in the afternoon after my parents had come home and I was sleeping, I heard the most gentle knock on my door.

Fuck off.

In the before, my mother would have slapped me if I ever said this to her. I think she had made her peace that her Canadian children would end up weak-willed and disrespectful, but there were limits.

Now this was my new default greeting and no one slapped me.

There was a pause outside the door and my mother meekly said, Please, Almita, open the door.

Her pleading tone rattled me.

Go away.

You have a visitor, darling.

I wondered if it was Marnie. We still weren't talking though she called sometimes and often sent me long, winding emails I deleted and fat letters I put through the shredder in my father's home office, turning her poison words into harmless confetti.

But I was still weak enough to think that maybe it was one of my friends from school. The blunt way they had all dropped me was somehow still sharp enough to cut through the pain of losing a limb, and every now and then, in moments of extreme weakness, I would open MSN Messenger and look at all the illuminated green lights beside my friends' handles, my own profile set to offline grey.

They were there onscreen and only a few blocks away from me, strewn around the Glebe, in their dens or their computer rooms or their own bedrooms, typing away at each other. I knew these rooms intimately, I had spent so much time in them, sat beside my friends at the computer, coaching them on what to say and not say to our friends and crushes in other rooms doing the same thing. And yet somehow, alone, I couldn't bring myself to open a box, to peck out a message letter by letter with my left hand. To ask where they were when I was alone.

I went downstairs in my sweatpants and my ratty old T-shirt with only one arm and there was the boy, Kowalski, Constantine Kowalski, holding a rather pathetic looking bouquet of drugstore roses. They were brown at the tips.

Hi, he said. I don't know if you remember me.

I do, I said and then I flinched because I had been about to call him Oliver's roommate and just at the thought, the thought of the word *Oliver*, I could once again hear the thud of his skull hitting the windshield.

Though my wound was cleaned daily I couldn't remember the last time I had showered. I was suddenly aware that my hair was matted and itchy and I stunk so much I could smell my own fug. My sleeve covered most of what was left of my arm but still I felt compelled to tug it down and then was annoyed at myself for this display of self-consciousness. I was also aware of my mother and father, hovering beside Constantine, looking back and forth between us with so much hope it terrified me.

We ended up watching *The Wizard of Oz*, which I had asked my parents to buy as soon as I left the hospital.

It was a movie I had taken to watching over and over again if there was nothing good on TCM and I was between downloads. Maybe after all the time watching it with the burn girl it should have driven me crazy, but instead I found the repetition comforting. I was so familiar with it I could walk away or fall asleep and when I came back, no matter what part of the movie was on, I knew exactly what had just happened and what came next.

Constantine had never seen it so I spent most of the time watching his reactions, his wide-eyed wonder at the tornado, his exclamations that Toto was cute, his skepticism about how janky the Cowardly Lion's face mask looked.

My dad sat with us to watch it, every now and then interjecting with a Did you know?

My dad was full of movie trivia. Sometime, somewhere, in the lost lonely childhood of his existence, his family murdered and his parents working to secure their future in the new country, he had comforted himself with movies and books about movies and now no matter what old movie I watched he had not only already seen it but more often than not had something to say about it.

For Constantine's benefit he started in on Judy Garland trivia.

She was sixteen when she filmed this, he said as she started in on Somewhere Over the Rainbow. Big voice for a little girl.

Around the time Dorothy was locked in the witch's castle, crying for auntie Em, I realized that I was leaning against Constantine. I felt revolting but he had an arm around me like I wasn't.

Did you know, my dad said, his pupils wide with wonder, that Margaret Hamilton also worked with Judy Garland on *Babes in Arms*?

I did know that, and I had heard him say about it a million times in the hospital and half a million since I left.

What's *Babes in Arms*? Constantine said.

We gaped at him.

He didn't notice. Instead he pointed at the screen and said, Which one of them is Margaret Hamilton?

Constantine stayed for supper. It was oddly nice. He talked a lot about school. He wanted to be a teacher and McGill had some special program for educators that he explained in detail to my parents. I studied him as he talked, as my father told him he was skin and bones and kept trying to sneak extra potatoes onto his plate. He could have been a friend of Marnie's driving through the city just to say hello.

After supper my father actually asked him if he had a place to stay but Constantine said he had to go back to Montreal. He was going to take the Greyhound.

I'll take you, my father said.

While he went to warm up the car, Constantine and I stood in the foyer.

I watched him kneel awkwardly to put his snow boots on and wondered how on earth I would ever do the same now that I was one-handed.

Suddenly, as if aware I had been watching the whole time, Constantine looked up from tying his boots.

I'm sorry about what happened.

I actually felt a pang of annoyance that he mentioned it. It had been such a perfect night until then.

Yeah, well, thanks, I said not particularly gratefully.

I'm glad I got to see you though, he said. I think about you a lot.

I hadn't thought of him once since I had walked out the door of his apartment. My mind was a swirl of other people—Oliver, my parents, my not-friends, Marnie. Maybe that was all life was. Thinking of people who didn't want you, and the people who did want you being the ones you didn't want back.

And I was worried, Constantine continued. When you weren't there at the memorial service.

What memorial service? I asked.

Which is how I found out that goys don't bury their dead right away. That while I had been living in the movies life had been going around outside of me and I had missed it all. Missed the memorial service arranged by Oliver's mother for some of his old teachers, a handful of friends who had stayed in Ottawa for university, and many of his McGill friends, people who had known him for three months at most, all of them saying goodbye to the man I had watched die right in front of me, the man I knew most intimately, the thump of his skull on glass the sound I heard every time I shut my eyes and which woke me up every morning.

THE MOTHER IN GRIEF

AFTER EVERYTHING THAT Constantine had said I started spending more time staring at Oliver's house, watching as winter deepened and a thick layer of snow fell over everything. Before Constantine I was getting to be brilliant at ignoring things quite close to me, of narrowing my already narrow vision and turning my head away so that I didn't have to see the things I didn't want to see. Now, at night, I turned off my lights and peered between the curtains at Oliver's house. I even unearthed a pair of binoculars from my father's brief flirtation with birding. I used them to spy on the house's sole remaining occupant, Oliver's mother. Mrs. Jentsch.

The windows to the back kitchen were wide and curtainless. All the better for me to spy on Mrs. Jentsch who, I discovered during my night watching, spent a lot of time in the kitchen, illuminated by the sickly yellow light of a naked bulb.

Sometimes she brought a book down to the kitchen table, sometimes she brought an item to tinker with, magnifying glasses on her head, her back humped protectively as she worked it over with her hands.

Mostly though she just sat there and smoked, staring out at nothing.

I admired her ability to simply be.

Some evenings I would peep out through the window, go downstairs, watch an entirety of a movie, get a drink or some food, go back upstairs, and peer through the curtains. She'd still be there in the same pose or one close enough that I couldn't differentiate it from her earlier one. Even her smoking was slow; she went a long time between drags and once I watched as she lit a cigarette, brought it close to her lips, and then just kept it there as if frozen. It was as though someone had hit pause on reality. I was far enough away I couldn't really see quite what was happening but I assume that at some point the cigarette burned itself down to filter, because after what seemed forever she dropped her hand towards an ashtray and then sat staring some more.

It was like watching a one-woman performance on grief that she was acting out every night, just for me.

I longed to join her.

I began to daydream about Mrs. Jentsch. Of being in her kitchen. Of talking with her about Oliver. For her I would lift up the long sleeve of my boyfriend T-shirt and reveal the raw scar, still bright red and jagged in all the places my flesh had been stitched together. I would tell her that Oliver had been nothing but good to me. I would tell her what I had never admitted to anyone before, that I loved him, that I had loved him since the time he ushered me across the fence between our two houses and held me in his lap. That I knew I was fourteen but I would have married him if he had lived long enough.

I could picture Mrs. Jentsch reaching across her kitchen table with the hand that didn't hold her cigarette and putting it on the only hand I had left, like a blessing. I would move into the house and take care of her and she would take care of me and we would grow old together like that, the not-mother-in-law and the not-daughter-in-law bound together by our love for this absentee.

I wanted to go straight to Mrs. Jentsch right away as soon as I had that thought. But there was one thing that prevented me from doing so. In all my daydreams I entered her home through the back door, just as I had done the one time Oliver had led me by the hand to his home.

That was what I wanted to do again, to cross over the boundary that separated our two homes just like when I was a child. But practicality got in the way. There was a fence between our two properties and unlike in fantasies or dreams I could not simply fly over it.

One night at three in the morning I put on my winter coat and simply went to her. I did not zip it up, for I still hadn't quite figured out how to do that one-handed, and instead went dashing out in the cold, out my front door and around the corner. It wasn't at all like I thought it would be. It wasn't romantic. It is hard to feel romantic about anything when running around in the cold of an Ottawan winter with an unzipped coat. The air you breathe in rattles your lungs, chills your bones, hardens your nipples. And instead of gracefully making the transition between our backyard and the Jentsch backyard as I had imagined in my fantasies, I had to run past several houses, around a corner, and then remember which was the Jentsch house. I was sure I would remember it but I didn't and it was only when I peeped around the unplowed driveway that led round to the back of the house and saw the back of my house that I knew where to stop.

I had to walk up that driveway to get to the back of the house. It was an incredibly arduous process; I was still not very good at being balanced and a few times I completely fell forward into the snow and had to struggle to right myself. By the time I reached Mrs. Jentsch's back door I was a sweaty, panting mess with frozen toes and a frozen hand, the cold making my scar sting like mad as if someone had sawn off my arm again, this time with a blade chilled in ice.

I pressed myself up against the back door and knocked. She was looking directly at me and for one maddening second I thought she would gesture for me to go back around the house and come back by the front door, or that maybe she would shut the light and refuse to let me in.

But she did neither of these things. Instead she gracefully unfurled herself from the chair and came towards me. We were face to face through the glass when I realized she couldn't see me, that from her perspective it would have been like looking in a mirror.

I knocked again.

It's me, I said. It's only me.

She opened the door and I stumbled inside.

Before I felt the warmth there was that ashy smell again, invading my nostrils, turning me into a time traveller. I was five again and Oliver was alive and just around the corner and I could feel my right hand, so small, in his bigger one.

And then I breathed out again and I was just there, myself, a mess, in Mrs. Jentsch's kitchen.

If Mrs. Jentsch was surprised that a teenager had come crashing through her door in the middle of the night she didn't show it.

She went and picked up her cigarette which was still smoking on the ashtray and took a puff.

It fascinated me how up close I could see details that I couldn't see from my room. That the ashtray was actually a plate, and underneath all the grey silt it was actually a bright blue. That the thing that Mrs. Jentsch was fiddling over was a circuit board and she had all sorts of unfamiliar things strewn about her kitchen table, tiny screwdrivers and strange wires and little metal machines that also had wires and clamps of some sort dangling from them. It all looked very interesting and electrical and too dangerous to touch.

It became clear that Mrs. Jentsch had no intention of asking me what I was doing there or offering any other conversational opening.

I ran my tongue over my lips which had split in the cold. The taste of blood hit my mouth and I began to talk.

I'm Alma Alt, I began.

I know who you are.

I'm a friend, I was a friend, of your son's.

No, you weren't, Mrs. Jentsch said.

I didn't know what to say to that. I supposed it was true, but this wasn't the way it had gone in my head.

I heard you were hurt badly, Mrs. Jentsch said. She was looking at my arm, or rather she was looking at my coat where it was clear my arm wasn't.

Take off the coat, Mrs. Jentsch said.

This I knew how to do. I shrugged it off and put it on the back of a chair, and then came closer to her, lifting up the sleeve, so she could look. I turned my head away, the way I always turned my head away when my mother dressed my bandages, and then I felt it, the tickle of smoke on my elbow. That was what made me turn around, made me look where Mrs. Jentsch was looking, made me see that I had no elbow, had nothing beyond the stump that came away from the pinpricks of my shoulder. I understood, more than I had when they actually cut off my arm in the hospital, or maybe for the first time, that this was the rest of my life, that there would be no miracle where I would grow an arm, no undoing of time, that my life would always be painful and people would always be shitty and I would always hurt, for no reason at all, for nothing.

The doctors thought I was healing nicely.

I was crying and I could see Mrs. Jentsch smoking and watching me cry. She didn't reach out a hand to my good one to comfort me. She did smile a little, the corners of her lips curving upwards, though there wasn't any glee in her eyes.

It was very embarrassing in the end to keep crying in front of someone who seemed, if not indifferent, almost happy to see my pain. Eventually my tears tapered off, and the need to blow my nose became more pressing than the urge to keep crying.

I started trying to stop my nose with my hand. I thought regretfully of Constantine and the toilet paper he had offered me, something which seemed like a luxury now. Mrs. Jentsch offered me nothing. I ended up wiping my snot on my own shirt. Just another gross indignity.

What a stupid little girl you are, she said. Coming here and parading your tears around and wanting absolution. Go somewhere else if you want that. Go to a church. You think I feel sorry that you lost an arm? I lost a son.

She reached out her hand towards me and I gave her mine, dizzy with what she had said. My fantasy and reality were all at once crashing into each other.

I looked at our joined hands and thought that I didn't want absolution. I wanted to atone. And to atone for something which could not be put right was the work of a lifetime. To atone was forever.

Alma Alt, Mrs. Jentsch said to me tenderly. I wish you were the one who had died.

ACCORD

IT MIGHT SEEM strange to anyone else, but the moment that Mrs. Jentsch told me that she wished I had died instead of Oliver, we became a kind of friend to one another. It was as though, stripped of all pretense, her hatred and my acceptance of her hatred laid bare, we felt kinship.

It wasn't what I had fantasized about, alone in my room, but it felt right. Hadn't I, in my darkest thoughts, wondered why I should have lived while he didn't? Who was I to begrudge Mrs. Jentsch for thinking the same.

And seeing that she wasn't going to be able to wring any more tears out of me Mrs. Jentsch became strangely hospitable.

From somewhere she unearthed a crumpled-up tissue and after I told her that the smell of the smoke was choking me to death she wrestled open a window and we sat there in the kitchen with the cold pouring in and talked of Oliver.

He was always nice to me, I said though *nice* seemed so small a word for the tenderness he had always shown me and the way it lit a spark under my flesh.

I told her about the way I could still hear Oliver's head thumping against the windshield, perhaps something I should not have told to a dead man's mother, but she took it as well as she could, even though her eyes fluttered closed and her hand rose to cover her face when she heard.

I wish that noise would haunt you for the rest of your life, she told me. I wish it would destroy you. But it won't. You'll forget it, just like you'll forget my son.

I love him, I told her. It was another thing I had not told anyone and just like everything else that night the confession did not go as planned.

Of course you think that, Mrs. Jentsch said. You're a very melodramatic child. You don't know anything about love.

I protested a bit, but the protests did seem very theatrical and so I stopped almost as quickly as I started. I didn't need to prove anything to her.

It was very late at night and I didn't want to go back home so I asked if I could stay there, in that awful smoky house. No, that's not quite correct; I asked if I could stay in Oliver's room and Mrs. Jentsch told me I could.

Perhaps the house was worse than I remembered it, or perhaps in the years that had passed I'd remembered it more generously than it deserved, but it seemed an even more treacherous and cramped place than it had been since I last had visited. Every room seemed crowded with haphazard piles threatening an avalanche if brushed, and when we got to the stairs there were steps I had to miss, stretching my legs over them, for these steps had all manner of books and clutter on them. If I fell I was liable to break my neck and Mrs. Jentsch would not rescue me, I knew. And even if we were in accord that I should have died and not Oliver, I still wasn't ready to die, not yet.

In the end I survived all this and Mrs. Jentsch brought me to Oliver's room, retreating without a word. Not to her bedroom, wherever it was located in that house, but back to the kitchen. I could hear her creaking around on the lower floor where she haunted my dreams the rest of the night, keeping up her vigil of grief and smoking endlessly.

I heard, in later years, that some people like to keep the rooms of the dead exactly as they were when their loved ones died. In their efforts at preservation they turn the room into a dead thing itself, like a piece in a museum or a set on a stage, something always calling out in the hope that its owner will claim it once more. But Mrs. Jentsch was not like that. Or maybe she was not like that with me, because she allowed me to inhabit the room, to change it with my being there.

When I walked in it was not clear at all that anyone had occupied it since Oliver. It certainly didn't seem that way, because the bed was made and all of Oliver's things were in their general places. It was not overly neat, there was still the sense that it was lived in, but it felt as if it was poised for him to return. If there was the smell of him somewhere in that space I couldn't find it. The smell of Mrs. Jentsch's cigarettes had penetrated the walls just as it coated the rest of the house and I found that I had to open a window and let in the icy night air just to survive in that room. Whatever trace of Oliver might have lingered, I aired it out that night.

I kicked off my boots, then lined them up carefully beside his own shoes which were slightly askew against a baseboard. Then I curled up on his bed, fully clothed, cuddling down in my coat as best I could, hoping I didn't freeze to death during the night. My eyes became accustomed to the dark; I was able to look around, to see the things Oliver had touched with his own hands. Worn books of the sort I would never read. His computer monitor, much sleeker than the one we had played *SkyRoads* on, glinting in the corner. I idly opened his night table which contained a tin. There was a kind of fruity smell emanating from it and I expected to find something like candy inside. But when I flipped open the lid I found a plethora of condoms. I had never seen any up close though they looked exactly like how they were depicted in the instructional videos we were shown in school. I could feel myself blushing at the sight of them and I shut the tin quickly, put it back in the drawer of the bedside table, and shut that too.

I found the smell of them crass, their presence in that room distressing in a way I couldn't articulate.

I fell into a fretful sleep and woke up sometime in the dark, feeling frozen.

Somehow I made it out of that house.

If my parents noticed my absence perhaps they chalked it up to another of my vanishing acts. Or perhaps they were simply frightened and did not want to pick another fight with me. It was almost time for me to return back to school, to go back and sit at my desk and pretend I hadn't been maimed, left friendless, been told I should have died, with the thumping of Oliver's head against the windshield dully echoing in my skull.

It was time for me to get on with life.

And, come January and the new year, that is exactly what I did.

THE HAND

SOMETIME AROUND SPRING my parents discussed buying Mrs. Jentsch's house. This was how I found out that she had moved away. It was dirt cheap, a good investment, because Mrs. Jentsch was selling it As Is. My parents went to the open house, allowing me to come. They were shocked by the state of the place.

Who knew she was a hoarder? they said.

It would have to be completely gutted. The only decent room was Oliver's from which, as far as I could tell, she hadn't taken anything in her flight. The wiring was bad on top of all that, but my parents were still interested.

I didn't want to let them know how pleased I would have been by the prospect of Oliver's house being ours but like so much of life this dream came to nothing but disappointment. Other people outbid my parents; a noisy rosy-cheeked white family with blond hair and a can-do attitude moved in. They were collegial neighbours, but even after years of being invited to their barbecues and seeing them at the grocery store I always thought of them as the new people who lived in Oliver's house.

They immediately began stripping the house to its bones, tossing everything that had once belonged to Mrs. Jentsch and Oliver into a revolving series of dumpsters that resided in their driveway for months.

That year when school ended Marnie went to Mexico for the summer and my parents bought me a cherry-red bike. They had a bar welded between the handles so that I could hold on to it one-handed.

I had never learned to ride before the accident so by the time I mastered it, riding one-handed felt like the most natural thing in the world. I couldn't imagine it any different.

I liked to ride along the canal, ringing the little bell my father had affixed to the handle to warn people to get out of the way, doing a loop around the borders of the Glebe before heading home. I always finished my rides not by going straight from the canal to Linden Terrace but by looping one block over and slowly cycling by Oliver's place, hoping to see what treasures the new people had thrown out.

It took until fall but one day, cycling by, I heard a dull sort of thumping from one of the dumpsters, too slow and rhythmic to belong to a living thing.

As Mrs. Jentsch had predicted, my mind had not been able to hold on to the memory of Oliver dying. It was just shy of a year since the accident and already the sound of the thump was something I didn't think of and couldn't call to mind even on the rare occasions when I tried. But the thump from the trash made me flinch. I circled back on my bike and parked it, climbing up the side of the dumpster and peering down.

It was there, just as I suspected. Among old bricks and rotted wood and twisted steel, the hand Mrs. Jentsch had made for Oliver, the perpetual motion machine, still drumming away. I lifted it out of the garbage and brought it to my mother who complained that I was a disgusting child for fishing things out of the trash like an urchin but who helped me clean it anyway.

She hated that hand but it didn't matter.

I kept it in my room on my bedside table. Every night as I looked out the window onto Oliver's backyard where the grass was now lush it lulled me to sleep.

My beautiful hand.

PART III
LOSS

THE YEAR MY MOTHER LEFT US

I SAW HER everywhere. Before this I would have sworn that Ottawa contained nothing but fat-bottomed white women, but now out of the corner of my eye I could see tiny fine-boned Mexicans everywhere. No, not just tiny fine-boned Mexican women. My mother specifically, her eidolons haunting the corners of my eyes. When they came closer they turned into something else: tall Indian women, short Indigenous women, particularly swarthy Italian women of no notable build whatsoever.

But my mind, missing my mother, was determined to find her and find her I did.

At night, in the humid unforgiving heat of the Ottawa summer, locked up in my new apartment, I took out a cigarette and then put it back in the pack, deciding the weather was too foul to smoke it. I called Marnie instead to ask her if she had noticed any false mothers.

I liked calling Marnie at night.

Since the accident I couldn't sleep more than two hours at a time without awakening with a shudder. Whether I remembered my nightmares or not I could tell I was still having them by the stiffness in my legs, the soreness in my throat, signs that my body had been vigorously active in my sleep. The advantage was that this left me sharp and awake most nights at three in the morning.

It also made it easy for me to call up Marnie when it was most inconvenient. To shake her from her peaceful sleep to join me in wakefulness.

She never let it ring through all the way to voicemail.

I thought I saw Mama today, I told Marnie with no preamble.

You didn't see her, Marnie said. Sleep coated her voice. It lulled me in, made me want to curl up and sleep myself.

You didn't see her, she's not here.

I said that I *thought* I saw her, I corrected meanly. Does that happen to you?

There was a pause on the other end. I could hear a gravelly sort of rumbling and the sound of Marnie getting up. I imagined Neil protesting and Marnie shushing him back to sleep, leaving the warmth of their bed and going into another room so she could whisper over the phone to me.

Far away in the same city a door clicked shut gently enough so that it did not wake up the other occupant of the house. But listening on the line I heard it.

At the bank, Marnie said softly, I grabbed the hand of the woman in front of me. I knew it wasn't Mama the second I touched her, it felt all wrong. But it looked so much like her that I was reaching for her before I knew it.

Oh, Marnie, I thought.

In that moment I felt grateful that there was one other person in the world carrying around the same grief I felt in my heart.

PLAYING PRETEND

FOR ALL HER magic Marnie never went far.

The fall after she went to Mexico she came back strange. It was only supposed to be another step in a prodigious artistic career: a friend of a friend of my mother's half-brother knew an artist there who was very respected and could help her.

I expected that, as with everything in life, Marnie would conquer Mexico, would come back full of inspiration and a million connections.

I half expected she would never come back, not fully, and the rest of her life would be spent in the U.S. or Europe, places where real artists lived.

But the Marnie who came back, who had all the markings of her former self in her straightforwardness, her ambition, her talent, was a different sort of Marnie.

She came back telling anyone who would listen that she wasn't going to be an artist anymore. She gave away almost everything, her pens, her pencils, the yellow X-Acto knife with the dirty handle she kept with her at all times for paper crafting.

All her childhood sketchbooks went into the recycling, and oh how my father cried when he found out. She would have thrown out the acrylic paints, but my father rescued them from the trash and kept them in his office.

I watched all this with indifference. That summer had been dull, filled with the sort of hot, humid weather we had more and more of in the valley, weather that caused our floorboards to warp and our doors to stick. It was too much to try to stay alive in that weather and react to Marnie's about-face.

School was on the horizon for us both, threatening me with more friendless days and boring lessons. Marnie was to go back to McGill of course, to her own apartment in the McGill ghetto, an apartment I would never see. Though she had been paying rent on it since July school didn't start until September and so she waited out the time with me.

We were sitting in the living room sweating one awful day, possibly watching *The Wizard of Oz*, which still remained a constant in the rotation. Possibly she was sick of *The Wizard of Oz* and had commandeered the VCR to play *The Red Shoes*. I was sitting on the couch, my prosthetic sticking uncomfortably to my body. This was my permanent custom prosthetic, the one that was supposed to be more comfortable than the temporary one, but it still chafed and aggravated, it still did nothing to assuage the painful numbness that spread out from the end of my stub to the top of my shoulder.

I hated wearing it. It was supposed to make me look normal though all it did was remind me that I wasn't.

I looked up from the movie at one point to see Marnie stroking the tips of the fingers on the prosthetic. They were motionless, sculpted in a way meant to look like a hand at rest. Perhaps far away the illusion held but up close I found it dispiriting and eerie.

Marnie noticed me noticing her.

It looks like a dead thing, Marnie said.

Well, it's not alive.

She went upstairs and I continued to melt into the couch.

Marnie came back with the rescued acrylic paints and some old newspapers.

Give me that, she said grabbing at my false arm.

It came off with a satisfying suction pop like a Barbie's arm dislodged from its socket.

What are you doing?

She didn't bother answering me but took the arm away, carrying it reverently to the kitchen where she got on with the business of turning it into something living while I turned to TCM where they were in the middle of a Buñuel marathon.

Has Marnie fed you yet? my mother asked when my parents came home.

I'm not hungry, I said. I'm watching Bunuel.

Buñuel, my mother corrected automatically, stressing the ñ.

TCM was still playing his Mexican-era films. It was funny to think of my mother being a child in DF at the same time Buñuel was making the masterpieces that would outlast him, masterpieces which would one day be played on a TV screen in Ottawa in front of that Mexican child, now a woman. I felt the same way watching Cronenberg films. While my parents were meeting and falling in love in Toronto Cronenberg had been making highly regional cinema in nearly the same place at the exact same time.

Were there geniuses at work in Ottawa? Would I one day look back on the pittance of my life and wonder how I could have walked the same streets as some brilliant unknown who had been able to translate their experiences into something that endured? I doubted it. Genius, like all interesting things, existed elsewhere. Ottawa had an unimpeachable track record of flattening the people who lived here into submissive ordinariness.

From the kitchen my mother screamed.

I ran to see what was the matter and saw my arm on the kitchen table now midnight blue, shining brilliantly on top of paint-splattered old copies of *The Glebe Report*.

I had no idea how she had done it but Marnie had added a full moon that actually seemed to glow.

I loved it.

Of course my parents were not impressed. They told Marnie to get a damn job and pay for my replacement which is not something they had ever told either of us to do before. One thing they had always been in agreement on was that money was their problem, grades were ours.

And yet because I was pleased with the arm Marnie bore the punishment willingly. She went back to Montreal where she did get a job at a coffee shop and sent my parents cheques they refused to cash, their anger having dissipated. I kept the arm as it was, with its moon and constellation of stars strewn like diamonds across it.

By the time Marnie came back for Christmas I didn't want a new arm.

She bought me one anyway.

She painted that one in reds so that it appeared to have flames licking up the side and she figured out how to rig it so that the ring finger functioned as a lighter. I got sent home from school with a note from the principal for that one.

But it started something between us, something private that continued well into our adulthood.

In public Marnie turned into someone else. She switched her general BA to a B.Eng. in mechanical engineering. She finished out her degree in the following three years, moved back to Ottawa, interviewed for several government agencies, and settled at NRCan, neatly sliding into the anonymity of a government functionary.

She married her university boyfriend, Neil, a placid white boy from an Anglican Scottish family. He had been with her at Montreal—he went to Concordia—but she never mentioned him until they were engaged, though he seemed familiar enough with all of us.

She became, in so many ways, what my parents had always wanted her to be, someone quite ordinary.

It was cousin Marnie who became someone, who went somewhere. After graduating from uOttawa she had gone to New York City for school and stayed there. My communications with cousin Marnie were severed by geography and her own busy work schedule but I was kept abreast of her increasingly meteoric rise by aunt Eshkie. She worked in finance at first and then in politics.

I saw her once on CNN (a *hit*, aunt Eshkie told me proudly. They call them *media hits*). Her frizzed hair had been flat ironed into a thick bouncy bob that gave the impression of a wig. She was wearing a ridiculous amount of makeup. But there she was, my cousin Marnie, miniaturized and on American TV. A star!

As for me, it became increasingly murky to remember but hadn't I once wanted to leave Ottawa, to go somewhere else, somewhere where things happened? I never did. It was like once I lost my arm I lost something else. How ridiculous that so much could be contained in a few twisted-up lengths of sinew and vein and bone. But there it was. I stopped being Alma with two arms, whoever she was. I even stopped being that half-Mexican half-Jewish girl. Instead I became the girl with one arm, the worst thing that ever happened to me worn on my body for everyone to see.

I went to university because my father demanded it, because that was what was expected of girls from the Glebe. But I was indifferent to which one I went to and flipped a coin to decide between Carleton University and the University of Ottawa. I went to classes, made no friends, and graduated with a degree in communications, unnoticed and with a mediocre average.

Afterwards I went straight to work for the family business. We were a family of accountants, my father and aunt Eshkie and uncle Bobby CPAs, my mother and I the supports. It was a pity job that paid a pittance: mostly I made calls, digitized files, and played solitaire while ignoring my father and uncle Bobby's increasingly pointed suggestion that I go back to school and become a CPA myself.

We worked out of the other house my grandparents had bought in the Glebe. There was an in-law suite at the top of the house which is where my grandparents had raised my father and Eshkie and where Eshkie and uncle Bobby had raised cousin Marnie. Now they lived there alone and came downstairs to work. Would probably keep doing so until they died. There was still a fully functional kitchen in the work half of the house, but more often than not no one actually ate out of it. For lunch aunt Eshkie would run upstairs and heat something she had pre-prepared for herself and uncle Bobby.

When we were little girls and my mother still stayed at home my father got in the habit of coming back home for lunch. He still did that sometimes but mostly he brought a sandwich and ate at his desk, working between bites.

My mother and I often left together and ate lunch at a restaurant along Bank. We would sometimes take long, ridiculous two- or three-hour lunches, coming back luxuriously late, aunt Eshkie apoplectic, my father pink-faced with frustration huffing, I called you.

I felt bad about it, but my mother always seemed to find their agitation amusing.

What are they going to do? Fire us? And she would laugh.

I saw her point though. We were family and there was no chance that they would turn us out. Besides, despite these indulgent lunches she was a harder worker than anyone, would stay in late in tax season, would calm the difficult clients, telling tame terrible jokes when they came in, nervously, to sign their forms. She had a box of tissues at the ready when people would cry over how much they owed and she would coo in sympathy even as, over their heads, she was rolling her eyes.

It was strange how in those years, tethered to my mother, instead of resenting her I grew to love her more. We knew each other in a strange and intimate way probably not afforded to most mothers and daughters, who were constantly separated by the circumstances of life: marriage, geography, their own children.

Over lunch she would tell me how miserable this country had made her in the beginning when she barely knew enough English to string together a full sentence. How she had chosen it after she saw a postcard of Niagara Falls as a young girl and fell in love with the beauty of the place.

She told me of driving through America and being terrified that her companions would rape her and determining that if it happened she would not fight it but simply let it wash through her and then go on with life. She told me of the time they stopped for gas in a sundown town and the gas attendant promised to lynch her companions if they didn't drive all the way through before dark.

I think she told me these things because she thought I would never leave her. My arm, or rather the lack of it, made her think of me as unlovable. Or maybe not unlovable—I believe she did love me. But she did think that the injury made me an unsexual being, a woman that no man would choose. It desexed me, rendered me into a perfect eternal daughter.

It was why she never was threatened by Constantine.

After that first visit he kept coming back. The first few times he mentioned that he had been to see Mrs. Jentsch, but after she disappeared he came only to see me. At first we talked about Oliver, though there wasn't much for Constantine to say.

He was a fun guy but a terrible housekeeper, Constantine told me. Couldn't even boil water without almost burning the place down.

Eventually we talked about me. He listened to my complaints about Marnie. He helped me with my homework. He was the one who sided with my father about going to university, who encouraged me to choose communications because at least I could watch movies for credit. The one who reluctantly bought me a pack of cigarettes so I could try them for the first time, a decision he came to regret when I became a casual smoker.

He moved to Ottawa after graduation so he could keep taking care of me. He became my only friend.

When we kissed for the first time, at my behest, it was only because I was of the firm belief that because of my arm no one would ever do it organically. Constantine was the only man consistently in my life I could practise on.

Our relationship staggered on like that for years.

I missed the first time he said he loved me, because I was trying to see if anyone was looking at my arm and caught a woman hastily turning her head away to hide that she had been.

I love you, Constantine repeated.

I laughed.

I thought it was a joke.

But even as my favourite boyfriend T-shirts migrated to his apartment the address on my health card never changed and my birth certificate and passport remained in my father's study.

I would rather live in a hundred-year-old house with creaky floors, leaky faucets, and doors to nowhere than a soulless condo, I told him every time he pressed me to move in with him.

You're a snob, Marnie told me.

She had long since moved to the Golden Triangle. Her home always had tarps and exposed wooden frames and I had to wear shoes indoors because I was always stepping on stray staples and nails and drill bits from the endless renovating.

I'm not a snob, I said. I'm a Glebite.

THE ONE WHO STAYED

BUT BECAUSE I was the deficient one, the one who stayed, the one who couldn't leave, I was the one who was there, one smoggy spring afternoon walking arm in arm with Mama, on our way to lunch, when she stopped in front of one of the big houses on Clemow and said, Marnie, I don't feel well.

It's *Alma*, I snapped at her.

I was always so annoyed when she did this, when she called me by Marnie's name or Marnie by my name as if we were the same by virtue of being her daughters instead of being two very, very different people, one of whom had one arm and one of whom was happy.

Then I looked at my mother.

My mother's death was something I thought about in an abstract way before it happened. But after it became reality I couldn't stop going over and over the details in my mind. It was something I wish I could forget but there is the brain again, that magnificent wondrous thing, and instead of protecting me and cleaving away from the pain it cleaved to it. It wanted to know exactly what happened, going over the details of that afternoon over and over again wanting to change the outcome in case it ever happened again.

But I couldn't change what had happened.

The second I saw my mother's face I knew immediately that something was wrong.

I told her to lie down on the fresh cool grass and she did so obediently. The lawn belonged to the Proctors, the mother of whom had led Marnie's Brownie group. Brown Owl she was called. I had never been a Brownie but I had tagged along to a few meetings and watched her set out a ceremonial toadstool in the centre of a circle as the Brownies all listed the good deeds they had done that week. I thought of all this as I called 911, a strange thing to call 911 since most of my life I had been worried about accidentally calling it, about clogging the emergency line by accident. And now, here was an emergency.

My mother lay down on the lawn neatly, her hands clasped over her stomach like she was playing at being the Lady of Shalott.

That was another sign things were wrong. My mother never liked doing anything that could be viewed as improper or attention-seeking. But there she was, lying down meekly, not caring that the grass was going to stain her cream-coloured shell.

All the natural copper colour had drained from her face leaving her with an eerie ashy pallor.

I was able to remain cogent as the 911 operator asked me questions. I told her exactly what street we were on, read the number of the Proctors' house, and privately prayed they wouldn't come out. I had a vague horror that they would ask me questions about what Marnie was up to as my mother lay dying and we would both be too polite to do anything but say, Marnie's doing well. She works for NRCan and is married now. And then we would struggle to think of something nice to say about Neil.

A woman in flip-flops with a lip of fat poking over the edge of her shorts came towards us, walking her dog. This blessed woman sat on the grass with us and took my mother's pulse, gave her some water, waited with me until the paramedics came. They bundled up my mother and me and took us to the hospital and then they left us in the hallway, my mother still tucked up tight in a stretcher with me beside her. I stroked her arm gently with my finger. She was shivering in the heat and I wanted to be tender with the only bit of her flesh available to me.

There were signs everywhere warning that we were not allowed to use cellphones in that part of the hospital. I was contemplating whether or not my mother was well enough that I could leave her for a minute to let my father know where we were, when I noticed that the numbers on her blood pressure monitor were falling.

It was so quick. A series of beeps on a monitor and then I looked up at her and something was clearly wrong.

Her eyes rolled back, no one was looking at her, and I called to the paramedics who were at the nurses' station, casually chatting, and when they couldn't hear my voice, strangled by my panic, I reached up my hand to tap the male on the shoulder, but I wasn't wearing my prosthetic that day, and maybe that cost me a precious second, maybe less, but it felt like forever till I was touching the paramedic on the shoulder and saying, Excuse me, and pointing at my mother.

Things happened very quickly then.

About five medical professionals descended on her stretcher.

She was rolled into a room.

Someone began to cut open her shirt and bra, exposing her breasts to the medical staff. The skin of her breasts was paler than the rest of her, and I felt a surge of protectiveness towards them as if they were not a part of her but their own independent entities, two frightened, quivering, helpless creatures. The last thing I thought before someone pulled a curtain between us was that my mother, who was so proper, who never let me swear, my mother would have rather died than have a group of strangers see her exposed like that.

Then a social worker and an intake nurse descended on me.

While my mother died they asked me all sorts of questions. What a relief it was to be able to punctually answer her name, date of birth, and her health card number which was on the OHIP card I retrieved out of her purse with shaking hands.

They asked what they could do for me. I told them I needed to call my father and they took me to a landline at the nurses' station where I called first my father and then Marnie.

Don't panic, I said to each of them even as I was panicking. Don't panic but Mom is in the hospital and you need to get here right away.

Then I was allowed back in the room to see my mother.

She was lying on the hospital bed, flat on her back, her eyes closed. Gravity was bringing in to relief the planes of her face, the bump on her nose, the cheekbones which had become sharp with age.

She didn't open her eyes when I walked in but when I reached down to hold her hand she clutched it back, so strong it hurt.

She looked dead.

She wasn't.

Her eyes fluttered open briefly.

Almita, she said.

Her grip was strong.

They had brought her back to me, you see. She had flatlined, right after they took her from me; she had died, and they had brought her back.

THE CHILD

HAVE YOU NOTICED, Marnie said not long after our mother's resurrection, that the heart attack has made her rather cruel?

We were in the kitchen of our parents' house, making a family meal the way we always did on Fridays, a sort of truncated Shabbat where we recited no prayers but turned off the lights, put our phones away, and talked by candlelight, an echo of an echo of something my father's family might have done in the past.

I wanted to dump the carrot peels I was sweeping up on top of Marnie's head.

Well, I said. She died.

It was true that when she came back Mama had become different. She had always told us unvarnished truths and been severe and demanding. But now her determination was single-minded.

You need to be independent, she kept telling me. You need to go off on your own. I can't take care of you forever.

This was how I ended up being evicted from my childhood home. At my mother's behest my father persuaded one of his clients, who owned a low-rise a few blocks away from our house and rented at dirt-cheap prices, to rent to me for a subsoil-cheap price.

I lived on the third floor of that rickety building. The floors slanted and there was no central air conditioning or in-suite laundry, causing me to return home every time I needed to wash my clothes. Every evening of that hot sticky summer after my mother died and came back I opened my windows and listened to my landlady and her adult daughter screaming vile things at each other, the kind of things no one should ever say to someone they loved but which only ever seemed to be said to people by people they loved, fuelled by a kind of anger only a loved one can provoke. I listened and understood why the rent was so cheap and thought of my mother and wished I could walk the few blocks back home, past the brick school and Patterson Creek till I was at our home in Linden Terrace where I could scream vile things at her till she let me come back to her.

But even though I hated the way she pushed me away I understood it. I imagined dying had a way of reordering a person's universe. I just wished she wanted to spend more time with me.

Marnie was different. With her job and her Neil and her life outside the confines of the Glebe, she didn't understand why Mama was so sharp. She always looked taken aback when she returned home. She didn't understand why Mama no longer took an interest in her career. She was puzzled when Mama no longer deferred to Neil when he was in the house.

Marnie, Mama said when Marnie asked her if he had done anything to offend her, he's just such a plain man.

That evening after we had eaten Marnie tapped her glass with her knife which was not something she ever did.

Excuse me, she said. Her voice trembled a little. I have something to say.

So say it, my mother said.

Neil fiddled with the edge of his placemat. Marnie glared at Mama.

I'm very happy—*we're* very happy to say that I'm pregnant.

Oh, I thought. Marnie had never mentioned wanting kids. I had begun to think that she and Neil didn't want them. I glanced at Marnie's stomach which looked the same as it always did.

Papa began to cry. He was shorter than Marnie but somehow he managed to pick her up and swing her around.

Stop it, she said laughing, you'll hurt yourself!

But he was so happy he couldn't stop.

I'm going to be a zaide.

He clapped Neil on the back.

I was grateful for his excitement. It allowed me time to structure my face in a grimace resembling a smile and gave my mother time to slip out of the dining room into the kitchen.

Congratulations to you, I said to Neil as Marnie dropped Papa's hand and went into the kitchen.

Have you thought of any names yet? my father said inanely to try to cover what was about to happen in the kitchen.

Aren't you excited about being an abuelita? I could hear Marnie's voice loud and demanding.

No, my mother said.

Neil nervously clutched his fork, the smile on his face sliding slowly downwards as he realized that whatever vision of familial joy he had imagined would not be forthcoming.

Um, Neil said. It's a bit early for names.

As far as I could tell he came from a family that never talked about anything real and any words or actions outside of pleasantries alarmed him to the point of mutism. The way we spoke to each other terrified him.

Mom, Marnie said, her voice rising. She only ever called Mama that when she was annoyed. That hard Canadian *Mom* instead of the Mexican *Mama*, with the emphasis on the last syllable.

Now, my father said to Neil, I'm not sure what your people do—

He was interrupted by Mama yelling from the kitchen, You'll understand when you give birth that the only thing in this life for your children is pain.

Jesus!

We all looked at Neil.

It's okay, my father said. You know it's been hard for Merced. With the sickness.

With dying, I corrected.

It was too much for Neil. He stood up abruptly and my father and I looked at him expectantly waiting for him to burst into the kitchen and rescue Marnie from my mother.

Excuse me. I need some air.

And with that he scurried off.

We didn't even wait to hear the door slam before my father and I were rushing to the kitchen, my father to berate my mother just as I rushed to defend her.

There was nothing wrong with what she had said. Life was pain. Monotony punctured by death with no respite in sight.

But Marnie took it so personally.

I didn't know how to tell Marnie, but I didn't particularly care for my future niece or nephew myself. The world seemed committed to suicide. Every year was warmer than the last; every season brought news of unseasonable floods and fires. It was unreasonable to have a child.

This was something I had been thinking more and more of as Constantine talked dreamily of the future. To my utter surprise, of late he had been talking about marriage. About children.

It wasn't just that I didn't love him. When I thought of bringing a child into this world, of being a mother, what came to mind were hospitals where arms were cut off and people died and were resurrected. Hadn't I experienced enough pain in this life and any other? Why did he want me to mutilate my body only to birth a death?

I said something like this to Constantine because it was easier than telling him that the feelings he had for me weren't ones I had for him. That despite the time we spent together I always expected that one day he would find someone real to settle down with and have his children. Someone who wasn't me.

He began to suggest that I should talk to someone.

I love you a lot Alma, he said, but I don't know how to fix this.

Fix what? I wanted to know. I'm fine.

But he kept persisting in his gentle Constantine way, suggesting the names of therapists, offering to role play asking the doctor for medication I told him I not only didn't want but didn't need.

So I cut off Constantine ignoring his phone calls and disinviting him from not-Shabbat where he and Neil had been allies of a sort. He would have hugged Marnie if he had been there. He would have followed Neil outside and tried to talk to him.

Eventually Marnie left, taking Neil with her. My father, furious for once at my mother, went to his study to angrily read.

I sprawled on the couch, waiting for my mother to find me and order me home.

You're still here? she said when she found me.

I was watching American news. Or rather I was watching commercial breaks between American news. An ad for a drug company began to list all its potential side effects. Restless leg syndrome. Bleeding rectum. Suicide.

Mama settled beside me on the couch where I ended up leaning my head on her chest, listening to the beating of her heart.

This was something I liked to do after her death. They had slit her open and installed a pacemaker, turned her into a clockwork mother. I thought after her operation her heart would tick like the Tin Man's but the pacemaker was only there as a failsafe to keep the beats steady if her heart couldn't do it. In ten years, they told her, they would have to reopen the scar on her shoulder and do it again. And again. Every ten years or sooner if the pacemaker failed before she did.

We ended up flipping channels. *Presenting Lily Mars* was on.

Don't you want to watch it? That Dorothea is your favourite.

But my mother had never understood I didn't care for Judy Garland as a person or as an icon. I cared for her as a sixteen-year-old drugged-up child star with bound breasts and prongs to change the shape of her nose, embodying Dorothy walking around Oz with wild-eyed wonder.

Alright, Mama said, when I declined *Lily Mars*. She flipped back to the news. To the Americans with you.

MEXICO

SHORTLY AFTER MARNIE announced her pregnancy, my mother announced she was going to Mexico.

I'm going to Mexico, she said one day at work. This news was somewhat startling. It had been years since she had made the trip, more since we had last gone as a family.

ALL ABOUT MERCED RUIZ OLIVARES DE ALT AKA MERCED RUIZ AKA MERCED RUIZ ALT

MY MOTHER HAD moved to Canada as a young woman. She had never learned anything but a pale sort of useless English at school, the kind of stiff and formal learning of perfectly plausible-sounding prepackaged sentences that no native speaker would ever use.

Which way to the library?

I like the colour blue.

So when she arrived here she had to learn the whole language from scratch, a new colonizer's tongue to replace the old one.

She learned how to order breakfast without a stutter and argue with parking attendants. She learned regionalisms: *chesterfield* and *loonie* and how to punctuate her statements about the weather (crazy weather, looks like snow, this heat) with *eh*.

Though her grammar improved over the years and she learned to fit her tongue around English phonemes (the hard *c* of the word *accent*, the subtle difference between *tuh* and *thuh*) she always kept a distinctive accent in English and eventually developed a twin one in Spanish as her words rusted with disuse.

Her life before Marnie and me always seemed hazy. And despite the evidence that she wasn't from here she was so present in every aspect of my life that the thought of her in Mexico seemed improbable, a work of fiction.

She had been born in DF, the youngest child of a rural family who had made the migration to city life, the only girl in a family with three strong older brothers.

She had lived in a rough sort of neighbourhood and sometimes she casually dropped details of the life she had lived there which was so different from my childhood that it seemed as if she was raised on the moon. She had stood out in her neighbourhood as a girl who wore pants (who didn't wear pants?); she had given a girl who had stolen her lunch a black eye (I went to a progressive school where I was given detention and a fifteen-minute lecture because I hadn't been generous enough when sharing pens during art class). While there had always been money in our home—money for clothes, money for books, money for taxes, money for trips, money for the candy I bought at the corner store across from school, dawdling on my way home—my mother had grown up in a land of want. Sometimes when she rained loonies into my outstretched hands she would tell me that when she was a little girl and had asked for money for a Coke her mother had whipped her with her father's belt.

I used those loonies to buy sour candies for me and my friends, sucking on the burning sugar until all I was left with was the sweet chewy centre, soft on my tongue.

My mother might have continued on in this rough sort of life, marrying a local boy, having tiny Mexican children, dreaming of something different perhaps but never knowing quite how to get it, except her father was hit by a car.

Traffic in DF is like no other traffic in the world, a stream of endless cars pouring forth like a river, each coming within kissing distance of the other. Somehow no one considers it a miracle that the vast majority of cars, day after day, avoid those fatal kisses and go to and from their destinations without incident. Those cars speeding along were what I pictured whenever I pictured my abuelo being hit by the car. Though that wasn't what happened at all; my abuelo was knocked over on a side street by one careless car going not too swiftly on an ordinary road on an ordinary day.

Because, like me, my abuelo did not die when he was struck by a car. He lay bleeding in the street and had time to send for his children. It was my mother who went to him first and it was she who clung on to his hand while he told her that before he died he needed her to know that, God forgive him, he was not her blood father.

Finally an ambulance came and took him away. To his embarrassment he only had some cuts and a fractured rib. He lived.

My mother loved her father, she always stressed this, as if we didn't know, as if she didn't keep a portrait of him on the wall at home, right beside Guadalupe, blessing us the way that saint did. Maybe she needed to stress it because what she did next was find her biological father.

She never referred to him by name, only as *He* and *Him*, with total disdain. He actually was dying by the time he agreed to see her. Cancer of the throat, though he wasn't a smoker.

They had one abortive conversation during which he didn't explain anything. Not how he had met my abuela, not how he had come to father a child by her, not if he knew my mother existed or not. He didn't ask about the rest of her family, not her mother, not her brothers nor her father either.

He said she seemed like a fine young woman. He wanted her to play happy families with his real wife and his son. But what use had my mother for a brother when she already had three she loved, who had taken her aside when they discovered the truth of her parentage and given her mescal till she couldn't feel her face and told her it didn't change anything, not for them, and then had never brought it up again.

My mother left the conversation and went home where it seemed as if all that happened with that man was a dream, too personal to bring up in front of her real family.

By the time she saw him again he was dead. He hadn't had time to amend his will if he had ever meant to amend it all. She was told this by her biological father's wife, a Spaniard with a chest like a plank of wood and blonde hair with black roots. She told my mother she was nothing and was owed nothing and then, after this little dehumanizing speech, she cut her a cheque.

You should have sued, Marnie and I, daughters raised by business people, daughters who knew lawyers, entitled daughters, said.

My mother was stubborn with pride and the stupidity of youth and besides that didn't know any lawyers and didn't trust anyone she didn't know. She took the cheque and cashed it at a bank and then took the cash and put it in a shoebox and then together with one of her best friend's ex-boyfriends and a cousin she put in one-third of the money to buy a car, packed up her things, said goodbye to the three strapping brothers and her proud mother and her weakened father, and got in the car and drove all the way through the cursed United States, came to Canada, fell in love with my father, and never left.

IT SOUNDED LIKE A FAIRY TALE

AND I SO loved fairy tales as a child. Whenever we went to visit I always wanted to meet my mother's other family, my rich tio and his flat-chested mother, the one who through her bribery was indirectly responsible for my existence.

I could never understand why my mother refused to talk to them.

I could never understand why we were always being schlepped to family reunions in the countryside which sounded quite romantic if you had never once set foot on a farm. That was where my abuelita lived, my abuelita who by the time I was born was a shrunken wrinkled doll-sized woman who complained endlessly that my mother was an ungrateful daughter and, when she came home, immediately set her to work in the kitchen.

I was also deemed a useless lazy child, but because I was a girl, into the kitchen I went, though my mother always set me in the corner on a stool and told me not to touch anything. Marnie, with her fair skin, was always treated with a sort of respectful fascination and sent, alongside my father, to sit with the men.

Though these divisions should have annoyed me I actually rather liked the kitchen. The kitchen was where food was, my tias feeding me the scraps and first bites of everything that was best. The kitchen was where, between my silence and my broken Spanish, I got to overhear the good chisme: wives whispering bawdy jokes, mysterious medical diagnoses that involved the removal of unmentionable body parts, which of my beautiful cousins had a new boyfriend or was on the verge of a proposal or was cheating on her boyfriend. The kitchen was inevitably where Marnie and my father drifted when the silence of the men was too oppressive and their feeble attempts at conversation faltered to an awkward end point. For though he loved my mother, my father had that same linguistic blockage that she had, Spanish never coming quite naturally to his Teutonic tongue. It was Marnie who could speak it quite well. Marnie the first child, the one my mother had actually spoken to in Spanish, who had an ear for the language and its rhythms. But my tios found it awkward to expect all their words to be interpreted by this strange blonde child. They always told us they loved my father like another brother, but because of this lack of communication it was a love that was more theoretical than factual.

These were the trips that I didn't enjoy. The trips that, when I was born, went from semi-annual, to once every five years, to nearly never.

I heard my mother making pained excuses over the phone every week. At first it was that children didn't travel well, and then the money was too much. Then Marnie and I were belligerent teenagers and then belligerent adults with our own lives and no appreciation for our family or their values.

ADIOS MAMA

BUT NOW IT seemed Mama was desperate to go back. She wanted to see her own mother, the one with the belt, the one who liked to tell me I was gordita every time she saw me, the one who, when she saw me post-accident for the first time, had said, Que lastima, and nothing else. There was a bump on my nose that might be a translation of the one on hers. This was the only thing we had in common.

I absolutely loathed the idea of my mother getting on a plane. What if the altitude wreaked havoc on her heart? Who was going to revive her if she died up there in the air? But not only was she not interested in being dissuaded, no one was interested in what I had to say.

I think she needs to do this, Marnie said.

At least *you're* not expected to go, my father said.

He had still, after all these years, never grown accustomed to anything Mexican. The food made him sick, the altitude sicker, and he would, I knew, return in a few weeks with skin red as a boiled lobster. But where my mother went my father followed.

The tickets were booked, the luggage was packed, one day my mother and father were there and the next they were not.

In their absence I moved back into the house. I ate my parents' food and didn't do the dishes and didn't think about Constantine who occasionally texted to ask if we were broken up. I answered only sometimes when Marnie called.

For all that she had seemed to diminish herself by taking on the mantle of an ordinary life, in private Marnie retained something of her old mystique. She never bothered making what *she* thought of as art anymore though sometimes I would pilfer one of her books and find marginalia tucked in the corners, a dragon here, a cat there, one time, disturbingly, a disembodied and too vividly detailed penis that I deliberately tried not to believe was modelled after Neil's. But these were done in Bic and I never saw any of her old instruments of beauty, those pastels, paints, canvases, and charcoal I remembered as ubiquitous when we lived in the same space.

Since their engagement she and Neil lived in one segment of a parade. The basement was still an undone space of crumbling brick that smelled of damp earth and never ceased to remind me that a house was a living thing. The basement was where she kept my arms.

While our parents were in Mexico she called me to her home to try on a new prosthetic. She had just bought her first 3D printer. (You don't want to know what it cost, she told me, and I didn't.) During the day, working her job at NRCan, she daydreamed up arms and in the evening she designed them and then set her printer to work so that all through the night as she dreamed, her little mechanical slave worked tirelessly to turn her visions into reality.

She had showed me the sketch of the one she was working on before she printed it.

The design was infused with LED lights that were temperature-sensitive so that, like a mood ring, it could change colour according to my weather. It was supposed to bend at the elbow and had a hand with articulated fingers that could make a fist.

The unveiling had been delayed because the printing kept going wrong, the machine going rogue and spinning out webs of plastic, creating deformed nodes and bumps that were too big to be sanded down.

We were on the fourth printing now and Marnie had told me it worked.

When we went down in the basement she had me cover my eyes while she moved around her workshop.

Ta-da, she finally said, and I moved my hand away from my eyes.

She had shut off the lights and there on her work table was the arm, already glowing.

Well, Cinderella, Marnie said, are you ready to try on your slipper?

It was blue, for cold, as she attached it, and gradually blushed into a light pink as she fiddled with it.

Comfortable? she kept asking as she hovered around me, even though she knew my measurements by heart now, knew this missing part of me maybe better than I knew it myself.

I raised the arm a little and it bent at the elbow, made a fist.

The LED lights, as if sensing my pleasure, flushed into a deeper red.

Of course it's not comfortable, I told Marnie. It's not a real arm.

THE FIRST SIGN

I HAD, FOR obvious reasons, never obtained my driver's license. Even to get in a car was, some days, an act of mental exertion that was not worth the effort. It was why I had gone to a university within walking distance and worked for my parents who also worked within walking distance.

Not being able to drive had fringe benefits though. I was often able to cancel plans I didn't care for, avoid Constantine whenever he wanted to have uncomfortable conversations about marriage, and, when my parents finally came home from Mexico, dodge picking them up from the airport.

Marnie, the daughter without the crippling car trauma, went to pick them up instead.

I was to join them for family dinner afterwards where we would talk about how the tios were and catch them up on what life had happened in their absence. Like a coward, I left their home askew and ran directly to my apartment after work. I knew that my mother, heart attack or no, would have no qualms about berating me for my laziness, but I also knew the more family members she complained in front of the more likely it was that someone would say, Merced, she only has one arm, and then Marnie and Neil, but Neil in particular, would feel bad and straighten things up with their own arms.

I dawdled on my way from my apartment to home.

I was feeling, if not happy, then something like the absence of sadness when I arrived. I was looking forward to seeing my father again. I was looking forward to seeing my mother and ignoring her complaints.

I opened the door which was unlocked, was almost always unlocked in that neighbourhood where we lived in the luxury of plenty, and no one came to deprive us of it.

The first thing I saw right in the entryway was Marnie, standing amongst our parents' suitcases which were open, the clothes spilling out like waves. She had one hand over her stomach, a classic maternal pose, and she looked so distressed that I almost asked her what was wrong before remembering that I hated Marnie and didn't care.

Oh, Alma, she said. It's all fucked up. Dad went and fucked up everything.

For one wild second I could see it all, my mother on the plane, clutching at her heart, my father oblivious in the seat beside her not noticing her face turning ashy until it was too late. They would have lain her down on the dirty airplane floor. She would have died without dignity as they stripped off her blouse and bra, exposing her this time not to a staff of medical personnel used to the varieties of the human body but to a whole cavalcade of passengers who didn't know my mother, who didn't love her or respect her, who didn't deserve the honour of being the ones to be with her as she died for a second time.

I had told her not to go.

I reached out to Marnie and we held hands and I could feel my heart beating ferociously in my ears, making it known that I, I, I was still alive.

But no, that couldn't be it. Because I could hear my father humming in the kitchen. I shook my hand out of Marnie's and went to the kitchen.

He was standing in the middle of my mess, adding to it in fact, putting the butter knife in the jam and smiling when he saw me.

Almita, he said. My baby. My bubbeleh. I missed you.

He bopped me on the tip of my nose.

I brought you those puerquitos you like so much.

For an instant I imagined a litter of rose-coloured piglets smuggled in his suitcase and then I remembered an apiary just outside my abuela's pueblo that sold pig-shaped cookies which I did like so much.

Where's Mama? I asked eyeing him suspiciously.

Marnie, he called to her, did you find the puerquitos?

Marnie appeared looking very dour, puerquitos in hand.

Tell her, Marnie said accusingly. Tell her what you've done.

For the first time I thought that Marnie would make an excellent mother. An excellent *Jewish* mother. Her eyes were on fire. I felt guilty just standing next to her.

And despite the fact that he had taken care of this formidable woman when she was a gummy little bald-headed baby who did nothing but sleep and shit, my father was cowed.

I didn't do anything, Alma, he said turning to me, his face full of guilt.

He gathered me up in his arms, pressed me close to his chest.

Your mother wanted to stay in Mexico.

THE SORRIEST DINNER

THE ONE I really felt sorry for was Neil, who had to sit there with a frozen smile pasted on his face as I yelled and Marnie raged, and my father obfuscated. Neil kept trying to divert attention back to the (excellent) roast chicken Marnie had made while the two of us, like dogs after the same scrap of bone, kept baring our teeth at our father, demanding to know what exactly had happened.

That my mother was not at home was clear. What was less clear was why exactly my father had let that happen.

I don't control your mother, he finally snapped at us.

Truer words were never spoken.

According to my father they had had what amounted to a fairly quotidian trip. The hermanos were visited. The sobrinas were gifted upon. A few of them had children and these children were appropriately cooed over and celebrated.

They ended their trip, as was usual, with a week-long visit to the pueblo to visit my abuela. My father, who did not enjoy country life, did his best to endure this time. At the end of the trip at the appointed time my mother and father got into their rental car to begin the six-hour trip to DF and as my mother looked in the rear-view mirror her mother waved goodbye at them.

I can't leave her, my mother said.

My father patted her on the back sympathetically. It was hard to leave a mother.

No, my mother said. You don't understand. I can't leave her. Stop the car. Stop the car. STOP THE CAR.

And like an idiot my father had stopped the car.

Then she had apparently gotten out of the car, grabbing a bag along the way, and gone back to her mother and not left.

And my father had done nothing.

No, worse than nothing. He got back in the rental car and drove back to DF.

I couldn't believe he had left her there.

I can't believe you left her there, I said to him.

They had been married for over thirty years. They went everywhere together. People I knew from elementary school would sometimes stop me in the street and after they expressed condolences over my arm the next thing they would say was always some variation of I remember your parents so well, they're the cutest couple. New acquaintances always thought it was miraculous I came from a household with parents who had never divorced. They were inseparable. And now they had separated.

I tried to get her to come home, my father said sulkily.

I watched him as he ate. He had a healthy appetite for a man who had abandoned his wife and then come home to his two disapproving daughters.

Does she even have enough heart medication? Marnie said before bursting into tears.

Neil patted her awkwardly on the back.

My father sighed.

I really did try to get her to come back, he said.

Whatever my father had done to try to persuade her to come home apparently hadn't taken very much time.

He had made his flight home.

RUMBLINGS

IT WAS AMAZING to learn how much of the fabric of our lives had been held together by my mother. Left alone I moved in with my father where we lived the lives of filthy degenerate bachelors. We forgot to eat and more often than not ordered in, the discarded packaging building into unwieldy towers.

Dust cropped up around the corners of the home as my father and I fell into a game of chicken he didn't seem to realize we were playing in which I refused to do any more cleaning than he did while he seemed perfectly content to live in dirt.

I had never lost respect for another human being more swiftly.

I hate him, I hissed to Marnie over the phone.

I called her constantly now, to rail against my father, to report another sighting of a woman who turned out not to be our mother.

Marnie sighed.

Once a week, to stop us from fully being subsumed by our own filth, Marnie appeared and did some cursory cleaning and cooking, a beleaguered older daughter trying to care for her inept father and crippled sister. It was a band-aid that did nothing to abate the slow-burning hatred of my father. I resented him for not bringing my mother home, for making her absence in our lives so notable, for exposing so cruelly the anarchy we would have descended into had she not been resurrected that afternoon when I watched her die in front of me. I resented him for telling his daughters that they could be and do anything, for telling us abortion rights were human rights, and paying for our school, beaming with pride when we brought home As, and yet not washing enough dishes to keep my mother at home when we needed her.

You're turning into quite the misandrist, Marnie told me in a jokey voice. But I could tell from her angry back as she scrubbed dishes and the way she avoided my father's calls that she resented him too.

A PLEA

WE ALL BELIEVED that it was a temporary situation and that sooner or later she would come back to us. But August turned into September with no sign of Mama. On one of those sick sweltering days that extended summer's reach into fall and reminded us all that climate catastrophe was now, Marnie came by after work and asked to speak with me alone.

We sat in the maple-red Muskoka chairs and looked in the direction of the Jentsch place, the sound of children's screaming laughter reaching to us from their yard. Marnie touched her stomach, and something soft flitted across her face.

I need you to go to Mexico, she said.

This was such an outrageous suggestion that I needed a cigarette. There was a saltbox on the porch where I hid my cigarettes and lighter; I took out a smoke, put it in my mouth, and then lit it in front of her.

Jesus, Alma. She immediately ripped it from my hand and ground it into the decking, a pitiful wisp of smoke trailing up from where she had stubbed it out. There would be a mark on the wood now, a memory of this moment, of my guilt and her anger. What right had she to be angry at me? Yet I still felt ashamed.

Since when do you smoke? she asked.

I can't go, I said. You know my Spanish is miserable, you know I can't convince her to do anything.

It has to be you, Marnie said. Mama has always liked you better.

She held up a hand to cut off my protests.

She loves us the same, but she likes you better.

She likes *you* better, I contradicted.

I played with my Bic lighter, turning the sparkwheel under my thumb gently so that it didn't catch.

Marnie was the loved child, the special child, the white child. But I couldn't deny that there was an accord between my mother and I, an understanding. A softness she had for me, even before my arm. The child she had prayed would look like her. The wanted child.

Don't make me do it, Marnie, I said, switching tactics. I can't.

She knew I travelled poorly.

Please, Alma, she said. She cradled her stomach with both her hands, playing her own trump card. The needs of her child taking precedence over my wants. I need her there when I give birth. She's the only one who understands.

Flesh of her flesh giving birth to flesh of her flesh.

For the first time I felt a flicker of empathy for Marnie's child, the doomed child about to be born into a world that would warm until it burned.

Poor thing, I thought. Poor thing.

I didn't agree to go but a few days later Constantine showed up at the house and my traitorous father let him in.

If you want there to be any chance of us surviving, you have to give me something, he said holding my hand. You have to try.

I didn't know how to tell him I didn't want to try, that what was between us was a dead man.

Okay, I lied to Constantine. I'll try.

I called Marnie that night.

Fine, I said. I'll go.

THERE ARE NO DIRECT FLIGHTS FROM OTTAWA, ONTARIO, TO MEXICO CITY, MEXICO

THERE WERE 4,479 kilometres between me, in Marnie's old bedroom, and my mother on the pueblo in Mexico. To cross that distance I would have to leave my home by bus, car, or taxi and get on a train or plane.

The train or plane had to stop at the airport in Montreal or Toronto where, along with thousands of other bodies, I would board a plane that would launch into the air and somehow, through the miracle of aeronautical engineering, take flight and, some five hours later, land at the Benito Juárez Airport in DF. Once I was in the city, Marnie had assured me, a tio or two would collect me. I would spend a night with them, habituating myself from valley to mountain air, and in the morning they would drive to the pueblo where my abuela lived which was five hours from the city.

Before she had even asked me Marnie had already booked a plane from Montreal to Mexico and a train from Ottawa to Montreal.

An astonishing number of seats were available. In September, the flight pattern of migrants flowed towards Canada for cultivating wheat and berries. I would be on a near-empty flight.

My job was to go to my mother on the farm and bring her back. After seeing the non-job my father had done to convince her home, both Marnie and I believed that I couldn't do worse than he had. Whatever the right words were I would find them.

That was what Marnie told me as she drove me to the train station.

It was our unspoken agreement that she would do this just as it was our unspoken agreement that I would not reimburse her for the tickets and that she would manage our father until my mother and I returned.

The day I left it was still eerily hot. I hadn't checked the Weather Network and was suffering in a grey sweater and loose lounge pants. As I looked out the window I saw people in linen dresses and shorts.

As Marnie began our drive out of the Glebe and towards the highway I looked out the window to say goodbye to the tree stump that was all that remained as a marker of my car crash.

And that's when I saw him.

HIDDEN OTTAWA

EVERY NOW AND then someone tries desperately to inject some culture into Ottawa. They work themselves to the bone putting on festivals and inviting exciting people from elsewhere to talk or dance or act. These events are always well-attended. Everyone loves them and claps fervently at the end. As they go home they wonder why there aren't more events like that and when the next one will be. And then afterwards the city sinks back to its usual stupor.

It resists all attempts to be interesting.

But what I and every other inhabitant of this city know is there is a magic in these streets.

That there is a giant spider called *Maman* that lives in front of the National Art Gallery.

That every single year we have seasons, four of them, and though I had lived my entire life within the confines of the Glebe I always felt grateful when autumn came and I stepped outside to see maple leaves burning red, leaving the ground aflame. That every winter, when the snow came, I knew it was a miracle that I was cozy inside while the world outside looked like someone had taken a snow globe and shaken it up.

Wasn't it a miracle that my mother had died and was still alive? Weren't my parents, children born from the survivors of the colonized and survivors of a genocide, proof of that?

I knew there were miracles hidden everywhere; I knew I was the child of two of them. That's why, when I saw Oliver standing on the street where I had last seen him dead, no older than he was the day he died, I knew he was real.

I PISSED MYSELF AT THE TRAIN STATION

NOT IN THE car. Not on the highway. Not while we unloaded my suitcase and wheeled it from the car park into the station. In the grand hall itself.

There must have been a point when I told Marnie to go because she wasn't there when it happened. The station was open concept, a single hall designed to easily accommodate the influx of travellers, large glass ceilings supported by broad iron beams and polished concrete floors. I was alone, standing in front of the vending machines, looking at over-priced bottles of water when I sensed the wet and when I looked down I had soaked myself completely, not a little trickle, which would have been embarrassing enough, but a full gush that puddled down my pants, into my shoes, and onto the floor.

I was so ashamed. I remember not knowing what to do and thinking that if anyone saw me, between the urine and my one arm, they would think I was mentally deficient and incapable of taking care of myself. I wanted Marnie. I wanted my mother. And then before I could move a woman came up to me. She had a stroller with her, and a toddler, a placid little girl safely buckled into her seat. She left the stroller trusting that her husband would be there behind her to take charge, and he did, moving swiftly to grab the handle grip. And then she took charge of me, taking my bag and ticket in one hand, and taking my one hand with her other. She led me away, to the women's washroom, my feet squishing uncomfortably in my sodden socks, my shoes squeaking the whole time.

We went into the disabled stall and she helped me look through my suitcase for new pants, new socks, new shoes. She commandeered wet wipes from another mother in the bathroom and discreetly looked away as I cleaned myself with them. When I didn't know what to do with my urine-soaked clothes she said, Just throw them out. She reminded me to check the pockets for anything important and saved me from throwing my phone in the bin.

When I came out of the stall, cheeks flushed, she smiled at me.

All good? she asked, and I nodded, too ashamed to say anything.

She checked my ticket and helped me queue up in the Ottawa-to-Montreal line and when my ticket was scanned she stood up on her toes and reached up and hugged me and wished me good luck on my trip.

It seemed as if the next thing I knew I was on the train. It was a weekday afternoon and so I didn't have a seatmate but until everyone was settled I was sure someone would sit down beside me and I hadn't properly cleaned myself with the wipes and they would smell the unmistakable whiff of urine upon me and, in that distinctly Canadian way, both of us would know what had happened but be too polite to remark on it and we would spend the trip in hell.

When the train tugged its way out of the station I, still seatmate-less, finally began to relax. I thought of the woman who had helped me. Her face was so distinct in my mind. I realized I didn't know her name.

The whole time we were together she treated me with infinite kindness. Infinite tenderness.

Wasn't that a kind of miracle?

TODO ES POSIBLE

IT HAD BEEN years since I had been to Mexico so I had forgotten that right before the plane lands in DF, there is a sort of swoop the pilot must do, a kind of circling where for one instant the windows on one side of the plane are facing the ground, the other side adjacent to the heavens, before the plane catches another current and the view is reversed. It must be necessary for landing, because it's never failed to happen every time I go. When I was lucky enough to have a window seat, as I did on this trip, I was able to look out the window and stare at the ground below, so neatly packed with roads and houses, buildings and bridges, all the general architecture of a city. Viewed from above, shrunken down to ant size, it resembled nothing so much as a circuit board.

It was always this view that made me feel I was entering into another world, one I would always and forever be hopelessly inept at understanding.

TIO DIEGO

I WOVE THROUGH the innards of the airport, a kind of no man's land that existed in Mexico but somehow didn't mean that I was in Mexico myself. I shuffled through this purgatory alongside hundreds of other passengers as we followed the signs I knew just enough Spanish to understand, which pointed me to customs, to luggage, to the set of doors that would finally loose me onto the Mexican streets.

I was impatient by the time I reached the final checkpoint.

The doors that separated the recently arrived from the outside world kept shifting open as people left through them. I kept catching whiffs of the dusty air of the city instead of the antiseptic too-clean smell of the airport.

I had held out some sort of hope that my mother would be there at the airport waiting for me when I arrived, but glancing through the door I realized that I was also looking for Oliver. That it would have made more sense to see him here, in this strange country, than on the street in Ottawa where I had left him behind a few hours ago.

Perhaps I hadn't seen what I thought I saw. Perhaps I was being haunted.

And then instead of seeing Oliver's ghost, or my mother, I saw my tio Diego, a lithe mouse of a man, my mother's favourite brother.

I was suddenly at the head of the line and airport security was pointing to a button and I pressed it and it flashed green, indicating I had not been chosen for a random search and I was in no line at all but free.

I stepped into Mexico proper, no longer beholden to the rules and whims of airport security. The Mexican part of the airport felt almost exactly like the liminal part of the airport, only I was, for the first time in many hours, close to doors that would finally lead me to the outside air.

Tio Diego and I regarded each other uneasily as I walked over. Unlike on previous visits there were no other tios, no tias, no primas with him. It set me on edge, reminded me that this was not a social visit but a mission. But then tio Diego was calling me sobrina and opening his arms. He gathered me to him in a crushing hug so that I had to bend over to return his embrace, his arms surprisingly strong. And despite the fact that he was tiny, about the size I was when I was twelve, I felt a relief at being in his arms. Here was a man who strutted around with straight shoulders and a cocky can-do attitude. Here was a man who lived in a hard city and refused to let it destroy him. Here was my tio, who knew what to do. I felt, for the first time since Marnie had implored me to go, that things might be alright.

And then he broke the embrace, clapping me on both shoulders.

You look healthy, he said and then picked up my suitcase like it was empty and told me we better get going.

Tio Diego took me to the car park where I realized that even though I had travelled for hours it was still day, the sun bright and brutal.

The DF air was not Ottawan air. There was a choking industrial thickness bred from too many cars and not enough trees. And even if this hadn't been the case my heart was beating erratically, my lungs hurting from the effort of having to breathe in mountain air.

There was a prickling in my head and I knew that there was a possibility that in the altitude I would faint and so I said, I need to lie down and rest.

Yes, he said in that distinctly agreeable Mexican way. Yes, we'll see Merced. Right away.

Right away? I echoed. I had that feeling, that feeling I always got in Mexico, of being pushed around like a child, while the adults did what they wanted to do. There was no time to ask to go to his apartment to plea for a nap, a shower, a break of any kind. Already I was being bundled into the front seat of his rusted van.

It was an effort to get in the car. I hopped in and reached my arm up to pull down the seatbelt. My hand met only air. I twisted my body around, looking for the seatbelt and realized there wasn't one. In my panic my mind completely voided of all the Spanish I knew.

The seatbelt, I croaked out. The seatbelt.

Tio Diego was busy turning the key in the ignition. English rap, which he didn't understand and which I understood all too well, poured out of the speakers, filthy and uncensored, a shock to my senses.

He gave me the universal look of deep exasperation that meant, What is it now?

Please, I said. I need the seatbelt. Ceinture, I said groping for the word again and landing on French.

Tio Diego shrugged at me.

I pointed to the absence of the seatbelt and the words came to me. La cinturón.

Tio Diego looked at me dead in the eye. *El* cinturón, he corrected.

He shifted the car into gear.

Princesa, he muttered under his breath and I felt my entire body falling back into the seat as we peeled off.

It was too much. The sensation of the van, and the way I had to cling on to the sides of my seat as the car shifted along. Nearly smashing into another car and then avoiding it. Being a passenger in Mexico was like being on a roller coaster that voided my head of all other thoughts, of even fear, as we skirted along, sailing past tall glass buildings, and short cement ones, and billboards with blonde Nordic-looking women with skin nearly as bleached as their teeth, selling toothpaste and cell plans.

We skidded to a stop behind a jam of other cars and I felt bile run up my throat as children came running out into the traffic. They were children the way my tio was a man, unaccountably small, even for their age. They had the taut worn faces of adults and were brandishing Chiclets, offering to clean the windshield, doing juggling tricks.

I had forgotten this part of Mexico, the part where the poverty was pressed right up against my nose the way it wasn't at home, the part that reminded me how, despite everything, my life was steeped in good fortune.

They came to the window and my tio waved them off.

In high school a girl had once brought a visiting childhood friend to a party. The friend was from a small town and she kept saying how disgusting Ottawa was, how filthy and large and frightening. I found her small-town fears deeply amusing. But here in DF I felt a wave of understanding. Here, I was the frightened one. The shivering small-town bumpkin, unsophisticated and provincial.

All around me life was flowing, millions of people hacking a living in this unforgiving city, surviving and even occasionally thriving in a way I knew that, if left to my own devices, I would simply fail at.

The lights shifted. The van lurched forward. We turned onto a wider street indicating we were in a richer colonia.

I asked tio Diego to pull to the side of the road and tried to breathe shallowly until he did. Then I opened the car door and vomited, the sour stench of stomach acid and plane food curdling on the sidewalk. Businessmen with shiny polished shoes and shellacked hair glanced at me in disgust then looked away.

I wiped my mouth.

It's the altitude, I said between heaves. I'm not used to the altitude.

A man hawking bottled water conveniently rushed up, my sickness enough to secure a sale.

As I panted, my body wrung out from the vomiting, the euphoria of wellness rushing back into my body, I heard the snap of the water bottle being opened and then water being splashed on my face, on my neck, against my forehead.

I spat the stale water in the street, and felt ashamed.

THE ROAD

IT WASN'T UNTIL nearly two hours later, when we made our way out of the city and hit the first of the toll highways, that tio Diego truly began to speak to me, in rapid Spanish that slipped through me like a river, impossible to fully grasp. It made me feel that the conversation was not something that was occurring between us, but something he was doing at me.

Looking back, the surreal part of this was how it was as if we had had a conversation completely in English, because my mind seized onto the language of comprehension: it translated what it needed to and erased everything else.

Tio Diego's monologue went something like this:

> God forgive me, but I always knew that your mother would do something like this. She runs off with money from that [rapist?] and she thinks she's too good for us.

Rapist, I thought. *Rapist???*
I had never thought of my mother's biological father in these terms. I had deliberately not allowed myself to. I couldn't bring myself to say the word. I was not sure I understood correctly and was afraid to ask for a corrective.

> It's good that you're here now, maybe you can meet a nice boy and settle down. Your mother told me you're running around town with a [redacted, likely anti-Asian slur]. You should find a nice Catholic boy.

I tried to tell him in a cold but firm tone not to talk about Constantine that way. I think instead I may have mixed up tenses and said something closer to I don't think you should talk to Constantine. Tio Diego took his eyes off the road and stared at me in some confusion.

Taking this pause as encouragement I drew breath and began to speak again.

I wanted to say that his anti-Asian sentiments were regressive and hurtful and unforgivable. Also to explain I didn't want to marry anyone Catholic as I did not relate to or understand Catholicism in any meaningful way. I didn't want to marry anyone at all; the only boy I had ever thought I wanted to settle down with, dead. Though if, as I knew through my lived experiences and as confirmed by those around me, he *was* dead, how could it be that I had seen him right before I came here? If this was all in my mind why had my fantasy provoked such a physically humiliating reaction? Had tio Diego ever urinated all over himself in a moment of extreme psychological vulnerability?

However, the linguistic complexities of trying to explain this in Spanish resulted in the following blunt statement: I'm Jewish.

This was true in my heart if nowhere else, and as I searched for the word for *urination* tio Diego began a new monologue.

> I've always liked your father. The Jews are a great people.
> We must never forget that Jesus himself was Jewish.

I was tired of Christians reminding me that Jesus was Jewish as it usually indicated the opening foray into an attempt to convert me.

> The Jews are a chosen people. I would like, one day, to go to Israel to see where Jesus himself was born.
> In fact, the first time I met your father I told him he was chosen and we had a long discussion about God. Your father is a very holy person, I always think of him as a great scholar . . .

I wondered what on Earth my father and tio Diego had actually discussed, as my father spoke and understood less Spanish than me. I could picture him nodding along amiably, his hand entwined in my mother's, waiting for the tios to stop talking, waiting to go to his hotel, waiting to go home.

The monologue began to drift away from my father to religion again, towards Catholicism now, and how the first time my tia Maria got pregnant with my prima Maria, she had wanted an abortion and he had convinced her it was a sin from which her soul would never recover.

I suppose that I ought to have argued what I believed, that it was a woman's right to choose and that what my tio had done was appalling and coercive, but not only did I lack the language to defend my point of view but it seemed mean-spirited to argue that my prima, who did exist, and was currently a living breathing person, should not have existed. I could recognize that this passivity was not something that existed in me in Canada when I was speaking in English or even French. But we were in Mexico now and I was already defeated.

Halfway to the farm the golden arches of a McDonald's appeared along the highway. From my first visits to Mexico as a toddler I had been so overwhelmed by the different people, landscapes, and language that I had refused to eat anywhere but at American franchise restaurants, which were the same in Mexico as they were in Canada. The hamburger buns in Mexico even had the same white circle on the bottom as they did at home, a fact which comforted me as a child but now, as an adult, I found a little disturbing. There is nothing quite like McDonald's french fries though, and over a Happy Meal for me and a black coffee for tio Diego, somewhere between DF and the farm where my mother was, I tried my best to communicate my thoughts on abortion, God, and the linguistic limits of communicating in a third language.

THE SAINTED PLACE

THE PUEBLO WHERE my abuela lived was so small that when I was little I didn't realize it was distinct from a slightly larger town we passed on the way over. That town had recognizable things a village might: a church, a laundromat, a grocery store, a community building that could be converted into a cinema or a dance hall as the need might be. Surrounding the centre were rings and rings of small streets made up of family homes. And then beyond that was a main arterial road surrounded by hills and shrubs. Occasionally a small dusty path jutted away from the main roadway. One such road, barely big enough for a car, widened into cobblestones and led to the pueblo where my abuela's farm was situated.

The pueblo was named after a popular saint, a name so common it rendered the pueblo indistinguishable from thousands of other little towns and hamlets hidden in the valleys of Mexico between the great cities. Marnie had long ago nicknamed it the Sainted Place and I still thought of it that way.

If visiting DF felt like falling into a technological future as it was already being lived, visiting my abuela's farm felt like falling back in time.

Part of my father's mania for film extended to a reverence for the endless BBC adaptations of nineteenth-century English classics. I found in the fetishization of the pastoral an echo of what it was like to visit the farm. Here too there were cobblestones and gossip and Christianity and neighbours upon whom we forced our charity.

The pueblo had its own church, a tiny thing that could contain perhaps twenty-five people. It also had a school, right beside the church. There was also a small building formerly used for grain, where the people gathered for festivals, fairs, elections, and meetings. In every aspect they echoed the larger town we had to pass through:

the Sainted Place was a town done up in miniature, everything scaled for a smaller group.

These buildings were all gathered around a small plaza. And whose home was among those abutting this zócalito? My abuela's.

It was originally built as a one-story, two-room bungalow. But over the years as money was scraped together addition after clumsy addition was added till it grew into the white-painted home I was familiar with.

Like most homes in Mexico it was built in an imitation Spanish style. There was no lawn to speak of, only a deeply unfriendly whitewashed wall adorned with broken bottles on top to ward off any burglars. The sole entry point was a green metal wicket gate that, when fully opened, was just wide enough for cars. And beyond this gate was, supposedly, my mother.

We arrived at this town at night.

There was no bell so tio Diego made me get out of the car and rap on the metal door until my knuckles were raw.

But flesh is no match for metal.

Right around the time when my hand was beginning to hurt and I switched to slapping the door I started feeling really, truly annoyed. That I had come all this way and I was about to be defeated by a goddamn piece of metal. How stupid. How ridiculous. I was just about to turn around and tell tio Diego to forget the whole thing and drive me back to DF so I could at least spend some time with the primas and have a halfway decent vacation when I heard a sort of shuffling from the other side of the gate. It was too deliberate to be a loose sheep or one of those awful turkeys my abuela used to raise. My heart beat wildly, impossibly faster, and I reached to put my hand over my breast to keep my heart inside my chest.

¿Quién es?

Alma, I said. Almita, la niña de Merced.

The voice considered this answer.

Tio Diego, impatient, hammered on the horn, disrupting the quiet of the village.

The narrow gate creaked open.

For a second, I swear, I saw my mother.

Instead I found myself face to face, or rather chest to face (my chest, his face), with a small mustachioed man, a hired hand, who took one look at me, shut the door, and then, before I even had time to feel affronted, opened the gates back up fully so that tio Diego could begin the nerve-wracking work of parking the car inside. There is an art to backing a car through the gate and there was about a centimetre of give each way. It was usually a pleasure to watch this sort of reverse birth, the impossibility of the wide car fitting through such a small space being overcome with no flair, no bravado whatsoever, only simple skill and technique.

But for once I didn't want to stand and watch my tio perform this uniquely Mexican magic trick. I wanted my mother.

So before tio Diego could begin to back the car inside I walked through the gate, each step bringing forth a memory of my abuela's home. It was like I had forgotten everything until suddenly there it was before me. There was the curved path that led around the house. There was the second, arched gate that led to the courtyard, another unique feature of Mexican homes that I loved so much. The floor of the courtyard was tiled over and there were plants everywhere.

From the courtyard I could see all the different parts of house, some of them stone and some cement, for as the years changed so did building materials. There was no common interior hallway. To get from the living room to the kitchen you had to cross the courtyard. To go to the bedrooms on the second floor above the dining room you would have to leave the kitchen, cross the courtyard, and go through the dining room, where behind that room was a storeroom which also contained a series of wooden steps that led up to the second floor where the beds were.

I was beginning to wonder where to begin my search for my mother when suddenly my abuela appeared.

She was a tiny, terrifying woman. Tinier even than tio Diego.

She had what appeared to be cataracts over her eyes now, a new development since I had last seen her, and she walked with a cane though as far as I could tell this was more for aesthetic purposes than to do with any visible limp.

She was upon me almost without my noticing, come to see who had disturbed the peace of her home.

She knew me at once.

It seems to me, she said, looking me up and down, you're Merced's daughter.

Then she took me by the hand and led me to the kitchen.

ABUELITA

IT WAS ALWAYS strange to me to hear people talk about grandmothers who pinched their cheeks and snuck them sweets and cookies. My abuela didn't think much of me as a granddaughter.

When she led me by the hand to the kitchen it wasn't to be kind or to feed me or to offer me a drink. It was to get me to make her tea.

It was hard to explain that I had never lit a gas stove before and was slightly terrified that if I tried with her 1970s model with half the knobs missing and a broken grate over one of the burners I was fairly sure I would light us both on fire.

Idiota, she muttered under her breath.

I didn't begrudge her this. By the time she was my age she had birthed all four of her children and was co-running the farm with my abuelo. She thought I was being difficult on purpose.

But this was Mexico, where the ephemeral nature of my anxieties clashed against brute reality and almost always lost.

My abuela wanted her tea and her tea she would have, even if I killed us both in the process of making it.

From a drawer she procured a matchbox with a picture of the Virgin on it and gestured for me to light it. I made my abuela hold the box while I struck the tip over and over against it until finally a flame sprang forth. She turned the knob for the gas and held it while I was able to light the working burner. A kettle was located and I filled it with water from the tap. I was staring up at the veritable apothecary of dried herbs attached to the ceiling when tio Diego came in.

Why is this strange man in my kitchen, my abuela asked me.

I couldn't tell if she was play-acting senility or actually experiencing it.

Tio Diego pulled her into a hug that seemed too rough for her fragile body. Leave her alone, he said, your grandchildren aren't your servants.

He reached up, grabbed some dried leaves, and threw them in the kettle without looking.

That's not what I wanted, my abuela began saying at the same time my tio began chastising her for turning on the stove.

Whatever you do, he said pointing at me, never leave her alone with fire.

Then he told me to go find my mother.

I went to the bedroom first. She wasn't there. There were traces of her: half-drunk plastic water bottles; her suitcase at the edge of one of the beds full of clothes that didn't smell like her; her gold wedding ring on the nightstand. I had rarely seen it off her finger and I slipped it on my own, for safekeeping.

Back in the courtyard my suitcase had materialized.

I can't find Mama, I told tio Diego who was in the kitchen, heating some tortillas.

I went to the shower which was a generous name for what it actually was: a concrete room, semi-outdoors. It had plumbing but no windows, a half wall that looked out onto the fields. This was enough, I supposed, for my abuela and my tios when they were at the farm. Even enough for my cousins, who were so short that they were covered completely by the half wall. But for Marnie and me, showering at the farm was a choice between hunching protectively in a painful crouch or standing upright and risking that someone cutting through the field might see our breasts.

My mother wasn't in the shower. No one was.

It felt like years since I had washed myself, and with shame I realized that I still hadn't been able to properly bathe since that morning.

I looked out onto the fields. The limitless-seeming land did not show how, like the house, it had been bought piecemeal, with money scrimped and saved over time, money from my father and mother, money from my tios that was supposed to go towards feeding my grandparents and instead had gone to this.

Crops no longer grew there. My abuela sometimes rented it out to local farmers so that they might graze their animals but aside from the occasional donkey or stubborn shrub the land went unused.

And yet who did I see as I looked out?

My mother, lit up by the light of the moon, standing at the farthest end of the field where the clear-cut abutted the wild.

MAMA

SHE WAS LOOKING at an outcropping of trees that bordered my abuela's estate, trees shaped exactly like giant pineapples.

I ran to her in a hurry, convinced that in the time it would take me to get to her she would disappear, a Mama vanishing act, not an Alma one. I was wearing overpriced name-brand running shoes, the kind that city-dwellers use to go from their homes to their offices. With each step, I could feel the stones dotting the field, the stray bits of plant stalk poking through the moisture-wicking netting, everything making me aware of how unwelcome my soft and tender feet were.

Mama, I called.

She turned.

For a moment, watching her look at me, I was struck by the memory of Marnie at home, looking lost amidst the suitcases, only my mother was surrounded by flora and was outdoors. No one ever said they looked alike, but I saw it then, the way they were both strange and beautiful and fierce.

Then her face changed to disappointment and she was coming towards me, walking in a very dignified way even though she wasn't dressed for the fields at all. She was wearing a green cashmere sweater and a black pencil skirt, her trademark skirt of choice for as long as I had known her. She was also, as I could see when she came closer, wearing loafers, leather loafers which were coated in mud.

She reached out her hand for mine and helped me balance on the rocky terrain.

It felt like a million years since I had seen her even though it had only been a few months. It felt like I had always been in Mexico looking for her. The shifting of locations, the strangeness of the language, seeing Oliver, all of this created within me a warped sense of time.

Mama, I breathed again. I leaned into her, letting my forehead fall to the top of her head.

My hand was still in hers. I wanted her to fall into my arms and tell me, Thank God you're here, I'm so sorry, Almita, I'm coming home.

Alma, she said instead in a hushed tone. You need to take a shower.

I felt my cheeks flame with shame but then my ankle was rolling because my mother was tugging me along back to the house, telling me the whole way there that cleaning myself should have been my first priority.

And why are you wearing my ring? she said yanking it off my finger and placing it in her pocket.

She said this to me in Spanish, which was odd because my mother never spoke to me in Spanish.

She shoved me into the shower cubicle and waited outside as I scrubbed myself clean in the freezing water, using only the dried soap I found there.

My mother brought my suitcase to the edge of the shower and I struggled in the dark to fish out clothes, to put the dry garments over my damp body.

You didn't even say hello, I said.

Hello, Mama said.

Aren't you surprised to see me?

No, she said. I've been expecting you.

Was Marnie able to contact you?

No of course not, she said. Your father told me you were coming.

It was news to me that she and my father spoke. He had given no indication that they did. Both were incapable of setting up a video chat and I had witnessed no furtive phone calls.

To entice her home I had depended on her surprise and my tears. Now there was no surprise, and standing there, watching my mother look at me with annoyance, I couldn't bring myself to cry.

DINNER IS A MEAL BEST EATEN IN SILENCE

IN THE KITCHEN tío Diego was cooking a bachelor's meal of eggs and Mexican rice. Between warming tortillas he was downing shots of mescal. He stopped when he noticed me.

His shoulders were hunched with the specific sort of tension that told me he had been around women all day and now that he had to cook for them too he was at his limit.

Go set the table, he said.

I found Mama, I told him.

That's nice, he said. The table.

Watch your manners, my mother said, walking into the room, her arm linked with her mother's.

My abuela had abandoned the cane but was now limping in an exaggerated way which both of her children pointedly ignored.

You tell your daughter to set the table then, tio Diego said and they began to bicker.

I could see, through their insults and their childish posture and the way my mother immediately cuffed her brother on the ear, what they must have been like as children. It was a tactile vicious love between them, a roughness that didn't exist between me and Marnie.

Then my uncle finished heating the last of the tortillas and they were being folded into a tortilla cover and the bundle was placed in my hand. My abuela put her hand, papery and fragile, in the crook of my elbow and together we went across the courtyard to the windowless dining room where a single naked bulb illuminated our meal as a moth danced around it.

My mother and tio Diego came in, their bickering falling away as they passed out plates and cutlery, handled hot dishes, brought out chairs. Then we sat down and set to eating, the only sounds our vigorous chewing. Every now and then one of us paused to ask for another serving and once each my mother and tio got up and went to heat more tortillas.

At one point after the meal, when we were waiting for our stomachs to feel as sated as we knew they were and tio Diego had switched from mescal to beer, I mentioned that in the field I had seen some beautiful pink-tipped reeds that I had never seen before. I wanted to know their name as I was sure we didn't have any of them in Canada.

It's grass, my mother said.

No, I told her. It's different. Your mother will know.

It's grass, my mother repeated with irritation.

The whole time my uncle had politely been minding his business, ignoring our English asides.

What is your daughter saying? my abuela asked.

Mama hesitated but finally she asked the question.

My abuela looked at each of us slowly in turn as if we were playing a trick on her.

It's grass, she finally said.

You see, my mother muttered under her breath.

Que tonta, my abuela said, not hiding what she said and I couldn't argue that she was wrong.

THE NIGHT MOVES DIFFERENTLY IN THE COUNTRYSIDE

WE DIDN'T REACH immediately for sleep. Instead by silent but mutual accord my mother cleaned the dishes and the rest of us went out into the courtyard, the cool of the country air like the best autumn chill. We sat on mismatched seats, my tio Diego settling on an empty metal drum that no one had found the time to throw out yet, his back against a wall of the house, his legs dangling off the ground like a little child's. My abuela sat on a '70s-style kitchen chair with a green paisley print turned muddy with time. When my mother finished with the dishes and came out she brought a battered wooden dining chair. For myself I chose a wooden bench with tiles embedded in the sides, a work of art that seemed incongruously beautiful beside the rest of our seating arrangement. We tilted our heads back and looked at the stars. It filled me with pleasure to see them. And I thought of how, by tilting my head up and looking at that diamond-filled sky and enjoying the wonders of the universe, I was partaking in an activity as old as humanity itself. For untold generations, my blood had, across the known world, been looking up into the sky at night and wondering about the people who came before and the people who came after. A rare treat to see the sky in this way instead of the inky grey clouds over Ottawa, muting everything.

As we sat in silence tio Diego lit a cigarette and the smell of the smoke floating through the country air was comforting. My mother told him he was disgusting before she plucked it from his hands and took a long drag herself. I wanted to reach for it but before I could she threw it on the ground and stubbed it out under her muddy loafers.

My mother and tio and abuela began to talk about the past in a dreamy sort of way that I could only half understand. My mother's anglo inflections, her simple words, were the conversational thread I clung to whenever I felt adrift.

Once, before they moved to the city, the fields had been brimming with chili peppers, row upon row of the stuff, and in those days the house had been nothing more than the gate and one room, the room that I thought of as the living room because it had an old couch in it.

Tio Diego told us a long winding story I only half understood about the building of the stone fence on one of the parameters. I had seen that fence before and to my untrained eyes it seemed an architectural marvel, immovable and built of a series of interlocking stones. But tio Diego along with his brothers, my abuelo, and a few other men had built it with their hands, lifting stone after stone, puzzling them together so that they locked and stood firm. I thought there was cement or some sort of sticking agent holding the thing together but that wasn't so. It was only rocks piled upon rocks and a very determined sort of person could, if they wanted, unbuild the fence, lifting the rocks away one after another, unspooling it the way a knit sweater could come unravelled by a very determined person pulling at a stray thread of wool and unwinding all the patient hours of labour that had gone into creating it.

This was a story that wasn't really a story, or rather a framework that held all sorts of little stories within it and tio Diego was forever digressing from the story of the fence to talk about how such and such a person had an affair with such and such a person's wife, or how a few years ago Diego had run into such and such a person who was his best friend when they lived in the village and whom he had lost touch with only to realize this friend too had moved to the city shortly after my tio did and they had actually spent their entire lives in the same neighbourhood only a few blocks away from each other, their lives running parallel without ever intersecting.

And though these stories didn't interest me and my limbs were heavy and I had a feeling that soon I would regret not being in a bed, it was nice to sit there and half listen to my mother and my tio kibitzing about people I would never know.

My abuela was the first one of us to give in to the night.

At some point she got up and started to drag her chair away, and we all half startled up and offered to do it ourselves, though in the end tio Diego won that particular battle. My abuela refused my mother's offer to help her and told her children they all talked too much, and left us, and the cane she proclaimed she so needed, for the comforts of her bed.

My mother and tio watched her go.

It was strange, but after their mother left they seemed to grow wizened and old, shrinking into their bodies with exhaustion. They were not young, but standing beside their mother, who was a full generation older, had done the trick of making them seem so.

For a while no one said anything, as if my abuela had been part of the essential magic that loosened her children's tongues and made the atmosphere of the courtyard so congenial.

The old lady doesn't have much longer, my tio finally said after a long period of silence.

This was addressed to my mother, who said nothing back.

I very suddenly had a clear vision of myself and Marnie in the kitchen at home, of me saying to Marnie, The old lady doesn't have much longer, while Marnie would say nothing back.

And one day this process would repeat itself. There would be Marnie's child or children saying, The old woman doesn't have much time left.

And maybe if I was lucky and they loved me too, maybe they would be the ones to say it for me.

I was the one who flagged next. I began to yawn, at first surreptitiously behind my hand and then boldly, the stretch of my mouth as I inhaled feeling deliciously wicked and good.

Tio Diego said to my mother, You had better put your Almita to bed, even as I insisted that I was well right where I was.

Neither one of them listened to me.

Tio Diego began shutting all the various doors to the house, which locked from the outside, walking about with a huge key ring and a flashlight, while my mother led me through the dining room and up the stairs to the beds. There were no distinct rooms on that floor, just a long dormitory-like space with empty beds lined up. In the dark it was frightening. I could see, in a corner, a little lump that was my abuela, breathing softly in the darkness. I wondered how after becoming a widow, she had slept in that huge space all alone night after night, year after year.

My mother wanted me to take my own bed, but I begged her to let me sleep with her, as if I was the girl tio Diego treated me as.

Of course when I was a little girl I was never allowed to sleep in my parents' bed. If I had a nightmare or was scared of the dark one of my parents (usually my father) would sit with me awhile in my own room and eventually, whether I fell asleep or no, would leave me no matter how hard I pleaded, telling me I had to be brave. It was Marnie who always took me in, tucking me in carefully and letting me curl up against her back.

And yet, as I lay beside my mother in the dark, I felt a wonderful sort of peace at being close beside her. I curled up against her back, placed my palm where her heart would be, and let the rhythm of her breath lull me to sleep.

That night I dreamed for the first time in years that Oliver was alive. When I asked him how this came to be he told me he had been alive the whole time, waiting for me to find him, and took my right hand in his left.

And there was no pain.

A ROOSTER CROWING LOUDLY

IN THE MORNING, I woke up to the light and listened to a rooster I never saw call out that it was morning. It was strange but between eating breakfast and unpacking my clothes and wandering about the farm, remembering how it looked in the daylight, it suddenly seemed less urgent to speak to my mother and tell her to come home. In this way a day passed and then another and then more.

There was no TV, no books, and no internet on the farm. There were no farm chores; it had stopped being a working farm long ago.

There was the regular business of life to attend to, eating to sustain a body, and going to the village to shop for food for that purpose. A morning walk to waken the limbs and an evening one to tire out the body. Even the act of dreaming of the future was impossible. The trees and the mountains and the sky rooted me in place so that it was hard to think of home or remember why I had come here at all.

In the Sainted Place, in the broad daylight, among fewer than a thousand people, I was scared to leave the comforts of my abuela's gated farm in a way I never was in the Glebe. When I walked past people, they stared at me, not because of my arm but because they, who knew everyone, didn't know me.

The streets were cobbled with large stones and even through my running shoes they hurt my feet. For a lack of anything else to do I sometimes went into the church, which was unlocked, sat in a pew, and stared at the altar where a two-foot-high white Jesus was nailed to a cross, dripping very unrealistic pinkish blood.

Mostly I stared at the Jesus and tried to hallucinate.

What I tried to hallucinate was Oliver.

Though he had seemed so real when I saw him, the more time passed the more I was able to convince myself that seeing him had been nothing more than a trick of my mind. And if I had conjured him without thinking on a street in Ottawa, I thought it would be easy to conjure him here, where all things felt wild and strange and possible, even in a little pokey old church in the countryside. Maybe especially in a tiny church. Catholicism was full of ordinary people having visions of Jesus and the Virgin.

If Oliver came to me again I could make my own religion of him. I could build an altar. Have a custom-made two-foot cast of him made and worship at its feet. Surely the money I had was enough to persuade a custom doll-maker to produce a figure of him.

Marnie could do it, I thought. But then of course Marnie would never do it.

I felt a deep urge to have this curio, this perfect Oliver doll I could touch and watch and stare at in the intimate privacy of my own home. A yearning that felt physical. But my attempts to conjure Oliver ended in failure. Every unsuccessful church visit ended with me going back to the farm to find tio Diego and persuade him to take me where there was internet.

To access the kind of computer I used back in high school tio Diego had to drive me to the grocery store in the bigger town where a storage room in the back had been turned into an internet café. I was always the only customer there, everyone else in the town busy with real work.

For the equivalent of two Canadian dollars I was granted an hour of slow-moving internet and as I sat in front of the computer I felt relief that for that hour I would not have to be alone with my own thoughts. There were emails to check (mostly messages from Marnie all of which I deleted unread). But what I really wanted was to log on to Facebook and to feel the secret, sick relief of looking at pictures of Oliver.

If he had died a few years later Oliver would have existed as a more fulsome phantom on the internet. Even on the Facebook page I had briefly cultivated and abandoned after high school anyone with Friend access could see me go from a chubby-faced teen to a young woman.

Somewhere, on the internet, on old forums, I was sure there were traces of Oliver. Comments and fandom arguments under handles I wouldn't have the first clue how to find. He had had a computer as a child and the lure of the internet, its potential for connectivity, its innovation, would have lured him to comment, but on what I didn't know.

That path to him was lost to me forever.

Yet other people were reviving him all the time. Marnie and I had a lot of crossover Friends, people who had gone to school with her and remembered me as a fearless child. And these people were careless with their nostalgia. These people uploaded class photos where I could trace Oliver's hair going from the bright blond of kindergarten to the dusty golden-brown I remembered.

There were photos of him in a nylon snowsuit on skis, from the annual Mont Tremblant elementary school trip. Photos of him at the Glebe Community Centre, doing a cartwheel in the back while someone mugged a smile in the front. In middle school he flexed his arms by the Jack Purcell Pool while two girls with wet hair plastered to their skulls leaned in pouting, their lips forever frozen just shy of his cheeks.

Someone from McGill, not Constantine, had set up a memorial page and this was where my favourite pictures came from. His brief life at McGill, a precious few months documented with enthusiasm by teenagers let loose in the digital world without supervision. The photos shifting from the beautiful grain of a camera with all its blurs and red-eyed imperfections to the pixelated smears of early digital photography.

Every time I checked there were new people who hadn't heard of his death before, who grieved anew. The latest comment on the memorial page wall, posted two months earlier, was from someone who had gone to summer camp with him, expressing shock and disappointment, punctuating their trite comment—Gone too soon—with an RIP.

On my computer and my external hard drive I had copies of all the pictures and screenshots of the Facebook memorial. But I didn't have any of that with me in Mexico.

Like an idiot I had thought I didn't need it.

I scrolled through the more recent photos of Oliver until I found what I was looking for, a photo of him at eighteen, taken shortly before he died.

I reached out and touched the screen of the computer, leaving greasy fingerprints all over. The man in the picture looked exactly like the boy I had seen in Ottawa.

Tio Diego arrived with groceries and I X-ed out of the browser quickly even though Oliver's face would have meant nothing to him.

Is it enough? tio Diego said. Are you done?

I paid the man at the till.

On the way home we saw people setting up in the town square, bundling pastries out of the back of a station wagon, ready to sell to the night crowd.

I wanted to buy mantecadas for the whole family but tio Diego brushed my money aside and paid for it himself. They came with the same red wrapper and the same light sweet taste with factory-like uniformity no matter if I bought them in the city or the country, from a chain panadería or a small local one.

Hamadi, tio Diego said as he took hold of the bag of mantecadas.

What is that? I asked him on the ride home. What is *hamadi*?

Hamadi, the only word of Otomi he knew, passed down from his grandmother to mine, to him and now to me.

An entire language now reduced only to *thank you*.

STRANGE LOOPS

AS TIME PASSED I was aware that I was supposed to have lured my mother home already or at least made some sort of progress or shift in her thinking.

Instead it was me that was being shifted. I was astonished every day to lie in bed and realize that, aside from existing, I had done very little that day, had not moved my mother an inch towards home.

My mind had emptied out: I was simply experiencing everything in front of me as it happened which left little room for rumination and worry. Even the grocery store internet café had lost its appeal; it seemed a way for the outside world to enter. I was deliberately not thinking of Oliver who, hallucination or not, was staying well away from the Sainted Place.

Well, what do you do here? I asked my mother.

I'm spending time with my mother, she said.

I supposed that was what I was doing too.

Every facet of my mother's life now revolved around catering to this woman. If my abuela had a hole in her sock we would go to town and spend all day looking for socks that looked and felt exactly like the old socks. If she wanted a special tea we would go to the market two towns over and amble from stall to stall until we found not only her favourite tea but the one sold and packaged by her favourite seller.

Today what she wanted was to go to the cemetery to visit her husband, so to the cemetery we would go. My mother and tio spent an hour arguing over whether they should drive to a store first to buy flowers for my abuelo's grave. My mother was of the opinion it was only proper, but my tio thought it was ridiculous. If she wanted flowers there were flowers in the fields, by the road or in the cemetery itself.

I let the waves of their argument wash over me, the Spanish so close to French I always felt on the precipice of understanding before the meaning washed away.

WE BOUGHT BOUGAINVILLEAS
TO LAY OVER OUR DEAD

IN THE SAINTED PLACE I saw bougainvilleas every day. The beautiful plant grew like weeds in shocking fuchsia and hot pink. I wondered at how seeing that beauty every day shaped the people who grew beside these flowers. I wondered what sort of people they were. Grateful people I thought.

And yet I didn't begrudge all this beauty existing apart from me. It seemed right that I had lived most of my life within the confines of a few blocks in little Ottawa, my eyes trained on blue sky, rust brick, and grey concrete. My heart wasn't built to know so much beauty.

I sided with my mother and insisted we buy an armful on the way to the cemetery. Somehow the transaction of money for beauty felt right. I couldn't repay nature for this gift but I could pay the woman who sold them to me.

When we arrived at the cemetery I was awed and overwhelmed in much the same way I always was when presented with a beauty I was unaccustomed to. It was true that my experience in Mexico was limited to a few places, but I think if I had travelled the entirety of the country I would never have found a place I loved as much as that cemetery.

I got out of the car first and opened the unlocked gate, waving the car through. I followed after stepping inside where all was lush and verdant.

The ground was too rocky to bury anyone and so remains were encased in stone mausoleums raised high above the ground. Some families had marked the graves of their loved ones with crosses or altars to the Virgin and these were easy to locate, but plain mausoleums were buried in a sea of that distinct chest-high pink-tipped grass I loved so much, giving the impression that the tombs in the garden of the dead were strangely few and far between.

I had no idea where my abuelo was buried and so I waited for tio Diego to park and for my mother and abuela to descend, to part the grasses and wade towards one cross in particular, the one that marked the grave of my abuelo.

When we arrived my mother began trampling the grass around the edges of the mausoleum, sometimes pulling up fistfuls in the Sisyphean task of trying to keep the living things from burying her father a second time. My abuela lovingly brushed some debris off the top of the mausoleum. The gesture was so careful it startled me, coming from my abuela. It put to mind a loved one brushing hair out of their beloved's eyes.

As she began patting the stone and talking to it I felt like I was witnessing something too private and looked away. There was something startling about the view and I raised my hand to shield my eyes to look out into the distance.

All I could see were low mountains and a pure blue sky. It was too easy to believe that this corner of the world was all there was, that there was no one but me and my ancestors, the living and the dead, in this cemetery.

I left to go mingle among them, to stumble across the graves of those who had been lost to grass.

It brought me pleasure to visit them, to try to read the names of beloved sons and daughters, mothers and fathers, brothers and sisters, who, by the sight of their markings, had not been visited in some time. Where they had names I tried to speak them aloud, a clumsy offering to the dead.

My mother eventually joined me, winding her arm around my waist and bringing me close to her. Side by side we walked from grave to grave. She pointed out a cousin here, a tia there.

At one point we stopped and I pointed out how beautiful the mountains were. My mother looked out at them with a jaded eye.

When I die, she said out of nowhere, bury me here. Please don't leave me in the cold.

Oh, Mama, I said.

There were bits of grass in her hair and I brushed them out.

She would die in Canada and I would keep her there, underground, in the cold, close to me.

I promise, I said, even though I knew in my selfish heart that I would do no such thing.

IN THE NIGHT SOMETHING HAD FEASTED ON MY FLESH

AT FIRST THERE was just a red dot on my underarm that I absentmindedly scratched against my side as I looked at the graves. Then there was another on my calf. By the time we returned to the farm they had evolved into full-grown welts that itched madly and covered my arm and both my legs. No one else had them.

Tio Diego was the first to be concerned. He and my mother argued about what the best course of action was. They both agreed that some sort of salve or tincture should be applied to the lumps. Which salve or tincture was a point of contention. Eventually they settled on something that came from a cactus though neither one of them could agree on which strain of cactus this supposed salve came from. My abuela who possessed this sort of practical knowledge decided at that moment to play at being deaf and answered all questions with upturned palms and a look of innocent stupidity.

Secretly, when my mother and tio were bickering, she would narrow her eyes at me and reach for the handle of her cane. I could see, as she fondled it, that she longed to beat me with it for the crime of being bitten by this mysterious pest, of being a weakling and a bother. Of not belonging.

In the end they persuaded her to at least look for aloe, my tio and abuela disappearing off into the fields together with a machete while my mother made a makeshift screen and stripped me down to my underwear in the courtyard.

My clothes went into the '70s-era washing machine that still chugged away viciously. I had to stand with my arm covering my chest, trying to get my mother to give me a modicum of privacy. She refused of course.

I'm your mother, she said with annoyance. I've seen everything.

When my tio and abuela returned, stalk of aloe in hand, my mother took to smearing the pulp of the leaf onto my body. Tio Diego at least fled to the fields, appropriately uncomfortable with my nudity. My abuela sat in the courtyard and when I asked my mother to get her mother under control, all my abuela would say was that this was her house.

She can't see anyway, my mother said as she squeezed more aloe onto my back.

I whimpered at the cool against the painful itch of my back.

My abuela, in the corner, smirked.

Gordita, she whispered as she looked at me.

Ignoring her I stared at a point on the outside of the house. The cement had been covered with an awful, flat Pepto-Bismol pink. I could just imagine my tio, in frustration, buying the cheapest paint he could find, something on sale, and spending an afternoon quickly painting the side of the building, cigarette in the corner of his mouth. It was hideous enough as a colour but it had started to flake, making the building look like a sickly scabied thing.

Round and round my mother went until every lump was covered in cool gel including an inconvenient one right on my scar which itched madly, and one on the bridge of my nose.

The aloe leaf worked more quickly than anything I had ever used before. Unfortunately pure aloe cut from the plant and fresh from the leaf has a disgusting smell, a smell that seemed to become less bearable the longer it was on my body. As the pain from the bites began to subside I wondered which was worse, the pain or the smell.

My clothes, still damp from the wash, were drying on a clothesline and my mother was too scared to put me in any clothes that had been in the house. So she draped me in a worn old blanket, ignoring the fact that it too had also been in the house, and we sat in the courtyard together.

Is that gold under that paint?

I got up and tried to scratch a bit of paint off the wall, only succeeding in scratching myself in the process.

Mama, my mother said. What's under there?

Your daughter made a painting, my abuela grunted.

Marnie was here?

It was surprising to think of her here, alone. I didn't know she had come to the farm during her time in Mexico, when she was supposed to be in the city becoming a great artist. The stupor that had enveloped me in the pueblo had lit a fire in her. Under all that paint was maybe the last real art Marnie had ever made.

I put my hand on the wall as if I could feel it, but all I felt was the warmth of the sun.

Your hermana, my abuela told me, came here one year and painted all the houses.

All of them? I turned around. I wanted to see all these Marnie paintings.

It's not what you think, Mama said.

My tio came back. No longer under threat by my nudity he went to the kitchen to make dinner. My abuela followed to berate him.

It was my mother and I alone and I realized that if I didn't take this moment there would be vanishingly few of them.

When are you coming home?

I said this unspoken thing between us before I could have a chance to regret it.

My mother sighed.

Not yet.

What does that mean, not yet?

Not now.

But eventually, yes? Sometime later?

She refused to look me in the eyes.

Are you going to divorce Dad? Is this what this is about?

No, of course not.

Why are you here? Why can't you just come home? Why can't you be with us?

Mama was silent.

What about Marnie? I tried, a final desperate gambit. What about when the baby comes?

Her body will know what to do, Mama said. And she has Neil. You.

She needs you, I said. She needs her mother.

I need to stay here, my mother said. I need to stay here until my mother dies.

And what could I say to that?

It was the most ludicrous thing I had ever heard. Despite the cane and the pretensions at being deaf or senile my abuela was still a well woman even though she was in her eighties. Longevity ran in her genes, she easily had another twenty, even another thirty years in her, God willing. I could more easily imagine myself dying than I could her.

My mother had a whole life back home in Canada, a whole family that could not be paused for twenty or thirty years. *I* still needed my mother even though I was an adult; my abuela seemed the most self-sufficient out of all of us. One by one her children and grandchildren would wither and fall away from her like petals on a cut flower and she would not only survive but thrive.

It seemed strange to me that my mother had such fidelity to this tiny, sometimes cruel woman but then my mother was to me also tiny, strange, and sometimes cruel and hadn't I come to fetch her back? And the truth was that even though Marnie had told me she needed our mother there when she gave birth, I didn't really care about that. I wanted my mother back for my own selfish reasons.

What about you? I asked finally. What about your appointments, your doctor, your medication?

I'm perfectly fine, my mother said squeezing me tightly. Then she pushed me away.

You're always so dramatic, Alma. I'm going to take care of my mother till she dies and then I'll come home.

She got up, smoothed her skirt, and went to the kitchen to help my tio.

ADIEU

IT QUICKLY BECAME apparent that however long my mother was going to spend on the farm, she would outlast me.

The bites became worse after the first night and I was forced to sleep first in the living room, locked in for the night and separate from my mother, and then, when the bites multiplied, in the courtyard, shivering under three stiff woolen blankets, under the stars. I began to develop a sinister belief that my abuela was right, that there were no pests at all. It was my body capitulating to my mind, creating problems where there were none, rejecting the farm and by extension the country itself. It knew I was not meant to be there.

I also could see that no matter what I said I would never be able to convince my mother to come back. And I realized something that my father had probably recognized himself when my mother had told him she needed to be with her mother. That while the impulse was generous and romantic, romanticism was no match for reality.

I had once found a letter from my abuela to my mother and had puzzled out the meaning using a series of dictionaries and my own rudimentary Spanish. It was shocking what mother wrote to daughter. She wrote that my mother did not belong in Canada. That she belonged back in Mexico with her mother and her true family.

And yet here, when she was supposedly in her natural habitat, my mother was awkward and unhappy. She had never seemed more Canadian to me as she did here, when she snapped at her mother that she was too critical of me, as she fussed over my bitten body, as she tested out food before I ate it to make sure her preciosa wouldn't burn her tongue on a dish made with too much heat.

She was tired, I could see. Even if she seemed relatively youthful beside her mother, away from her she looked bored and worn down. She would come home in her own time.

One day my tio said he had had enough. It was time for him to go back to be with his wife and see his daughters and live the life he generally lived when he was not catering to his mother, his sister, and his niece, the three of us driving him mad with our endless demands that he chauffer and cook and entertain us.

I could have stayed. Every day I did I learned more about the rhythms of the place. The bus routes, the roads to and from the Sainted Place to the other towns. I saw how, despite my initial feeling that I was in the middle of nowhere, the Sainted Place was one minor vein connected to major arteries all of which led back to DF.

But I didn't want to stay. I had taken all the time I needed to be in that place, that place where I would never belong even though my blood and my mother's blood and her mother and the mothers who knows how far back came from those hills. It was time for me to go.

Before I left, my mother took me to see the houses Marnie had painted. They were just that: painted houses. There were no secret murals, no fanciful patterns. In the slow sleepy days of village life she had made herself useful, painting for free. Many of the people whose homes she had painted still remembered her, La Rubia.

I don't get it, I told my mother.

Oh Almita, my mother said, combing her hands through my hair. The accident was difficult for all of us.

Tio Diego and I left late at night.

I said my goodbyes to my abuela, hugging her even though we were not close. I had to bend to hold her and in my arms she felt more fragile than she looked. It occurred to me that maybe, between the distance and my indifference, this was the last time I would see this matriarch.

It was different with my mother. When I hugged her I tried to commit everything to memory: the point of her chin on my shoulder, the way I felt protected by her even though I was the bigger of us two.

When I returned home I would have to subsist on memory alone until she came back to me. And she would come back. There was no future here amidst her past.

I said a more private goodbye to the gift of the night stars. I didn't know the next time I would see them.

PART IV
HOMECOMING

THE AGE OF REPRODUCTION

AFTER I RETURNED I spent a great deal of time on my computer looking at Oliver.

At first, relieved to be near my computer, I simply pulled up the photos I had saved of him. I did it in the dead of night, with a blanket pulled over my head. A quick glance at an Oliver photo and then guiltily I closed out of the box, turned off my laptop, rolled over, and tried to sleep, his digitized image stamped on my eyelids.

This wasn't enough.

Soon I was lining up pictures of me and Oliver together. I took a recent and semi-flattering picture of me, taken at the pueblo by tio Diego and put it beside a blurred photo of Oliver, sweaty and wearing a rugby top in the field behind Canterbury. I wanted us to look like we belonged together, but we didn't match, not at all. It was more than the change in camera quality, the switch from film to digital. I was older than Oliver had ever gotten to be. I didn't feel older than myself at eighteen. I didn't look much older. But I had lost that fat-cheeked lustre of youth, that too-round smoothness of a growing child.

I was, for better or worse, a woman now.

I dug up some pictures of me at eighteen, to put beside my Oliver pictures.

Better now, even though we never would have been eighteen at the same time. But there was something unsettling about lining up those two eighteen-year-olds together. He was dead and I wasn't her, didn't want to go back to that time. I remembered eighteen as bewildering and unpleasant, a year when I reluctantly entered university and had to be the-girl-with-one-arm to a whole new campus full of people. There were always new people doing double takes, looking shocked, being overly interested or pointedly uninterested.

I spared a thought for the girl with the burned legs, my former CHEO roommate. She must have been a teenager herself now and going through the worst years.

What I wanted from the photos was an older Oliver. Not Oliver as I had seen him but Oliver as he never was.

The miraculous part of the internet was that I could pay someone to make him for me, someone who specialized in photorealistic imagery, who didn't ask too many questions when I said I wanted an aged-up image of Oliver. Not too aged, not too different. We communicated in a chatbox about the art I commissioned, the bomb of what I was doing neutralized by the fact that I had reduced my desires to text, my sickness paid for in dollars and cents.

I paid too much and waited.

Marnie could have done it of course.

But of course I never would have asked Marnie and anyway, at that point we weren't talking again.

MARNIE WASN'T PLEASED TO SEE ME

INSTEAD OF TELLING her when, exactly, I was coming home, I dodged her texts and emails and took a taxi home from the train.

It felt so good to be home. The air tasted different. And more than the sound of people speaking English, it was the bilingual announcements that made me want to weep, the French reminding me that I was back among my people.

The whole way home, from the moment I got to the Benito Juárez airport, to the flight, to the train, I could feel my body relaxing, unwinding.

And then I got home and Marnie was there.

It was disorienting to see her in front of me. After a few weeks of seeing nothing but brown-skinned people she seemed startlingly pale. Jaundiced even. Being away had felt longer than it was, it always did. I was expecting that, to match the change in my mind, everything at home would be different. That Marnie's stomach would be comically round, like a beach ball had been stuffed down her shirt. Instead she was much the same as when I had left her, in that awkward in-between phase of pregnancy when it was impossible to tell whether she was pregnant or a bit fat.

I brought you puerquitos, I said, hoping to provoke a laugh.

She looked at me much the way my abuela had looked at me in the courtyard when I was covered in bumps.

How amusing it was to see that same level of condescension translated from my abuela to my sister. If she had had a cane I was sure Marnie would have given me a good thwack.

I asked you to do one thing, Marnie said. One thing. I told you how much I needed this and you failed me.

I felt the blush of shame painting my cheeks. I hadn't wanted to go, had promised Marnie nothing, and yet it was terrible to be a disappointment.

It was embarrassing to feel this humbled in front of Marnie. Marnie who should have been blushing in front of me, who should come to me humbled and on her knees begging me for my forgiveness every day of her life.

I'm sorry, I said sarcastically. I'm so sorry that I didn't acquit myself perfectly on the little task you sent me on. But our mother is her own person and she doesn't care about the baby no one told you to have or coming here on your timeline. Now if you'll excuse me I am half sick to death from being trapped at altitude with a bunch of disgusting people who wouldn't stop staring at my arm.

Fuck you, Marnie said, stepping in front of me, blocking my way.

Her face was flushed as pink as mine felt. I inhaled sharply as she breathed out, her hot little gust of anger choking me as I breathed it down. The intimacy of the moment was revolting.

I'm so sick of you acting this way, Marnie said. I could see every fine wrinkle in her face, the way her pupils were dilated with anger, the way a little vein stuck out of the side of her temple. I didn't want to be this close to her, hadn't really looked at her in years. Even older, even angry, she was still infuriatingly beautiful, my Marnie. I felt the urge to apologize, to plead for her forgiveness.

Instead I made a motion to shove her away and then stopped, my body remembering before I did that Marnie was pregnant and that it wouldn't do to go shoving around a pregnant woman. That a miscarriage I provoked would be worse, somehow, than the loss of an arm, would make us unequal in a way that favoured Marnie.

But Marnie had seen my intention to strike her and she was standing, one hand on her belly, looking unbearably smug. The thought of trying to strike her while she was pregnant was going to be used against me till the end of time. Marnie would take her little baby and coo in their ear, You're so lucky to be alive, you know your tia Alma tried to kill me while I was pregnant with you.

You have to stop it, Marnie said.

I'm not doing anything. Just because you're perfect pregnant Marnie doesn't mean I can't tell you to fuck off. Just because I tell you the truth—

I don't give a fuck about any of that and you know it, Marnie said. It's the way anytime you don't get your way you wave your amputated arm around in my face. I've tried to tell you I'm sorry a million different ways a million different times. You don't want to be my sister anymore, fine. But how are we supposed to keep going when I have the baby? How are you supposed to be an aunt this way?

If it was possible to black out with rage I felt it then, the heat of my anger taking me like a wave, the emotion possessing me. There was a tiny box in my brain, the part that always was in control even when the pain hit, even when I felt lost, the part that knew what to do, the part I thought of as being the most me. That part was screaming to calm the fuck down. But I couldn't calm the fuck down. There was no part of me that felt in control of myself. I wanted to backhand Marnie. So I did.

Or rather I tried. It was the missing hand that let me down again by virtue of its not being there. I felt the ghost of it connecting to Marnie's cheek with a satisfying slap but of course that didn't happen because in the end nothing at all hit Marnie. It was just the stump of my arm reaching for her in a pitiable way, only rather than look at me with any pity Marnie's face remained hard and angry.

There you go again, she said.

I pushed past her then. I wanted to leave before I actually did something stupid like kick her or slap her with the hand I did have. But then, because we were tied together forever, because, even if I hated her, she was my sister, I turned back.

I'm so sorry my pain is inconvenient to you, Marnie. I'm so sorry that every day I'm reminded of the worst thing that ever happened to me, that I'm trapped in a body with the worst thing that ever happened to me and that by association you have to remember that what happened happened because you were selfish and cruel, that you can't go on thinking that you're a perfect, good person who would do anything for your sister because when it mattered you didn't.

Marnie was blinking very quickly, both her hands clenched, and bright patches of red where her jowls would be. It was just so Marnie that even when I was excoriating her her glossed-over eyes shone bigger and brighter than ever, catching the light. And the stain on her cheeks, the same one my father sported when he thought he had made a mistake with a client or when someone told a joke too lewd for his taste, made her glow with health.

It was unfair that I loved Marnie in that moment, but I did.

I'm sorry, Marnie said. I know, every day, what I did, and every day I try to apologize. But you do wield your arm like a weapon against me, Alma. You do. I know that I don't know what you lived through. I know that you've seen terrible, unimaginable things and have suffered pain I can't understand. But you hold on to your anger against me so much that we're not even sisters anymore, not really. Our family isn't really a family anymore. We do whatever you want to do; we tiptoe around your pain. Even Constantine does it. And you keep it like a pet that you fawn over, that you love more than any of us.

Her voice broke.

You're still a little girl, Marnie said. You're still a little girl.

THERE IS A FEELING BEYOND RAGE
AND THAT FEELING IS JOY

IT WAS LIKE I had ascended so far past my anger towards Marnie that all I felt was an overwhelming sense of bliss. How dare she? was replaced with a quiet peace.

I started to laugh, quite loudly, and Marnie looked at me startled and afraid which made me laugh harder.

What could I say?

I no longer wished to injure Marnie, to make her see or understand my pain. I wanted Marnie to continue to live her blissful stupid life with not a care in the world. And I wanted her to do it as far away from me as possible.

Goodbye Marnie, I said. I hope you enjoy the rest of your life.

SOMETIMES I FEEL LIKE EVERYTHING I KNOW ABOUT JUDAISM IS GRIEF RITUALS FOR THE DEAD

IN NOVEMBER, on the anniversary of Oliver's death, at sundown, I lit two yahrzeit candles, one for Oliver and one for my arm.

I was back in my apartment with the landlady and her crazy daughter though the screaming between the two had mostly abated. Now, whenever I saw them, they were always hugging affectionately, the daughter smiling fondly at her mother, zipping up her coat all the way to shield her from the cold and giving her a kiss on the cheek every time she said goodbye. It was quite touching actually. On recycling day there were orange prescription pill bottles in the blue bin which probably explained the change.

Marnie was still pregnant and we were still not talking.

I wouldn't have thought I would miss her, given our years of respective coldness, our inability to talk to one another about anything real since the accident. But I did miss her. The way we bickered at one another, the arms she made in her basement, the way sometimes, over not-Shabbat dinners, when Neil mispronounced a Spanish word we would lock eyes with one another and try not to snicker.

Every time I looked at the calendar and saw another day had passed I felt my throat close up. Now, in addition to not sleeping, I was also not eating, my throat too tense to swallow. There needed to be an end date to this estrangement, one that coincided with the birth of Marnie's baby. I couldn't not be there for the birth. And yet Marnie was not playing her part, was not calling me, was not repenting, and even if my heart was soft my body was not. I couldn't have called her if I had tried, my fingers cold and inflexible, my feet unwilling to go beyond the Glebe. I cut out the Golden Triangle from my walks the way I cut out everything else unpleasant to me.

Whether it was because of this argument or for her own private reasons, my mother had come back, with absolutely no fanfare, shortly after my own return, banishing me once more from the family home. She blamed my father for what had happened between Marnie and me. When she had left, things had been if not perfect, then status quo.

In apology to the women in his life my father tried, in a clumsy way, to mediate peace between us, inviting us both to the family home.

But Marnie had ceded not-Shabbat dinners. She was demanding apologies from me and Mama. Mama quickly capitulated but I refused to talk to her, demanded an apology of my own. Every time I tried to wheedle my father over to my side he blustered out some half-hearted defence in which he said that Marnie was, herself, going through a difficult time as she was quite heavily pregnant which had made her very emotional.

It was a sexist milquetoast defence. It made me half angry on Marnie's behalf that my father would be so spineless.

For the first time in my life, Constantine was not there either. He had come to my apartment while I was in Mexico and taken back his hoodies and boyfriend T-shirts and the best of the books I had borrowed from him. In return he'd left a cardboard box of all the possessions I'd left at his place, a box which I refused to open. It said enough that I couldn't even remember what was in it.

So when I lit the yahrzeit candles I was alone. In deference to my landlady's No Candles rule I lit them in the kitchen sink so they could burn without potentially burning down the building.

Then I called Constantine.

I felt his absence in my apartment. After I first moved there he would come over and occupy the space, moving in his fluent way, cleaning up the coffee I spilled in the kitchen, straightening the sneakers I had kicked off by the door. He sorted through my mail and left it in two neat little piles, junk and not junk.

Without him, without the order of living at home, I began to understand the tangle of Mrs. Jentsch's home. How privacy quickly could slouch into laziness.

He answered the call on the first ring.

How are you today? he asked, a more generous question than I deserved.

Constantine had seen me enact this ritual for years.

I've been thinking of him a lot lately, I said. Of Oliver. It felt strange to say his name. I hadn't said it aloud in so long.

When I was a little girl it had struck me as a romantic masculine sort of name, the name of the man to whom I would one day matter. But now as I said it, it seemed like the name of a little boy. Oliver Twist pleading for more porridge.

You know the funny thing is, when I realized what today was I ran out and bought a candle too, Constantine said.

Do you still think of him?

There was a pause. I pictured Constantine in his ugly condo, alone in the city.

No, Constantine said. I don't really remember him. Now, on this day, I only think of you.

Oliver was all I thought about, the background to my years. The pulse around which I operated, the thing that connected me to Constantine and also what kept us apart.

I'm thinking of leaving, Constantine said. You know, Montreal is a great city. I had good years there. And rent is cheap.

I think that would be good, I told him. I think that would probably make you happy.

I waited for him to ask me to come with him, to be happy too.

Thank you, he said. He sounded relieved.

That night I slipped from bed and went into my living room to peer out onto the street. November, when the trees had been fully stripped of their leaves but there wasn't yet any snow on the ground, was a miserable month. The little brick buildings looked far apart from one another, like they were shivering in the cold.

I waited for Oliver to appear on the street but there was no one out there, the city properly asleep. Seeing him had been so different from when my mother left us and I kept seeing her everywhere—those instants had been split seconds of confusion that clarified the second the actual women came closer, reality asserting itself over my wishes. In all the time he had been dead I had never mistaken anyone for Oliver, found his form in another. I had seen Oliver once. Despite my later attempts at denial I had known it was him.

My parents, out of respect to their religions, had raised Marnie and me mostly godless, but bits of Catholicism and Judaism had infiltrated our childhoods. The not-Shabbats. A very gift-based Christmas. I knew more of Christianity—it was impossible not to know about Jesus in a Christian-based society—but I had always liked the sense of mysticism and agony and raw lust in the Torah. Those open-ended stories seemed to have been written in a time full of wonder and I thought perhaps in our age of technology, of cloning and animated limbs and internet and social media, we were returning to wonder again, a time when all things were possible.

The changes I had seen within my lifetime were baffling, the changes my parents had seen even more so, the changes that my abuela had seen ten times that.

Why could the world not create a blessed mistake, bring Oliver Jentsch back to me, alive and well, folding time so that we could co-exist once more in the same space.

I missed him. I wanted him.

It had taken me years to admit it but if a multi-eyed seraph had appeared to me in a vision and told me that it would give me whatever I wanted back in this life, the miracle I would ask for would not be my body made whole but Oliver brought back to me.

I wanted to find him, whatever it took.

I did not have to travel very far.

ACCORDING TO THE MOST RECENT CENSUS
THERE ARE THIRTEEN THOUSAND AND
FIFTY-FIVE PEOPLE WHO LIVE IN THE GLEBE

ONE OF THEM was Mrs. Jentsch.

THE GLEBE

DESPITE THE FACT that I lived in a city, living in the Glebe all my life held many echoes of living in a small town.

On a regular basis going grocery shopping or running any other errand I was stopped by the mother of a childhood classmate, usually someone I had been friends with in elementary school who had abandoned me after the accident. They were always so happy to see me, treating me with a kindness which in my late teenage years I sullenly misread as pity. As I aged I recognized it as the affection all people feel towards anyone younger than themselves, a sort of protective parental instinct I had started feeling myself when I saw the little siblings of my old school friends walking about in newly adult bodies.

At the same time I regularly met people I had never seen before, neighbours who let me pet their dogs or said hello on morning walks, or who opened doors for me when I went to the bakery. Sometimes we would get into little conversations and many of these people commented they had lived in the neighbourhood even longer than I had. They were perfectly friendly, ordinary people, people who had loved and lost and thought and worked and got papercuts and stared out windows and yawned and lived whole lives. People with whom I shared a short conversation before they disappeared back into those lives, our paths never to cross again.

And I, in all my misery, had been living my life of tragedy and anger and grievance and strangeness within this community. A life within the borders of the Glebe. No, a life smaller than that, a life lived on a few streets. Smaller than that: I could not enter any house I wanted, for example. And even within the houses I was allowed to access, this access was limited, my life lived in even smaller corners. I was not forbidden from but seldom went into my parents' bedroom on Linden Terrace. The attic, where the things we didn't want went to their final resting place, was a space I hadn't seen in years. I almost never went into aunt Eshkie and uncle Bobby's upstairs apartment even though I worked in the house they lived in, visited it nearly daily. The apartment I rented was in a relatively small building but I had never been inside the other units, never stood on the roof or even ventured into the backyard which was the domain of my landlady and her now tamed daughter.

If only I had been more curious, ventured out more, perhaps I would have found Mrs. Jentsch earlier.

It turned out to be alarmingly easy to find her.

I typed her name into a search engine and there was nothing, as I expected. No digital trace.

But I thought she might have stayed in Ottawa, I hoped for it even. The White Pages were going the way of the landline; my parents recycled their copy just as soon as it was delivered, but there were old copies at the office, in the client archives.

When everyone went to lunch, my father and mother going home, aunt Eshkie and uncle Bobby upstairs, I claimed Constantine was coming to meet me, waited till everyone had left, and slunk off to the basement. Down there were old typewriters, defunct computers, and boxes and boxes of old client files which I kept arguing should be digitized.

I knew exactly where the White Pages were, in an untouched stack in a corner. I pulled out the year after Mrs. Jentsch had moved, sneezing at the dust it unleashed, and paged through the tissue-thin pages. I found the Js, kept searching through the Janes and Jansens till I got to the Jenkinses and there, suddenly, a Jentsch. There was only one. Dr. Jentsch. She was still listed as living on Monkland even though that year she had left it. I pulled out the next year. No Jentsch. I pulled out the third year, hoping against hope that she had stayed in the city. That she hadn't moved to some other city or, worse, a tiny hamlet. That she hadn't fled the country or renamed herself. But there it was, again. One Jentsch. The only one in the entire city.

She lived on Broadway Avenue.

Dr. Jentsch, or someone by her name, had moved to Broadway Avenue three years after Oliver's death.

Mrs. Jentsch, who had wished me dead when I was a little girl and wanted nothing more than to be told I deserved to die, my beloved cruel Mrs. Jentsch had not disappeared into the night but had simply moved to what amounted to a fifteen-minute walk away from me.

I remembered all that clutter I had seen in her house. The things that she had kept, seemingly for years, only abandoning them when Oliver died.

She was not a woman who moved easily. She was a woman who stayed.

I thought you were meeting a friend, aunt Eshkie said.

I jumped in the air.

Yes, he cancelled, I said carefully. I snapped the phone book shut and tucked it under my arm. Aunt Eshkie watched me, but said nothing.

I feel sick, I have to take the afternoon off.

We moved together to go upstairs and I paused at the base of the steps. Though we saw each other frequently we were so seldom alone.

Aunt Eshkie, I said turning to her, do you think the family treats me differently because of what happened to me?

She wet her lips with her tongue before she spoke.

We all love you very much, she finally said, and reached out and patted me awkwardly. If this is about your CPA certification of course Bobby and I would be happy to help—

It's not that, I said. I'm just not feeling well. And then I ran up the stairs.

I wanted to run all the way from work to Mrs. Jentsch's home on Broadway Avenue and knock at her door until my fingers were bloodied and either the police came to drag me away or she finally let me in.

But then sanity, and my father's voice, telling me it was rude to impose on others, prevailed. There was another softer option. I went to my apartment and sat among the things I lived with every day and I called the landline listed in the White Pages.

It rang.

SHE SOUNDED EXACTLY THE SAME

A FEW DAYS before, gun to my head, I would not have been able to describe what Mrs. Jentsch sounded like or even call to mind her voice. But somewhere her voice had been preserved in my memory, ready to be called forth, so I could say, Ah, yes, *that* is Mrs. Jentsch. That is the voice I remember.

Yes, hello, she said.

There was a wheeze to it from the smoking that might have gotten slightly thicker. That was all. Still that voice, slightly deep for a woman. An adult's voice. A voice of authority.

This is Alma Alt, I said.

There was a little pause and for one frantic moment I thought over and over again, She doesn't remember me, shedoesntrememberme, shdsntrmbrm, everything sliding together in a panicky gust. I wanted to run to Bank and let a truck run me over, purge me of my humiliation.

So, you're still alive, she rasped. I thought you might have died.

I felt a blush crawl up my face. I remembered that last conversation we had had where I had confessed my love. I was embarrassed to be alive, embarrassed not to have let the grief take me away. The smallness with which I had lived my life seemed, when talking to Mrs. Jentsch, indecently sprawling and vulgar.

Well, no, I said.

Hmm.

Over the phone I heard a match being struck, the intake of breath that told me she was inhaling from a cigarette. The scent-memory of smoke drifted through my nostrils.

You've certainly taken long enough to find me.

Can I see him? I said.

You can come on Wednesday, she told me.

Then she hung up.

WE HAD SET NO FIXED TIME TO MEET

AND AS THE days went by I had a sinking feeling in the pit of my stomach, every thought that came to me consumed by the fact that I was, on Wednesday, going to see Mrs. Jentsch at some point. By Tuesday I was such a miserable, jumpy mess that even uncle Bobby, notoriously tactful, made note of it. At work aunt Eshkie wondered if perhaps I was still sick and, seizing on this possibility, I said, Yes, I thought I was, and then had to endure everyone stopping their work to come and poke and prod at me, three neurotic Jews fussing over me with such concern that I almost retracted my lie.

I was permitted, by my father, to come back to Linden Terrace for the night.

I knew this meant a concoction of vitamins and wretched camomile tea from a bag and limeonade made by my mother and bizarre Mexican home remedies and attention when what I needed was to be left alone but I couldn't resist the lure of being home again.

So halfway through the day, with a sudden exaggerated limp (what was I limping for? I didn't know, only that once I started I couldn't stop) I headed home, leaning heavily on my mother, who had also taken the afternoon off and promised the three neurotics that she would fuss over me as much as needed.

In the end it was nice to be home even though I wasn't sick.

My mother did make me drink the hateful tea but after I chugged the thing down she looked at me with a glint in her eye and asked me if I wouldn't like pizza for dinner.

And when I admitted I would, instead of chastising me she simply ordered it in.

I was too full of anticipation for my rendezvous with Mrs. Jentsch to concentrate properly on anything, so when my mother suggested we watch something I asked that she put on *The Wizard of Oz* so we could talk over it if necessary.

We skipped to the part where Dorothy began to sing Somewhere Over the Rainbow.

Do you remember the girl in the hospital? This was her favourite, my mother said right as a tree slapped Dorothy on the hand for picking one of the apples on its branches.

Of course I remember, I said. I always think of her when I watch this movie. I always wonder how she's doing. I always hope she's doing well.

I didn't tell my mother about the list I kept in a notebook that was filled with every burn survivor I came across in fiction and in life. There were more than one might think. I wondered if somewhere that girl was keeping a list of amputees when she came across them. Mr. Rochester in *Jane Eyre*, a burn survivor and amputee, would have made both our lists.

Pobrecita, my mother said.

I ASKED MY MOTHER BEFORE I WENT TO SEE MRS. JENTSCH WHAT SHE WOULD SAY IF I SAID THAT I HAD SEEN OLIVER

DID YOU SEE Oliver? she asked.

We were still sprawled in front of the TV. We had switched to *The Matrix*, her choice.

I think I saw Oliver, I said.

I still pray for him, she said.

I still think of him, I said. At first I could only picture him the way he was when I last saw him, but now— I couldn't bring myself to finish the sentence. To explain. Instead I asked my mother if she too had ever seen a dead body.

I knew she had seen my grandmother in the hospital after she died but she surprised me with her answer.

Too many.

Too many?

In the way she said it I could tell that this was a part of the life my mother had lived as a woman before she became my mother, something that reminded me that she didn't belong to me or Marnie or even to my father but only to herself.

Why did you come back to us, Mama? I asked.

I hadn't been brave enough to ask her when she appeared but now I felt I needed to know.

She smoothed the top of my hair, my waves growing wild and frizzing with the humidity of the coming rain, and planted a kiss on the top.

I love you, she said. Which could have been an answer or a diversion.

It was clear she didn't want to talk about it anymore and so we didn't.

I WOKE UP IN THE EARLY HOURS OF THE MORNING CONVINCED THE WORLD WAS ENDING

I WAS SO disoriented by the sky, glowing orange outside, and the fact that I was in Marnie's old bedroom. I wasn't sure what was going on or what year I was in. I looked outside and the sky was a smoky orange with lightning flickering in the distance. The denuded branches of trees looked charcoal-black against the light.

I'm going to die, I thought. It didn't alarm me at all. Accepting my fate, I closed my eyes again and fell back into dreamless sleep.

When I woke up again it was day and I knew myself and the world around me again.

I had intended to wake up early and go see Mrs. Jentsch as soon as I could, but the second awakening took place close to noon and was caused by a rumbling in my stomach and a dryness in my throat.

I brushed my hair into a frizz and ran about the house getting ready. I had a feeling that I was late for something, that I had missed my one opportunity to see her, that I would arrive and instead of the house that I had looked up on Google Maps there would be a gap between two houses, a gap of nothingness. Or there would be a house but it would look different than the one I had seen, with a different number affixed to the door and when I knocked someone who was not Mrs. Jentsch, someone who had never known Oliver, would open the door.

As I walked the familiar streets I had walked all my life, an unseasonable rain that should have been snow beat a soft pattern on my umbrella. With every step that took me closer to my destination I chastised myself for believing that finding her would be so easy, that she would be there, that Oliver would be.

I was sick with nerves by the time I rounded the curve of the pathway around Brown's Inlet. The water was mostly drained away and I could see the inukshuk that someone had built at the base of the pond years ago and which neither nature nor man had knocked down. There were still little pools of water in the basin of the pond and a few ducks, stragglers on their way southward, swam about in pairs as they must have been doing since the inlet was carved into the earth and flooded with water, to please the people of the Glebe.

I went to Broadway Avenue and there, just as the address had promised, there was Mrs. Jentsch's house.

I could tell immediately which one was hers. It was a little shabbier than the rest, with a porch that tilted in a way that did not look quite architecturally sound and guttering that was broken so that rather than the rain making its way all the down the house and landing harmlessly in the driveway, a torrent poured from the second floor all the way down to the garden, making a mud puddle right below one of the windows.

Instead of the pretty little English gardens that had become so favoured by Glebites in recent years, replacing the outmoded grass lawn, Mrs. Jentsch had a sandy-looking patch of dirt in front of her house, echoing the state of her backyard when she had been my neighbour. I wondered why she did not get someone to come and seed it. But then, she wasn't the sort of woman who would have done a thing like that. She was not a woman who cared for grass or gardens, or what her neighbours might think. She didn't take care of her lawn because she simply didn't want to and no amount of coaxing or censure would cause her to change her mind.

For one second I thought, This is enough.

To be near her, to know that she was alive. To see evidence that she was still the same woman I remembered. I let myself dream a dream in which I turned in my rain boots and ran home, cuddled under the covers and, at a normal hour, called Marnie and asked her to be my sister again, called Constantine and asked him to marry me, and then called a doctor, told them I had been experiencing hallucinations and allowed them to drug me until I never thought of Oliver Jentsch again.

I imagined kissing my parents goodbye and taking the hand Constantine was always offering me, the two of us fleeing far from sleepy Ottawa to Montreal or Toronto or maybe even somewhere European, a place where things happened, where by virtue of my arm and my accent and my skin I would always be other, but at least I wouldn't be here.

I imagined leaving Ottawa behind without a backwards glance and salting the earth behind me so that it was forever a place I would stay away from, not even coming back when my father and mother died. I imagined forgetting everything I knew to be true and having a child or two, dumping them into a miserable future that was none of my concern and being so preoccupied with raising them that I wouldn't have time to miss Marnie and her children.

I imagined a lot of things but even while I was imaging them I was knocking and the door was opening and there was Mrs. Jentsch.

IT SEEMS THERE ARE ONLY SO MANY WAYS TO MAKE A HOUSE A HOME

AND THE ONLY way Mrs. Jentsch understood to do it was by turning hers into a nest. If she had left behind all her worldly possessions when she left her old home she had more than made up for it in her new house.

There were stacks of boxes filled with what looked like old magazines, newspapers, and binders in the foyer that made it difficult to get in.

The entire home had that familiar choking scent of ash, stronger than I was used to but, now that I took the occasional puff, subtly pleasing to me.

As we moved deeper into the house the smell was not as overpowering as I remembered but this was because the windows were open.

Unfortunately this allowed insects to come and go as they pleased and while I was there I noticed various ecosystems of flies and spiders and the like busy establishing themselves in the corners of the living room, the room where Mrs. Jentsch brought me.

She didn't seem to mind that between my rain boots and my umbrella and my coat I had half brought the rain in with me. As I looked about helplessly she shuffled forward and cleared away a corner of a couch, gruffly refusing my offer of help, moving a matted lump of cloth and sweater on top of a different precarious pile of books and clearing away the vase, scissors, and puzzle that appeared from beneath. At last it was cleared down to cushion and I sank into the corner of the couch, springs digging into my back.

As she sat down in a chair opposite me neither of us said anything. We were older than we remembered each other. We drank in the changes that had accumulated since we had last been in the same room. She could not have been much older than my parents, was probably younger than them in fact, but unlike my mother whose hair was bottle black, Mrs. Jentsch's hair was undyed and pure white. She was the same woman but there were more lines around her face and I noticed that when she greeted me our eyes had met each other on even territory. Whether this was because I had grown or because of the slight stoop she was starting to develop or a combination of the two I couldn't tell. But all of these superficial changes seemed meaningless compared to the light in her eyes. She looked happy, something she hadn't been the last time I had seen her or really anytime before that.

There were many things I had planned to say to her but what came out first was: I never left.

She nodded when I said that.

I never thought you would, she said. I did see you from time to time.

You did?

You're easy to notice, she said, with a look at my arm. When you were in school I saw you often. These last few years, not so much. I did think, over time, she continued, that you might have killed yourself. You'll understand that it gave me some pleasure to think of you that way. But the way it worked out is fine. Perhaps even good.

She paused a moment and looked at me.

I can tell you never forgot him.

No, I said. I did forget some things, but I never forgot about him. I don't know how to forget a thing like that. I didn't want to.

She looked almost gleeful when I said that, like she was feasting on my pain.

I couldn't leave either, she said. As you can see. The old house was too near you, I couldn't bear it, but this was just distant enough that I could be near him without drowning in the grief. Do you know I still don't cross over to the other side of Bank Street? That whole territory? I chose this house because the grocery store is on my side. If it wasn't I could have gone elsewhere, I suppose, to do my shopping. Or maybe, she said reflectively, I would have let myself starve.

I never married, I told her. I thought it was important she knew that.

Oh well. Many girls your age don't marry nowadays.

I never will. No children either. Not after what happened.

No. She closed her eyes and leaned back in the chair, dislodging some clothes from the back, which fell in a clump to the floor. She ignored them.

What a lucky girl you are to have choices, she said, still with her eyes closed. I think about it all the time. If I had known what I know now about Oliver would I have chosen to have him? No, she said not waiting for my answer. No, I don't think so.

The mention of his name felt so precious and gave me the courage I needed to speak of him.

I saw him, I said.

Mrs. Jentsch's eyes opened slowly, her lids lazy. She did not look in the least flustered by what I had told her.

My mother died and then left and she's fine now, but it was a heart attack and she died and—I saw him. Where he died I mean. I saw him. Standing there.

He's often there, Mrs. Jentsch said. He knows he died. I didn't put the memory of his death inside of him, but I didn't hide that it happened. I thought he should know. Since then he's often there. Maybe it's inevitable he'd be drawn there; in this neighbourhood there are only so many streets, so many places to walk. Sometimes I like to believe it might mean something. That he's trying to remember. That would be phenomenal.

I didn't think remembering dying would be phenomenal at all, but I didn't really care about that because she was talking about Oliver like he was a person.

How can that be? I asked. How can he be alive?

I remembered the incident at the train station, losing total control and pissing all over myself, and I dug the nails on my hand deep into my thighs to try to keep myself alert and in control of my body. I felt a twinge as the nail on my ring finger split and kept digging anyway.

She didn't answer me. Nothing was ever easy with Mrs. Jentsch. She made me ask twice. I got the sense that she would have enjoyed it if I got on my knees on the dirty floor and debased myself, desperate for her knowledge.

I thought of the sound of his head thumping into the windshield, my lost arm, Mrs. Jentsch telling me she wished I had died, all those stupid fights with Marnie and Constantine and everyone else. The bitterness of spirit which had invaded my whole life from the time of the accident forward.

Take it away, I thought. Take it all away.

I kept trying to put everything together in my mind. All the arms Marnie made for me in her basement. All the pictures of Oliver I made in the dark. Mrs. Jentsch not ten minutes from where I lived. The three of us relentlessly creating in secret.

The Oliver I had seen was neither old enough to be the Oliver I had grown up with nor young enough to be an Oliver conceived and birthed in his wake. He was an in-between Oliver, an Oliver at eighteen, perfectly crystallized at the moment before his death.

What did you do? I asked her.

Oliver, Mrs. Jentsch called. Oliver, come here and say hello to Alma.

The tread of a man in the other room coming closer.

Then he was there.

It was Oliver in the flesh, as he was, not a day older nor a day younger than the day he died in front of me.

Hello, Alma, he said. He smiled at me. He even had that soft line of wavy ridges on the bottom of his front teeth from where they had been pushed through the gums. I had the same ones. My dentist had once offered to file them down for aesthetic purposes and I, thinking of how the most beautiful man I had ever seen in my life had the same ones, refused the offer.

HE LOOKED LIKE OLIVER

HIS EYE CAUGHT the light in a twinkle the way Oliver's did. There was a thin silver scar on his brow bone that cut through his left eyebrow. I had forgotten that that scar existed and suddenly there it was, on his face, like an old friend. It was too fine to show up in the school photos in Marnie's yearbooks or the scanned photos of him that were uploaded on his memorial page, copies of copies that had failed to translate him faithfully.

He smiled at me, a lopsided smile. His eyes regarded me with the easy amiability that Oliver's eyes always held.

I was standing without meaning to, reaching for him and he reacted with innocent geniality, his hand meeting mine. It felt like flesh. I touched the pulse point and found the beat that indicated he still had a heart. I buried my face against his shirt the way I hadn't dared when I was a little girl and half in love with him. I heard it again, the steady life beat that meant that he was alive. I inhaled and there was ash from living in this house but under that his smell was Oliver: some pleasant cologne under which was the smell of skin and sweat and humanness.

I stood there, nuzzling him, in a way that was totally inappropriate to do in front of his mother, his creator. I clung to him with my one arm as if he were everything, as if through sheer force of will I could merge our flesh, turn us into a monstrous one. He responded by tentatively placing a hand on the back of my head.

When I reached for him it was without thinking but if I had been forced to speak I think I would have said that I wanted to be with him forever.

It is hard to stand entwined with someone who is not twining you back with the same force. At a certain point reality set in. My eyes were leaking on his shirt and my breasts were mashed up under his breastbone while he was awkwardly trying to angle his hips out of the way to try to keep up the modesty of our hug. And Mrs. Jentsch, who in my eagerness I had forgotten, was in the room. I could hear her breathing and when I finally detangled myself from Oliver I could see she was watching this scene with a glimmer in her eye.

His eyes took in my missing arm.

Alma, he said with concern. Did that happen to you in the accident when I died?

He both was and wasn't my Oliver.

MRS. JENTSCH SENT HIM AWAY

WHEN MRS. JENTSCH and I were alone, later, I saw her looking at me with a pleased smile on her face like a cat with a mouse between its paws feeling very smug with how clever it was compared to the mouse.

If I was the mouse I would have been very pleased for her to end my suffering and kill me. But of course the delight of the cat isn't in the killing but in the teasing, the toying. It feeds just as much on the misery of its prey as it does on its flesh.

It is very gratifying, Mrs. Jentsch said, to see how you reacted to him. Tears are such a natural, beautiful, spontaneous response, much like laughter. When Oliver was done I felt as if I had gotten him right but I had spent so much time building, creating, destroying, tinkering. You have no idea the sheer number of prototypes I went through on the eyes alone. So when he was quite done it was a bit anticlimactic. I wasn't sure whether I had done a good enough job or whether I had created something that was only the memory of a memory.

Motherhood is a kind of godhood, don't you think? I created a child, with my body. And then my child was taken away. I couldn't have a second child the way I had my first, but I could become a stronger god. And so with my brain and my hands I made a new child. A better one.

The words she was saying didn't make sense to me. Or they did and I couldn't believe it.

You made him? I said.

I remade him, Mrs. Jentsch confirmed. I put in every little thing, up to the point of death. We live in a great digital age. I had diaries, chat logs, film, videos. A tape of him singing Alouette that was surprisingly phonetically useful. And my own memories of course. I know my son.

Only here did I detect the faintest sense of humility in Mrs. Jentsch. She knew her son but only as a mother knows a child. We are, all of us, different people to different people. I wondered if she knew about the condoms in Oliver's room. About his drives with Marnie. About the kindness he showed me when I appeared before him, distressed and crying.

But I had touched him. I had had him in my arms, solid and real. As real as the perpetual motion machine I had fished out of the trash. As real as the arms Marnie made me that she kept in her basement. As real as the phone in my pocket.

That Oliver existed was all that mattered now.

Can I see him again? I asked Mrs. Jentsch.

Yes, she said. Come to us again.

IT HAD STOPPED RAINING WHEN I LEFT THE JENTSCH HOME

PEOPLE WERE WALKING by in light fall coats. A black squirrel with a plush tail was busy burying a nut in the ground, patting the dirt to make sure it was sufficiently hidden. A car zooming by hit a puddle that splashed me and soaked my feet.

All of these things, things I saw every day and typically took next to no notice of, were baffling to me now. Were they the real and everything that had happened as soon as I entered the Jentsch home some sort of incredible fever dream? Or was everything in the outside world a fever dream and Oliver and Mrs. Jentsch the only things that were real?

I had that feeling again, the one I had when I was a child and crawled through the fence to the Jentsch place, that somehow I had walked through a portal and become Alma Alternate. Or maybe Alma Alternate was the one who had experienced all the terrible things in my life and now I was becoming who I always should have been, the child who had never crawled through the fence, the original Alma Alt.

I kept starting at things I saw on the way home. Children being let out of school, running towards their parents, their backpacks flopping to the beat of their steps. A particularly frightening tree, its branches bent and arthritic-looking. Birds that flew away at my approach.

When I arrived at the door to my home I was so out of sorts that I knocked until my father answered despite the fact the door was unlocked.

What's the matter with you? my father asked, laying a hand to my forehead. You look like you've seen a ghost.

GHOST STORIES

OLIVER HAD DYSLEXIA, which I hadn't known until I began to spend time with him and Mrs. Jentsch again.

She had him read to us, like a pet performing a trick, some sort of technical manual on electronics, something I truly couldn't grasp. It was a jerky, lifeless reading, full of pauses and occasional stutters, so different to how kind and attentive he was in conversation. But I was grateful for it, because it gave me an excuse to stare blatantly at Oliver, to examine those long lashes I loved so much, to experience a desire to reach out and touch his hand, without actually giving in to that desire.

He was never diagnosed when he was alive, Mrs. Jentsch said fondly. I only discovered it this time around. I always thought he wasn't trying hard enough.

Oliver looked down at the manual, thumbed a tissue paper page away from the rest, and fretted it between his fingers.

I try, he said. I always try.

I know you do, I said, quick to soothe where Mrs. Jentsch was about to sting.

I had spent so many years talking to Oliver in my mind, imaging just this sort of scenario, one in which logic was suspended and I could reach past death to talk to him. I would be his stalwart companion, his kind angel.

It was alarming to find that he talked back. He wanted to know what I had done in the interim between his death and the now, and I found I didn't know how to answer. How to describe that barren field of time in which I had done nothing but mourn him. When I ran into other people from my life, old acquaintances and their parents, Marnie's friends, they seemed to understand and expect that I had nothing much to say. The accident had frozen me. I had no real accomplishments, professional or personal.

I stayed in touch with Constantine. I finally settled on a topic I could bear. You remember Constantine.

Of course I do, he said softening gently. Constantine Kowalski. He had no idea how to cook and once set water to boil, took a nap, and I came home to licks of fire around the pot. Could have burned the whole place down.

I had heard that story so many times, but the way Oliver told it was all wrong. In Constantine's version it was Oliver who had fallen asleep, Constantine who, deciding to skip a lecture, had come home to a pot on fire.

And that phrasing, licks of fire, that was something that Constantine always—

Tell Oliver more about yourself, Mrs. Jentsch said, returning to a topic she had seen embarrassed me. What do you do with your friends?

What do *you* do? I asked him.

Computer engineering, it turned out. There were online courses that Oliver could take and was taking, learning how to turn strings of os and 1s into decipherable text, colour images.

It's what I always wanted to do, he said. Before I died.

I didn't know that, I said.

It occurred to me there were many things I hadn't known about him. Like what he went to Canterbury for.

I played the cello, he said, surprised.

Do you still?

He looked at Mrs. Jentsch and she looked away, embarrassed.

We don't have time for that, she said.

It pained me that she was depriving him of things.

I was almost grateful when our time came to a close. Mrs. Jentsch began to shift in her seat and told me with her typical abruptness that I should return home. Oliver, quick to smooth over her impertinence, smiled at me. Goodbye, Alma. I hope to see you again soon.

You will, I said struggling to get the words out. So long as Mrs. Jentsch let me, I would always return.

A CLOCKWORK BOY

HE SEEMS LIKE a person, I said to Mrs. Jentsch one day when Oliver was not in the room.

He's better than a person, Mrs. Jentsch said, defensive of her clockwork boy.

Mrs. Jentsch told me that, if she really wanted to, she could one day move Oliver into the body of a man and then an older man. He could not age naturally as a human could but she could age him in steps. His mind would continuously grow but she would transfer the Oliver of him into different bodies as she pleased.

For now though, she had chosen to keep him at eighteen, the age at which her Oliver had left her. It brought her comfort to see him that way. She'd had him that way for five years and it seemed as though she would never get enough of it.

To be sure, Oliver did look human, from what I could tell. He didn't act like a stupefied golem, designed to obey, but a thinking creature with something like free will.

His kindness in reacting to my discomfort—that felt real. But some of his stories were strange. I kept wanting to call Constantine, to ask him to tell me the story of the boiling pot. Had Constantine been mistaken or was Oliver? It had been many years since that incident and I could see how, in the drift of time, stories bent their way out of shape; characters shifted; memory, tired of repeating itself, varied in unpredictable ways.

But Oliver was young, he talked about Constantine and the accident as if no time had passed at all.

I kept trying to return to the past, to bring up things I knew were true. Do you remember when you used to drive Marnie home from school? Do you remember when I crawled from my backyard to yours? What was significant about that day?

He was never annoyed, only increasingly puzzled, answering my questions with a preternatural patience.

When I was with him I believed but every time I was away from him, even only when he stepped out of the room, my faith crumbled.

I know what you're doing, Mrs. Jentsch told me one day. Oliver is real. He is as alive as you and I are alive. He will keep learning, analyzing, making choices based on the new information just as you are changing based on your experiences. To disbelieve is an insult to us both. You are here specifically to believe.

Me? I said. I had never thought too closely about why Mrs. Jentsch had allowed me to be near Oliver. In my less charitable moments I imagined it was simply for someone to marvel at her genius.

I was half convinced, she continued, that after being alone for so long I had deluded myself as to how human he was. I truly thought that perhaps he was an abomination. That if others saw him they would stone or burn him. Come with pitchforks and destroy my poor boy. But he passed. He passed for one of them. Even though he is superior in every way those others couldn't see he was something created instead of born.

Still though, allowing him to walk by people was one thing. Mrs. Jentsch began to become bolder in her tests. She had him talk to people in the street, at first only a polite good morning or good evening. Later she let him run errands. He could pick up her medicine at the apothecary and buy groceries.

But still this wasn't enough for Mrs. Jentsch. She was greedy for the test of someone who had known him. And the person she was greediest for was me.

I began to hope you weren't dead, she told me. It would have been such a pity if you were in the end. The way you talked about him. The way you remembered him was different from the way I remembered him. I wanted you to see him and see if he seemed right to you. I knew that if you were still alive the pain would have imprinted him in your brain. That even if you had lost the feeling for him the pain would always bind you to him, would make you remember him and be eager to see him now, as he is, rather than as he was. And I was right, wasn't I?

A TRUE BELIEVER

IT SEEMED TO me that if Mrs. Jentsch had made a creature, a creature of flesh and bone, she was as close to a living god as I could imagine.

In an age dominated by atheism, where it was no longer en vogue to believe in God, it seemed quite plausible that the gods should be us; that is that clever people, people like Mrs. Jentsch, the creators, would be the ones on our damned planet to make whatever it was that came next, to wind it up and set it free.

I did not have that sentimentality of God as some benevolent benefactor. I knew God could be as temperamental, fickle, and sometimes needlessly cruel as the most dysfunctional of parents. In this way I accepted Mrs. Jentsch could be a god. Her cruelty and her hoarding, the jealous and possessive way she bound her new Oliver to her, her hatred of me, none of this struck me as particularly disqualifying. In fact, it was affirming. All the women I revered, from my mother to my abuela to Marnie herself, all treated me with a sort of disdainful arrogance. It did not surprise me that a god should find me lacking in the same way.

Are all life-creators gods? Mrs. Jentsch asked. Should we kiss the feet of every mother who pushes life out of her body?

Maybe, I said. It seems an awful burden to me. I've never done it in any case and I probably never will.

Love is a powerful inventor, grief even more so. I just happened to be born at the right age and time with the right talents to resurrect the dead. If you think I'm the only one on this planet to have done so your mind is too small. There must be others working away all doing the same things, finding how to re-translate dead flesh into a more easily reconstructed body. Someone someday will come forth about it and then . . . Well then maybe at last we'll become less attached to needlessly breeding ourselves over and over.

It sounded like potential eugenics nonsense to me, but I didn't dare interrupt Mrs. Jentsch when she was like this, bloviating on her favourite topics, her attitude irenic.

But, like all temperamental lesser gods, Mrs. Jentsch was soon made aware that I was not as enthusiastic as she was about being taken over by automatons, and she became quite annoyed.

You of all people should be happy about this, she snapped. Don't think I don't know that it causes you undue hardship to move through life with only one arm.

As if in sympathy to Mrs. Jentsch's point, I felt a sudden cramp that shuddered unpleasantly down my arm. It wanted nothing more than to be kneaded thoroughly, a hand running over the muscle until it relaxed.

It's not difficult at all, I told Mrs. Jentsch, lying smoothly, enjoying the way her nostrils flared in irritation as I contradicted her. Yes, in the beginning there was some pain, but rehab worked wonders. And switching from my right to my left hand was only a matter of practice and endurance. I can do nearly everything that someone with two hands can do and for the very little I can't, well, there is usually someone around to help me and if not, there is always a prosthetic.

A prosthetic which you don't wear, Mrs. Jentsch said, catching me out.

I was always fumbling in front of her and she was always there, with her reptilian eyes, noting every mistake, quietly taking joy in it. I suppose that part of the reason I kept trying to deceive her was the very pleasure she took in always evading my traps. On the other hand there was a very real competitive part of me that was determined that one day I really would make her look the fool.

You know, Mrs. Jentsch said, looking slyly at me, I could make you whole again.

I wished that she could. That she would take her Tinkertoys and soothe my addled mind. I had a vision of her puncturing my brain with a needle, my bad thoughts and worse deeds escaping in an evil hiss. But then I realized that she meant my body.

I thought of what Mrs. Jentsch could make that Marnie couldn't. Maybe she could truly create a second arm out of some wonder material. Something that would bind to my sinew and graft to my bone, that would blend the unnatural and the natural seamlessly. The thought didn't appeal to me as much as it once would have. What price would she extract for this?

I could make a new you, she said.

I felt the hairs on the back of my neck stand up. A new me.

An Alma for Oliver. An Alma at eighteen with two arms. A person who had never existed, not in this world at least.

I'm sure that you could, I agreed neutrally.

I watched her for signs of suspicion, but there were none. Pleased with herself, she called on Oliver to come say goodbye, her habitual signal that our time together was at an end.

DRIFTING

THAT WINTER THOSE around me began to complain that I wasn't quite there. It was hard to dispute this with any conviction because I *wasn't* there. I was always thinking of the house on Broadway Avenue where Oliver was.

Mrs. Jentsch continued to wield access to him as both carrot and stick. This was the unspoken reason why I never spoke about Oliver to anyone or even mentioned that I had seen, and was continuing to see, Mrs. Jentsch. She controlled the time we spent together completely and we both knew that this was simply for the best. If I had told anyone, if I had convinced anyone that Oliver, as I had known him, existed in some way, no one would believe me. They would accept germ theory, the internet, cellphones that worked as mini-computers, aliens, but not the extra-evolutionary step that Mrs. Jentsch had made. If they believed that *I* believed it, at best I would have been drugged and institutionalized like so many truth-speaking women before me. My time with Oliver, or what remained of him, would have been completely lost.

So I endured Mrs. Jentsch's conversation the same way I endured eating, talking, sleeping, existing in general, counting down the moments when I could catch a glimpse of Oliver again, when he would smile at me, say hello or goodbye, read, or, on one memorable occasion, brush his fingers against mine as we both moved to keep a stack of books from collapsing onto a pile of tools that had completely taken over a corner of the Jentsch living room.

The heat that crawled up the nape of my neck, the way the hairs on my arm stood on end. Were not these all signs that he was realer than real?

And then in late December an ambulance came and took away my landlady. A week into the new year, as people were still writing down the old year, crossing it out, and writing in the new one, she died. I knew because my father went into the office on a Saturday, a day of rest, for a personal consultation with her formerly erratic, now medicated daughter, now orphaned and the sole heiress to her mother's fortune.

The snow came thick and powderful obscuring pathways and roadways. School was cancelled.

I loved the snow, particularly because, with the excuse of having only one arm, I never had to shovel any of it, leaving me to enjoy its phenomenal beauty. On the other hand, much like the rain, it always caused a peculiar ache in my arm, and this morning, as I woke up, for the first time in quite some time the ache told me that the only thing that would cure the sensation was if I put on a Marnie arm and felt its tightness around my right arm stump, felt its weight, solid and true, balancing me out.

I needed the heaviest Marnie arm. But the heaviest ones were the old ones that hung in Marnie's basement, my winter arms that I hadn't had time to collect before we stopped talking in the autumn. I settled for the next best thing, one I had at my parents' house that was structured of aluminum and titanium, heavy with internal circuitry and copper wiring.

The metal warmed to my body as I put it on. It had a screen inserted in the forearm and during the period when Marnie had been designing it she had found my old book on Morse code. I remembered her finding it particularly amusing to code the dots and dashes into os and 1s that flashed pink and blue. When the arm was charged, if I remembered correctly, what all that engineering spelled was Alma Alt, in International Morse.

Despite the cold and the general stupor of the city, it was an Oliver day and I could not bring myself to miss something so precious. So while half the city stopped working and cars stayed in their garages and people lost power and made do with candles and extra blankets, I bundled myself into my large down coat and, feeling more like a sleeping bag than a woman, trudged my way to the Jentsch house where Oliver was already in front, helpfully shovelling a path for me to enter.

OUT OF BREATH

IT TOOK ME quite some time to catch my breath in the Jentsch home. Fighting the snow drifts had left me sweaty and panting, and trying to inhale deeply in that house led me to cough and sneeze. The windows had mostly been shut and the ash and dust were at an all-time high.

Mrs. Jentsch smiled at me as I tried to breathe in normally.

Quite likely an underlying heart condition, she said. Or maybe weak lungs. The sort of thing that would make someone die quite young.

Thank you, I tried to say sarcastically, but it was difficult to say anything sarcastically while out of breath.

Didn't your mother have a heart attack? she said continuing along her theme. A hereditary condition. People think they can live however they want but each trauma to the body weakens it, bringing it one step closer to death.

Sometimes, I told her, I cannot quite believe you aren't Jewish. That is just the sort of thing my father is constantly telling me just when I am beginning to feel half alright. It's the smoking, anyway, I said, collapsing into my habitual carved-out corner of the couch. I don't do it much but it's the smoking probably.

Since she so delighted in running me over, conversationally speaking, it felt wonderful to do the same to her. She looked quite shocked.

Why would you do something so stupid?

Why do you? I asked. Why does Oliver?

Oliver came back inside. The effort of shovelling had brightened his eyes, rouged his cheeks to a charmingly bright glow, and made his hair loose and sweaty in a way that reminded me of some of the athletic pictures I had saved.

Oliver doesn't smoke, Mrs. Jentsch said with a frown.

I tried to keep talking as he arrived but he was stamping his boots, shaking snow and salt out on the wooden floor. A shock that he would desecrate a wooden floor this way. It was a beautiful natural elm similar to the floors in my parents' home. They were made of wood from trees that would have been hundreds of years old when they were cut down and planed into floorboards, elms that had flourished plentifully before they were devastated by fungus and became rare in this part of the world. They had been there as part of the house for a hundred years, and if they were treated correctly would last longer than my lifetime.

But then Mrs. Jentsch wasn't one to care about things like floorboards or preservation. She couldn't keep a house. She couldn't keep a son.

He does, I said, confused. He did. He smoked on the drive before the accident.

Mrs. Jentsch was still frowning.

Oliver smiled at me and it felt as though life had been breathed into me.

OLIVER JENTSCH

AND THEN OLIVER was looking at my arm. I had been so dazzled by him I didn't notice what he was looking at but all the expression loosened from his face. It wasn't simply that he stopped smiling, it was that some muscle or fibre slackened in a way that made it seem that, although his eyes continued to move, he was no longer alive.

I followed his gaze and saw that he was looking at my prosthetic arm which was flashing cheerily ALMA ALT.

Mrs. Jentsch looked where we were looking. She too seemed startled by my prosthetic.

It was the first time, I realized, I had ever worn one in their presence.

Perhaps since the default assumption is that people have two arms, the fact that I showed up with two struck them not as strange but as a return to a norm, and it was the noticing that was discordant, this reminder that I was broken, the two arms a lie.

I felt an embarrassing sense of hurt at the thought. I had believed that, out of everyone, Mrs. Jentsch and Oliver were the sort who would understand a prosthetic and not be alarmed. But rather than ignoring it, as most people seemed to (the presence of an arm, even an obviously synthetic, mechanical one, was usually more comforting than an absence where the second arm should be), they both seemed visibly ill at ease as if angered.

Marnie, I knew, would have had some way to smooth out the conversation but I wasn't Marnie, I was only me, and I felt my shoulders rounding up protectively, my throat closing up, my mind voiding of anything but discomfort.

Eventually Mrs. Jentsch said, That's quite a pretty piece.

Marnie made it, I said. My sister, I said, clarifying. I wasn't sure, in spite of how closely our lives were tied, how much she remembered about my family.

Oliver came towards me. There was something not quite right about the way he was moving, something that frightened me in how he looked at me. He came very near and opened his mouth and said something—no, didn't say, *communicated* something I didn't understand, something that didn't even sound like words, but like mechanical clicks and whirrs. I kept staring at his mouth, searching for understanding. Beyond his perfect white teeth I could see the dark cavernous hole that led to his throat, a human throat making inhuman sounds.

I felt scared. I had never been scared of him before.

Mrs. Jentsch said, I think it's time for you to leave.

Now I looked to Oliver for help, though why I had no idea. He had never expressed any sort of interest in whether I stayed or left.

Oliver? I said. It was his name but it was a plea for intervention. To let me stay.

But now his smile was back and he was standing upright instead of leaning towards me.

He said, Pardon me. He said, Let me get your coat.

His voice was the same as it always was and the musculature had reconstituted to make his usual face, lively and emotive and alive.

My coat was by me, because Mrs. Jentsch's closets were full of Mrs. Jentsch's things and there was nowhere to hang a coat by the door, just piles and piles of more of Mrs. Jentsch's stuff strewn about in layers. But Oliver, like a gentleman, plucked my coat from my side and walked me to the door and then held the coat out so that by turning my back to him I could slide my arms into the sleeves. A very thoughtful gesture as it was difficult for me to get the coat on without jostling the prosthetic painfully.

The funny thing was I didn't want to turn my back to him. Reluctantly I did it and felt a frisson as he exhaled onto the nape of my neck. Three short puffs followed by three long exhalations and then three short puffs again. He did this quickly in one breath without needing to inhale more air.

Goodbye, Alma Alt, he said as he opened the door for me.

I knew that signal.

I thought of it the whole way home, my arm under my coat flashing Alma Alt, Alma Alt.

Three dots followed by three dashes followed by three dots was the International Morse distress signal. SOS.

I DIDN'T GO BACK TO THE JENTSCH HOUSE FOR SOME TIME

I KEPT CONVINCING myself that I had imagined those breaths on my neck. Or it was an accident, my mind finding patterns where there were none. Every time I thought of seeing Oliver again, I remembered the strange way he had approached me when he noticed my prosthetic, the way, in that moment, he hadn't seemed human at all. I thought of that SOS, that plea for help, and felt fear. I didn't want to believe it was real. I didn't want to believe that he wasn't Oliver.

Real life, prosaic and ordinary, intervened and I allowed myself to become quite busy.

LIFE, DEATH, AND TAXES

MY FATHER HAD a favourite expression that ran like this: There are only three certain things in this life; you're born, you die, and you pay taxes.

My landlady's daughter was suddenly in possession of a large amount of wealth and it was our duty to help her with it, for a fee of course. We were instructed to drop everything the second she walked through the door, not only because she was a valuable client but because of the connection between our families. She was a third-generation client. Her grandmother and my grandmother had met each other while seamstresses in Montreal. Her mother had been my landlady and now she would be.

She would show up to our offices more than once a week looking shell-shocked, sometimes crying as we presented her documents to sign, bills coming at her from all directions, the CRA waiting in the wings to claim its share. (Thank God, aunt Eshkie said in private, that she died in early January. Thank God, she has a whole year to file. We all nodded.)

The landlady's daughter was suddenly spending a glut of money, but it was a glut she could well afford given the vast amount of property, stocks, bonds, investments, and cash that was slowly being transferred to her name.

I was never tempted to begrudge her her cash though. She often would look at the documents we handed her and would bite her lip and say, I would give it all so that she would come back. It reminded me too much of my bubbe, of Oliver, of my mother's heart attack, death inevitable and creeping closer every day.

You see, bubbeleh, my father said, hugging me close between reading the tax code and calling up lawyers and money managers, money doesn't solve everything.

I wondered if Mrs. Jentsch had claimed the death benefit for Oliver the year he had died and then pushed all thoughts of Oliver and Mrs. Jentsch away.

Marnie had her baby.

I learned of it through Neil, who called us from the hospital to tell us of the birth of Sonia Olivia. Sonia, after our paternal grandmother, and Olivia for Oliver. I found the gesture incredibly touching.

Should I call her? I asked Neil. Once I would have known the proper steps to take but now, our relationship fractured, I wasn't sure.

Not yet, Alma, he said.

I didn't meet Sonia Olivia Alt until Marnie, on maternity leave, came by the office to say hello.

I was nervous meeting them. I felt my palms sweat, felt unsure about holding Marnie's gaze.

Do you want to hold her? she asked.

And even though I didn't want to I obligingly put my arm out to receive her.

The baby was impossibly small, as babies are. I cradled her close to my chest and Marnie stood close by, ready to help if my one arm wasn't strong enough for her bird weight. It seemed impossible to believe that we all started life in this way, perfectly miniature seedlings, ready to bloom.

Marnie, I said, did you want to get a coffee?

A CONVERSATION WITH MARNIE

IT WOULD HAVE been impossible, I now knew, to talk to Marnie before Sonia Olivia.

I was too obsessed with point-scoring, with maintaining my upper hand as the scorned child. But seeing her humbled me. Seeing Marnie humbled me.

I'm sorry, I said as she was saying the same thing.

I'm sorry, I'm sorry.

We both began to cry.

We were sorry for the ways in which we had grown embittered, been cruel, cut each other down in our most vulnerable moments. We were sorry for how we had failed each other and would do so again. Even in our reconciliation we knew that this great feeling of peace would not last and that we could only hope to be brave enough women to apologize when we transgressed again and then be braver still and accept those apologies.

After we had cried and we had told each other everything, from my trip to Mexico to her final days at the office and the pain of labour,

I found myself wanting to ask her what to do about Oliver. The longer I stayed away the more distressed I felt about ignoring him. So I told her something I had thought I wouldn't be able to tell anyone.

I saw Oliver.

Marnie hummed a little in response. I waited for her to ask me if it was a dream but she said, Did you?

Yes. He was—he seemed alive.

He's dead, Alma.

I know but I saw him. Alive, still eighteen.

When he died, I told Marnie, eighteen seemed so grown up and now it seems so young, like a child. Like baby Solvita.

But that was the last time you saw him, why would he look any different?

He should be older, I said. The one truth I could articulate.

Did he say anything to you?

I hesitated. I didn't know how to explain Mrs. Jentsch, my conversations with Oliver. Admit that I had seen him, talked to him, touched him.

He wants me to help him.

And did you?

This is what's so annoying about you, Marnie, I said exasperated. This is what's wrong with our whole family. I wish you would just tell me something normal like I'm cracked in the head or you're going to have me committed or it was just someone who happened to look like him. I wish you wouldn't treat me seriously and keep asking questions.

Is that what you want? she asked. Yet another question I should have chafed at.

I want some bullshitty soft spiritual answer that makes it okay that I saw him.

Fine, Marnie said. Then I'll tell you this. I wouldn't worry about seeing him at all. Because if you saw him you saw him.

You believe me?

Yes, I believe you.

You shouldn't, I said.

Why not? Marnie asked. We're probably living in a simulation anyway.

Marnie! I said. I couldn't believe that of all the things she could have said to me that's what she would choose. It was utterly ridiculous.

It's true, she said. Look it up. There's a fifty percent chance that we're all just living in a simulation and nothing we do really matters anyway.

Why would we be in a simulation? I asked.

To figure out how to solve large-scale climate catastrophe, Marnie said. Whoever is running the simulation is probably running an infinite number of them. I think we're living in one of the ones where we don't figure things out.

Marnie, I said, heartbroken. I didn't know that she thought about things like that too.

Why did you have her then, Marnie?

I love Neil so much, Alma, she said with an intensity that surprised me. I love him so much and I think it's the most beautiful, most true thing in the world, to take the love between the two of us and turn it into one living breathing person.

That's not ethical to her, I said.

No, she said. But maybe I'm wrong and it will all work out. I think about that a lot too. I hope for it.

We looked at her doomed child and she yawned and blinked awake, this beautiful child, and then she began to scream, hungry for food.

There was a conversational drift. I helped Marnie with the awkward business of adjusting her clothes and her child for breastfeeding and then we talked about a crystal arm I wanted her to build and she promised to try if I would send her the pictures I had seen.

Even as the hours stretched and Marnie started yawning around sentences, I couldn't bring myself to say goodbye.

If Oliver needs your help, Marnie said at one point, I think you should help him.

But what if I lose him? I asked.

Oh, Alma, Marnie said. He's already dead. How much more lost could he be?

THREE MOTHERS

DESPITE WHAT MARNIE might have hoped our mother did not soften towards her only grandchild. She was ambivalent about being an abuela, and often would hold the child for a minute or so before passing her on to my father who was the misty-eyed, doting zaide we'd never experienced. From somewhere in the attic he unearthed all sorts of books holding the Jewish folk tales I had grown up with and we all learned again of the village of Chelm and Zlateh the goat and the golem of Prague.

To my great surprise the one who melted the most towards the baby was me. I still had no desire to have a child of my own. Constantine did get a job in Montreal and with him went the likeliest future father of my fictional children. But I liked little Solvita. She had eyes like a grey storm cloud, an uncanny mimic of Marnie's baby eyes, and skin that was white but more olive than either of her parents'.

I recognized that her life would be different from my own, harder in some ways perhaps, but I felt in my bones a deep desire to protect her, the way I imagined everyone felt about new life.

When I held her to me and she snuggled deep against my chest, I realized that she would grow up with my body as it was. The accident would be something so far in the past that it would exist only as a fairy tale to her. If we raised her by my side, as I knew we would, she would always see me as tia Alma, never Alma with one arm or Alma touched by tragedy. She would see me as myself.

We would love each other, I could see that now. And even though I knew that teaching her to love me would only be offering her a painful future, one in which she had to mourn me when I died, I couldn't help but think that maybe it would be worth it. I was grateful to Marnie and Neil for bringing her into the world, in an act of loving delusion.

Even after our reconciliation things between Marnie and I were imperfect and sometimes tense. We bickered, as we always did, but there was a shyness even through our annoyance as if we were aware that at any moment we might break apart again even over something so stupid as a sarcastic You're welcome, or a dress shrunk in the wash. But I saw the way she tried, with her daughter, to speak to her in Spanish. She kept a picture of the Virgin of Guadalupe in her home and a mezuzah on the door frame even though she didn't believe in God. I tried to remember she was trying.

Between washing endless loads of laundry for Marnie and Neil and baking casseroles for my landlady's daughter (now my landlady), I couldn't stop thinking about Mrs. Jentsch and Oliver. To my relief, since my tentative confession that I had seen Oliver, Marnie had not mentioned him at all. Despite Marnie's suggestion that I help Oliver I had continued to avoid the Jentsch house.

Oliver did not reach out with a second plea. If Mrs. Jentsch noticed I was gone she never communicated it. She was a very proud woman and I think very committed to the idea that she hated me. I think she was so committed to that idea that even if she had missed me she would never have admitted it.

I pictured her with her books and her Oliver, waiting for me to come back. For time moves differently for the lonely. The days are agony but the months and years a smudged-out blur. And with nothing to fill their days, no new life, only the drudgery of taxes and the increasingly welcome prospect of death, they hold close in their hearts the friends and enemies of old, people who are living in a different time, who have moved on, who have forgotten them. They sit in cold rooms and entertain themselves with books, or lose themselves in the vast quarrelsome waves of the internet and they wait to be remembered. And I knew that all too well, because I had felt, for years, that desperate biting loneliness.

It was spring at this point, well and truly months since I had properly seen Mrs. Jentsch and Oliver. We had just finished the April rush of filing taxes for our clients. Marnie and Neil were beginning to settle into parenthood with Solvita sleeping through the night for the first time earlier that week.

There was no reason for me to not go to the Jentsch house and so I went to see if I could free Oliver.

HELL IS OTHERS

MRS. JENTSCH WAS, as usual, unhappy to see me. In the time since I had last seen her she seemed to have shrunken down, like an applehead doll, collapsing into herself.

She made more of a fuss than I expected, berating me for showing up on a weekend, telling me she had plans, even though she clearly didn't, beginning to rant about my forgetting her son. She was so pleased with her displeasure I let her go on for a little bit.

Oliver was beside her, and he was smoking.

He would have never smoked in front of her was my first thought. She changed him.

I looked at her in her usual chair, surrounded by the detritus of a former life, alone in her genius. A musty odour had begun to intermingle unpleasantly with the smoke.

Oh, Mrs. Jentsch, I thought.

I tried to open a window, to let the fresh air in. It did little to cut through the smell, but I thought it might do Mrs. Jentsch some good.

She complained about the sudden cold, an exaggeration. It was actually unseasonably hot for a spring day, much closer to the choking swelter of summer than the cool airiness of spring. On my way to Mrs. Jentsch I had sweated through my spring jacket and had passed half a dozen people in shorts and sundresses, eager to slough off any memories of the cold.

If it had been my own mother I would have draped my coat over Mrs. Jentsch to stop her complaints and warm her bones. But my coat was drenched in my own heady sweat, a smell too personal to drape over this mystifyingly terrifying woman. I also happened to like that jacket and I did not want Mrs. Jentsch's own odours invading it.

I told her I would go find her a sweater or a blanket or something and she seemed quite alarmed that I should go, on my own, through the rest of the house, but I hushed her the way I would have hushed Solvita, and to my surprise, she did not come chasing after me but settled deeper into her chair, contentedly grumbling to herself about my rudeness.

Oliver, I said, could you please help me?

He led me to the kitchen.

It was in a sorry state, as I knew it would be. Even so it made me gasp. It wasn't the sheer quantity of things, though the kitchen was crowded with dusty-looking jars and cans and appliances on every surface and more tools and ashtrays and other objects that shouldn't have been there. It was that the kitchen showed more obvious signs of neglect than the rest of the house. There was a large scorch mark on the wall, an accident from a pot left burning. The plaster from half the ceiling was falling off in chunks and the paint was coming down in strips as if some giant had started peeling it and then abandoned their work halfway through.

I tore my eyes from the carnage and looked at Oliver. The sight of him made me sick.

I realized, after a moment, this was because he was not breathing, not moving, preternaturally still. It was not like he was dead; it was like he was an object. A human-shaped object. I hadn't known until then that the breathing was something he did for Mrs. Jentsch. For me. Something to comfort us. It is alarming to stand beside someone who looks human, who acts human, who smells human, but who is not breathing. It took all my effort not to rush to him and try my best to revive him. But there was nothing to revive.

For perhaps the first time, in this attitude of not quite being alive, this Oliver seemed to me the most like the real Oliver as I had last seen him. The dead child. The child I had surpassed in years and experience and wisdom.

This clever mimic, whatever it was, was not him.

Oliver, I said. I didn't know what else to call him.

He moved. Again he had a strange expression on his face. His mouth slacked half open, his head flopped, tilting obscenely at an angle that looked almost broken. He looked like what I imagine a stroke victim would look like, what humans look like, I suppose, when they are alone and have not schooled their expressions for others. But worse.

He looked, in short, like a human-shaped thing that was tired of pretending to be human.

I wanted to tell him, Be Oliver, pretend for me again.

But I couldn't do that. There were no lies clever enough to cover up the truth.

Oliver, I said, what are you?

I don't know, he said.

I reached out and touched him and held his hand.

You have to help me, please, Oliver said.

Not Oliver. The thing Mrs. Jentsch created. And in honour of the Oliver that died, that boy whose face this thing wore, I agreed that yes, somehow I would.

NOT OLIVER

ONCE I HAD breached the kitchen it seemed as if something had been breached in Mrs. Jentsch too. She no longer set the rules of when I could come or for how long. I began to tidy up around the house and though she hovered fretfully she didn't put up as much of a fight as I might have imagined.

Most of all she did not seem to find it at all amiss that Oliver and I began to spend more and more time alone and out of her presence planning how he was to leave her.

There was another language he was more fluent in, a kind of machine language which he was disappointed to find I didn't know and couldn't imitate at all.

I'm sorry, Oliver, I said when he tried to speak to me in it.

He hissed and clicked at me in the machine tongue.

Don't call me that, he said in English.

But there was no word in human language for what he was.

He resented speaking English, but conceded that to communicate with me at all he had to compromise and taint his mouth with the imperfect and foul.

He hated Mrs. Jentsch for giving him a consciousness, a life of sorts, and then trapping him in a human body.

Sometimes when we were alone he rolled his ankles as if they were broken and walked on top of them, his feet flopping uselessly like extra appendages. It alarmed every fibre of my being to watch something that looked so human walk in such an unnatural way. I could tell that, to him, this unnatural way of walking was closer to natural than the way Mrs. Jentsch must have taught him to walk.

Sometimes when we were alone he just collapsed inside of himself, his eyes freezing, unblinking, unfocused.

A doll drained of life.

I wish she'd never been born so that she never would have made me, he told me.

I had a sudden vision of him sticking her in the face with a knife or picking her up by the ankle and smashing her into a wall. I was cursed with expressive eyes; he read the fear in them right away.

There is no part of me that wishes her harm, he said. He gave a little mechanical whirr almost like chimes twinkling. It was an incongruously beautiful sound but I understood it to be something close to a scoff of derision.

You wish her well, I said. But for her to be as far away as possible from you.

It was what I had once felt towards Marnie.

For *me* to be as far away from her as possible, he said. She dabbles in my mind. Changes me to be more or less like him. I want to leave here and be free.

I wish I could rip off my face, he said. That's what I really want to do. Just completely peel it off. Break my arms and legs so I could crawl on all fours like a beast.

He took one of his fingers and bent it.

Stop it, I said. Stop it, Oliver.

It snapped. Not a little break but something I had never heard before.

It was purpled and at an angle.

I screamed without meaning to and then cut myself off, rushed to head off Mrs. Jentsch.

What happened? she asked trying to get into the kitchen.

I almost knocked over one of your precious piles, I said. But Oliver saved it.

Mrs. Jentsch looked over my head and smiled, a true smile, but one I could not have imagined her giving to Oliver when he was actually alive.

I turned back to look at Oliver. His hands were behind his back. But more importantly he had resumed his breathing, so that he seemed, once again, like the boy he had been modelled after.

HEAVEN IS OTHERS

I TOLD OLIVER that perhaps he wouldn't survive on his own. Maybe, like the jealous mother she was, unable to accept that she could be parted from Oliver by death or anything else, Mrs. Jentsch had planned for his obsolescence.

There was a thing I kept reading about more and more: planned obsolescence. *Obsolescence*, what a beautiful romantic word. A word much more melancholic than *death*, which signalled finality; *obsolescence* indicated a fall from grace, the act of existing but becoming obsolete.

The technology to make things last forever, or at least longer than their current shelf life, existed somewhere in the minds of engineers or in the vaults of tech companies, but their insatiable need for money, and more money on top of that, made them make things that, after a certain point, were designed to fracture, break down, malfunction. It was why my parents' avocado-green Kenmore fridge that was older than I was still hummed along happily while the security software they had bought for the office had one day ceased working and when I was given the task of finding out why, I discovered that the company that sent the updates for the software had simply folded quietly and without notice the previous month and the security cameras, cut off from that software, had puttered along for a while before suddenly and abruptly giving up.

I was no engineer; I could not tell Oliver whether leaving Mrs. Jentsch was death or how long he might live apart from her. I had a half-formed thought of bringing him to Marnie.

Marnie understands these things, I told him. Marnie makes my arms.

He was so charmed by the arms, their mechanisms and machinery. The fact that I was bionic was what had caused him to trust me in the first place.

No Marnies, he said.

I knew he meant no engineers, no more human hands tinkering with his body trying to make him more like them instead of accepting that he was something else.

He was very clear about what he wanted and what he wanted was to be away from humans, to peel off the human skin that bound him, and traipse around until he fell apart and became one with the earth.

I don't know why this surprised me but it did.

I would have thought he would want to run away from Mrs. Jentsch and perhaps begin to find others like him or live a human life, not as Oliver but as someone else.

I don't need that, he told me. I want you to be the last human I see.

I told him I was not a magician nor even particularly clever. His options were limited to Canada and even then it would be hard for me to transport him because I could barely drive.

Let me worry about that, he said, which was not exactly the reassurance I wanted.

I brought him a map of Canada. I told him we were less a country and more a collection of beavers and trees and this became his favourite idea, the thing he never tired of hearing. He would touch the upper limits of the provinces, the water, the islands and I could see that he was imagining all the places humans weren't. All the places fit for him to inhabit. He wanted to go off in the north, or as far north as I could get him.

When he looked at all that stretched-out territory his face would go even more slack than it usually was in my presence and I came to recognize this as undisguised longing, his body already feeling how it would be free when it would no longer have to present itself to a human gaze.

What if you die? I asked him.

I had laptops and phones and tablets that had died, taking with them pictures and phone numbers, saved websites and screencaps. I remembered the feeling of panic when faced with a black screen. I called that death. This would be worse.

Oliver was ambivalent about his human skin; I couldn't imagine him keeping clothes on once I had left him wherever he wanted to go. He would run his body ragged on nature. Predators would tear pieces off his flesh. He had no sense of self-protection.

Oliver was unfazed by the idea of dying.

If I cease to work, he said, it makes no difference to me. Before that woman made me I was nothing; if I become nothing again what does it matter?

I could have told him it mattered very much to Mrs. Jentsch and also to me. But I knew this wouldn't dissuade him from leaving.

Another thought kept occurring to me as I sat up at night, indulging in the very worst of my insomnia, reading news article after news article about the extinction of flora and fauna, the impending doom we were all hurtling towards seemingly sans cesse.

What if, in her vast cleverness, Mrs. Jentsch had built her clockwork boy so that he might endure? By my bedside I still had that hand which continued to beat the same steady beat as when I first saw it in Oliver's room. That was the one thing that was missing from all these articles about the upcoming climate catastrophe. People kept referring to it as killing the planet but it was not the planet we were killing, only the ecosystem which allowed us to thrive. The Earth would be inhospitable to us. But we were not the beginning nor the end of the story of life.

I did not doubt that after the last humans choked out of existence there would be life. Something would survive, some living thing. And maybe that thing was whatever Oliver was. The eternal son, the inheritor of the Earth, the whole world cleared free of humans so that he could exist for all time, the sole witness when the sun finally flamed out.

I kept these thoughts to myself. I wouldn't betray Oliver by asking Mrs. Jentsch any questions that might lead her to suspect her son was close to fleeing. And I did not bring up the possibility to Oliver who I feared might damage himself in some irreparable way if he thought that life eternal was in his future. I secreted these thoughts in my heart and never told a soul about them.

THE DEAD

I LEFT BEHIND my phone and stole my father's car in the dead of night. I was terrified of getting behind the wheel. My father, mother, sister, and even Constantine had all given me lessons at various points in my life, enough so that I was familiar with the mechanics of the machine. But my body still remembered the crash. I shook as I turned the key in the ignition but I thought of Not Oliver, waiting for me and steadied myself.

No one could ask for a more placid driving environment than the streets of the Glebe at night but still I was afraid that a car would come out of nowhere, would plow into me, taking my other arm, or perhaps finally my life. But the avenues were wide and completely deserted. I drove a little slower perhaps than was strictly normal, but no one was around to take note of what was normal or not.

Drenched in sweat, I arrived on the corner of Broadway Avenue in the same amount of time as it would have taken me to walk. I parked the car as best I could and then turned it off, getting out and slipping into the passenger side.

I didn't have to wait long. Drifting like a ghost, not bothering to walk in a human-like way at all, Oliver came towards me.

I was thankful there were no late-night dog walkers on the street. He would have terrified them. He half terrified me even though I was expecting him.

He settled into the driver's seat and it felt familiar. Oliver and I driving into the night.

Then he took a screwdriver and peeled off the entire top of his scalp. Skin resists the urge to rip and that tension creates a hideous noise. I gagged even before the blood started to run. Whatever he was made of, it smelled real. There would be explaining to do when I brought the car back.

Refrain from your butchery until you're free, I told him.

And then we were off.

My father often told me that when Marnie was a baby she used to fall asleep quite easily. She was, even then, the perfect child. But like the stubborn thing I grew to be, for months after I was born I would go to bed fighting against sleep. Eventually one of my parents heard a tip from a neighbour that difficult sleepers often enjoyed the thrum of a car engine. So it was for me. To lull me to sleep my parents would strap me into the car seat and drive around and around the neighbourhood and the street lights and the hum of the engine would always rock me to sleep before we got home. There must have been something of this I had lost when the accident happened. Back in the car I found it again.

Before we had left the Glebe I fell into sleep.

I DREAMED A DREAM SO PERFECT

IT WAS DAYLIGHT and we were parked by the edge of the highway, a treeline before us. I sat in the passenger seat and looked out the window. Oliver walked towards the treeline. First he shed his clothes, and then he shed his skin, and then his muscle, and underneath there was no bone, no intricate system of veins, but titanium and wire. With his hands he took off his feet and then, no longer needed, his hands fell from his body. Whatever he was now, he was beautiful. And he dropped to all fours and disappeared into the wilds without once looking back. And I knew that I would go see Mrs. Jentsch and hold her hand and cry with her, but I would never regret having helped the thing escape. It might be the only good thing I ever did in my life. The only right thing.

I was very disoriented when I awoke because it was morning and I was by the side of the highway and Oliver was gone, the only sign that he had been in my car the blood spatters on the driver's seat. I wondered if I could pass them off as menstrual blood. I felt the kind of stiffness a body feels when it has been cramped too long in one place and I got out of the car to stretch myself.

I wasn't sure where I was. The landscape was unfamiliar.

There were some trees about but they were not very thick, some only saplings with trunks the size of my wrists. There was also a rocky wall to the left which had not been in my dream.

Although the car was in my possession I knew I would never be able to navigate home alone.

I got out and began to walk.

After about ten minutes I found a truck stop.

I sat down at the diner and ordered an open-faced chicken sandwich.

Mrs. Jentsch would forgive me in the end, I thought. She would forgive me for taking her son a second time as long as I kept showing up to her house, busying her into remembering that she hated me, bickering with her over the broken lamps and cracked mugs she couldn't be persuaded to throw out. I would keep her occupied with her hate so that she wouldn't feel so maddeningly lonely, wouldn't be driven to breathe life into a third son, a fourth, a fifth, all of them leaving her in the end, the way healthy children should.

After I paid I asked for some change and went to the back of the diner where I found the first pay phone I had seen in years.

I fed my quarters into the machine and called Marnie, who I knew would come and take me home.

ACKNOWLEDGEMENTS

DURING THE COURSE of writing this book, I lost two family members: Larry Hirsch and Ursula Benitez Ortiz. I thank them and all the dead, for all that they taught me about life.

Thank you to my family, Tanya, Trudi, and Aris Garcia, for always believing I could do this.

Thank you to Jen Albert. This book exists on paper and not in my head because of you.

Thank you to my agent, the wonderful Ron Eckel, for shepherding me through this process.

Thank you to Nicole Messina who, from her home in New York, was there every step of the way while this was written from my home in Ottawa.

Thank you to everyone at CHEO, past and present. Special thanks to those who did a wonderful job sewing this author back together during an unlucky childhood.

The writing of this book was funded by grants from the City of Ottawa's Cultural Funding, the Ontario Arts Council, and the Canada Council of the Arts. I thank these arts bodies for their continued generous support of my work.

And finally thank you to the entire ECW team who, whether I have met them or not, have always treated me and my work with the utmost respect and care:

Editor: Jen Albert
Copy Editor: Peter Norman
Proofreader: Crissy Boylan
Editorial Manager: Sammy Chin
Art Director: Jessica Albert
Cover Artist: Liz Ranger

Publicist: Cassie Smyth
Publishers: David Caron, Jack David
Sales Director: Emily Ferko
Production Team: Jennifer Gallinger, Victoria Cozza, Christine Lum
Marketing Team: Elham Ali, Caroline Suzuki, Alex Dunn
Operations Team: Aymen Saidane, Michela Prefontaine, Sarah Laudenbach

REBECCA HIRSCH GARCIA lives in Ottawa, ON. An O. Henry Award–winning author, she has been published in *The Threepenny Review*, *PRISM international*, *The Dark*, and elsewhere. Her debut collection, *The Girl Who Cried Diamonds & Other Stories* (2023), was the runner-up for the Danuta Gleed Literary Award and shortlisted for an Ottawa Book Award. *Other Evolutions* is her debut novel.

Entertainment. Writing. Culture. ─────────────────

ECW is a proudly independent, Canadian-owned book publisher. We know great writing can improve people's lives, and we're passionate about sharing original, exciting, and insightful writing across genres.

───────────────────────── **Thanks for reading along!**

We want our books not just to sustain our imaginations, but to help construct a healthier, more just world, and so we've become a certified B Corporation, meaning we meet a high standard of social and environmental responsibility — and we're going to keep aiming higher. We believe books can drive change, but the way we make them can too.

Being a B Corp means that the act of publishing this book should be a force for good — for the planet, for our communities, and for the people that worked to make this book. For example, everyone who worked on this book was paid at least a living wage. You can learn more at the Ontario Living Wage Network.

This book is also available as a Global Certified Accessible™ (GCA) ebook. ECW Press's ebooks are screen reader friendly and are built to meet the needs of those who are unable to read standard print due to blindness, low vision, dyslexia, or a physical disability.

This book is printed on FSC®-certified paper. It contains recycled materials, and other controlled sources, is processed chlorine free, and is manufactured using biogas energy.

FSC
www.fsc.org
MIX
Paper | Supporting responsible forestry
FSC® C103567

ECW's office is situated on land that was the traditional territory of many nations, including the Wendat, the Anishinaabeg, Haudenosaunee, Chippewa, Métis, and current treaty holders the Mississaugas of the Credit. In the 1880s, the land was developed as part of a growing community around St. Matthew's Anglican and other churches. Starting in the 1950s, our neighbourhood was transformed by immigrants fleeing the Vietnam War and Chinese Canadians dispossessed by the building of Nathan Phillips Square and the subsequent rise in real estate value in other Chinatowns. We are grateful to those who cared for the land before us and are proud to be working amidst this mix of cultures.

ecwpress.com